Bree's hands curled [...]
home, Rylan."

"We're going to my ranch—"

"Take. Me. Home." Although she tried to disguise it, anger, hurt and sorrow quivered in each word.

Rylan must have heard it, too. After a brief sidelong glance in her direction, he checked for oncoming traffic. The road ahead was clear, and he swung the car onto the opposite side of the highway. They completed the return journey in stony silence.

When Rylan halted the vehicle in the Diamond parking lot, he turned to face Bree. "I respect what you must be feeling right now, but I can't let you risk your personal safety. Someone fired a shot directly over our heads. Because we left the scene fast, I have no way of knowing what happened next. Was that a single incident, or was it an active shooter situation? I have to find out if we were the only target or if other shots were fired."

Through the fog of her competing emotions, Bree's initial reaction was fear for his safety. What if the person who fired that shot had intended to kill one, or both, of them? What if he was waiting for their return?

* * *

The Coltons of Roaring Springs:
Family and true love are under siege

* * *

If you're on Twitter, tell us what you
think of Harlequin Romantic Suspense!
#harlequinromsuspense

Dear Reader,

I'm so happy to bring you another Colton story, this time set in the scenic Colorado resort town of Roaring Springs.

I love the dynamics of these epic family dramas and I get wrapped up in the lives of the characters. I'm always waiting impatiently to read the next book in the series!

In this story, the hero, Rylan, is caught in a dilemma from the very first page. He is forced to fight the overpowering attraction he feels toward Bree Colton because he is not being honest with her about his identity. Bree, meanwhile, is being threatened, and the only person who makes her feel safe is Rylan. If she discovers his deception, her trust will be shattered...

Many of you will already know how much I enjoy including animals in my books. Well, this book has a whole host of them! Rylan's ranch is a sanctuary for a multitude of misfit creatures he has rescued. There's Merry, the sheep who thinks she's a dog; Cindy from Finance, the cat who has fostered a brood of orphaned ducklings; Boo, the heartbroken goose... The list goes on.

Although the ranch provides a safe and entertaining place for Bree to escape her fears, danger pursues her. Rylan has sworn to do everything he can to keep her safe, but he's fighting a hidden and devious opponent.

I'd love to hear from you and find out what you think of Rylan and Bree's story. You can contact me at:

Website: www.JaneGodmanAuthor.com

Twitter: @JaneGodman

Facebook: Jane Godman Author

Happy reading,

Jane

COLTON'S SECRET BODYGUARD

Jane Godman

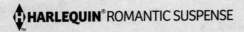
HARLEQUIN® ROMANTIC SUSPENSE

Special thanks and acknowledgment are given to
Jane Godman for her contribution to
The Coltons of Roaring Springs miniseries.

ISBN-13: 978-1-335-66193-7

Colton's Secret Bodyguard

Recycling programs
for this product may
not exist in your area.

Printed in U.S.A.

www.Harlequin.com

Jane Godman writes in a variety of romance genres, including paranormal, gothic and romantic suspense. Jane lives in England and loves to travel to European cities that are steeped in history and romance—Venice, Dubrovnik and Vienna are among her favorites. Jane is married to a lovely man and is mom to two grown-up children.

Books by Jane Godman

Harlequin Romantic Suspense

The Coltons of Roaring Springs

Colton's Secret Bodyguard

The Coltons of Red Ridge

Colton and the Single Mom

Sons of Stillwater

Covert Kisses
The Soldier's Seduction
Secret Baby, Second Chance

Harlequin Nocturne

Otherworld Protector
Otherworld Renegade
Otherworld Challenger
Immortal Billionaire
The Unforgettable Wolf
One Night with the Valkyrie
Awakening the Shifter
Enticing the Dragon
Captivating the Bear

Visit the Author Profile page at Harlequin.com for more titles.

This book is dedicated to my very beautiful,
very tiny new granddaughter.
Welcome to the world, little one.

Chapter 1

Bree Colton had stopped trying to reprogram herself. Some people were larks, others were owls. Larks were cheery rise-and-shine morning people, the sort who started yawning once darkness fell. Owls were the alarm-clock-smashing, dance-till-dawn types. Bree was a night person, at her best between midnight and 4:00 a.m.

Which meant that right now, at eight thirty in the morning, she was having trouble remembering her own name. Over the years, she had developed strategies for dealing with her daybreak intolerance. The first stage was caffeine. Rocket fuel strength, without a trace of cream or sugar. Bree had trained her assistant to keep the coffee coming until she was ready to face the world. Most mornings, it took a long time.

Her other tactic solved two problems. One of her

most precious possessions was her digital recorder, which, as well as helping overcome the morning brain fog, was also an aid to coping with her dyslexia.

Every evening, before she left the gallery, she would record the following day's to-do list. Her first task each morning was to link the recorder up to her laptop, so she could upload her list into her voice-activated diary. Then, of course, she had to get her newly caffeine-fueled body moving and *do* the things she had planned.

After taking a long slug of coffee, she pulled open the top left drawer of her desk and reached inside without looking. It was where she always placed her recorder and when her fingers didn't automatically close around it, she frowned. A quick search through the contents of the drawer confirmed her worst fears. The recorder wasn't there.

She bit back an exclamation. The forthcoming art show was taking up all her time, and she'd worked late the previous night. It had been almost nine o'clock when she'd finally left the office. Scrunching her forehead, she made an effort to remember. She could recall dictating her list. Then what?

I'm sure I put the recorder in the drawer.

If that was the case, where was it now? Bree had locked the gallery doors last night and opened them again this morning. No one else could have gotten into her office. No one had any reason to. Even if they had, why would they remove her device and not take anything else?

The answer was simple. It hadn't happened. Her memory was just playing tricks on her, fooling her into thinking that, because she always followed a certain routine, she had done it again last night. Clearly, she had put the recorder somewhere else. The question was…*where?*

Huffing out a breath, she drank the rest of her coffee while emptying her purse onto the desktop in the hope that she might have picked up the recorder with her cell phone. Even as she did, she remembered that she'd been talking on her cell as she left the gallery.

Reassuring my mom that there haven't been any more threatening emails.

Briefly, she rested her chin on her hand and gazed at the screensaver on her laptop. It was a view across the valley from the beautiful farmhouse where she had grown up. Evening sunlight glinted on the snow-covered fields of the CC Farm, while Pine Peak dominated the scene. The towering mountain provided the skiing and natural springs that made the resort such a popular tourist destination.

Normally, the tranquil scene soothed her. However, today, it made her feel restless. It was a reminder of her Colton heritage, and that was what the menacing emails had been about. Even though the anonymous sender had called her hateful names because of the color of her skin, the underlying message had gone deeper. *You Coltons are only good for using and taking advantage of those who are less fortunate.*

Furthermore, the sender had said that if she had any sense, she would pack her bags and head back to her life of privilege on her parents' farm. If she didn't? The most recent emails had included some sickening images of what would happen to her if she ignored the warnings.

Small wonder she had lost concentration and mislaid her recorder. It was a minor lapse, unimportant and only slightly inconvenient. She could remember what she needed to do today. It was just…

What did *I do with it?*

Pushing her chair back from the desk, she went through to her assistant's office. The two rooms were separated by a short corridor that included a private bathroom and a small kitchen. Inside Kasey Spencer's office, the floor on three sides was piled high with programs for the forthcoming show.

"Have you seen my digital recorder?"

Kasey looked up from the pile of papers she was collating. "No, but I can leave this and help you look for it."

Bree shook her head. "It's okay. I probably took it up to the loft without thinking." Her apartment was above the gallery. "I'll check when I grab some lunch later."

She turned toward the door that led to the main gallery, only to be halted by Kasey's voice. "Since you're here…"

"Yes?"

"Rylan Bennet asked if you could spare him a few minutes," her assistant said. "He's in the promotions office."

"That man spends more time here than all the other artists' managers put together." Bree was aware that her smile was slightly self-conscious. "He sure is dedicated."

"Dedicated?" Kasey raised an eyebrow. "That's a new name for it."

Bree was tempted to ask the other woman what she meant, but it was fairly obvious, particularly since

Kasey gave her a teasing look before returning to her task. So much for Bree's speculation about whether the attraction between her and Rylan was real or just a pleasant daydream. Kasey's words implied that her assistant had noticed it, which meant it existed outside of Bree's imagination. The thought sent a pleasurable shiver down her spine.

The promotions office of the Wise Gal Gallery was a long, narrow room at the rear of the reception desk. Rylan Bennet didn't know much about the art world, but he had soon learned that it was a luxury for visiting artists and their managers to be provided with an area of their own in which to work. He figured it was because this gallery was located in a former warehouse, where space wasn't an issue.

Rylan seemed to be the only person involved in the prospective show who was interested in taking advantage of the hospitality provided by Bree Colton, the gallery owner. Most of the time, he had the office to himself. The situation suited him just fine, although he was aware of the curious glances directed his way by the gallery staff. They were obviously wondering what he found to do there all day, every day.

If he was going to be convincing in his role as a manager and promoter for a group of local artists, he clearly needed to work harder on his disguise. His initial goal had been to get through the door and establish contact with Bree. After all, she was the only reason he was here. But now that he had gotten to know her, he needed to maintain her trust.

Deceiving her didn't feel comfortable to Rylan, but

his old army buddy Blaine Colton had been resolute. He'd told Rylan that his kid cousin was in danger, and he needed someone he could count on to watch over her. While Blaine was in DC, getting his discharge finalized, his uncle Calvin and aunt Audrey, Bree's parents, had contacted him.

A week ago, a gallery show at Wise Gal had been interrupted by someone throwing a brick through the full-length front window. Kendall, who was married to Decker Colton, another of Bree's cousins, was hit in the face and seriously injured. Shaken by the incident, Bree admitted to her parents, and her brother, Trey, who was Bradford County's sheriff, that she had been getting threatening emails. Instead of taking action, she had apparently been ignoring the problem, hoping it would go away.

Calvin and Audrey were going crazy with worry about their daughter, but according to Blaine, Bree had refused their requests to return home and stay holed up at their farm. In desperation, they had asked her cousin to find a bodyguard, someone he trusted to keep her safe. The only problem? Rylan, the person Blaine had selected to be her protector, was sworn to secrecy about his role. If Bree found out, she would point-blank refuse to let the situation continue.

Reluctantly, Rylan had agreed. Although he'd recently sold the private security consultancy he'd been running since he left the army, he had the skills and experience to watch over Bree. He also lived close to Roaring Springs. Add in the fact that he owed Blaine a few favors from their time together in Afghanistan…

The only minor difficulty had been his cover story.

Fortunately, Bree's mom had helped him out with that. Audrey Douglas Colton was an attractive African American woman, whose love for her daughter and fighting spirit shone through in equal measures. The day after Rylan had expressed his doubts about his ability to blend into an artistic setting, Audrey had called him with a solution.

"Bree's next show is called Spirit. It's a celebration of African American art. A friend of mine is a professor at the University of North Colorado School of Art and Design. She has a group of graduates who are looking for someone to promote their work."

When Audrey outlined her plan for him to pose as the manager of the artists in question, Rylan had expressed his reservations. "I don't want these people to get their hopes built up. I have nothing long term to offer them."

"No one loses from this arrangement," Audrey had assured him. "These young African American artists will have their work displayed in a prestigious gallery. Wise Gal is becoming very well known." There had been a note of pride in her voice. "All I ask of you is that you do your best to promote their art to a wider audience."

Since he was planning on being in the gallery anyway, that seemed like a reasonable request. He would have time on his hands, so he may as well use it productively. Then Rylan met Bree…and reasonable became a distant memory.

Because, for the first time in his thirty-four years, a woman had taken his breath away. He'd seen her formal picture on the gallery's website when he had done some research. In it, she appeared cool and quirky, with a distant expression and a bohemian dress sense. In reality, she was a ray of sunshine, with a huge smile that, despite a slight shyness in her manner, quickly became a throaty laugh.

One look at Bree's flawless golden-brown skin and amber eyes had Rylan questioning everything he thought he knew about himself. And he tumbled deeper into enchantment each time he saw her. That block of concrete in which he'd encased his heart? It might not be as impenetrable as he'd always believed.

The problem? Even if Bree felt the same way—and he thought she might—he was lying to her about who he was.

"That's quite a frown." Rylan looked up from his laptop screen to find Bree leaning one shoulder against the door frame as she watched him. A slight smile curved her full lips. "Anything I can help you with?"

Since he'd been studying a floor plan of the gallery, checking the entrances and exits for weak points, he snapped the lid closed and got to his feet. In an attempt to be objective, he had speculated about the possibility of getting Bree to confide in him about the emails her parents had mentioned. If she did that, he reasoned, then he could legitimately offer her his protection. Maybe that way he could get past the feeling he was a cheating, lying jerk.

He got straight to the point, not easy when all he wanted to do was gaze into the honeyed depths of her eyes. "Your mom mentioned the incident when a brick was thrown through the window."

Bree already knew that he'd met her mother. One of

Audrey's many charitable causes was the cover for the inclusion of Rylan's group of young artists in the show. The fact that Bree had accepted the situation without comment confirmed that her mom regularly involved her in similar activities.

Even so, he caught the shift in her expression, maybe because he was watching her so closely. Gone almost as soon as it had appeared, it was a flare that could have been annoyance or impatience.

"I should have guessed she wouldn't be able to resist sharing that information." She hunched a shoulder. "Actually, that's unfair. It was a nasty incident."

"Have the police arrested anyone?"

"No. My brother, Trey, is the sheriff. He's been investigating, but so far he doesn't have any leads." Her face was troubled. "Our family has been having some problems lately."

Blaine had alluded to this but hadn't gone into detail. The focus of their conversation had been on what was happening with Bree. Rylan knew, of course, that Blaine's older brother, Wyatt, had recently been investigated when the body of a young woman was found on his ranch. Things had gotten nasty when the press put a spin on the story, leading the townsfolk to believe that Wyatt was guilty and getting preferential treatment because he was a Colton and his cousin was the sheriff.

Rylan had heard that the case had been closed with all charges against Wyatt dropped. However, from the way Bree was talking, it sounded like they had problems that were about more than one family member.

"You think those issues could be linked to the attack on your gallery?" he asked.

She hesitated, and Rylan hoped she might be about to confide in him. Then she smiled. It was a little too bright, as though she could be trying hard to convince him, or maybe herself, that everything was okay. "I'm sure they're not. And please don't worry about the safety of the artists you represent. I've had the front window replaced with toughened glass, and the alarm system has been upgraded."

The moment was lost, and Rylan bit back his frustration. Instead, he tried another approach. "I hear you've been working late every night."

"You hear?" This time Bree's smile was genuine. "Now, whoever could have told you that? Surely, Kasey, my super-discreet assistant, hasn't been telling tales about me?"

He grinned. "Actually, I overheard her talking to the security guy. He was asking if the reason you were staying so late is because of the big event coming up. I guess that's because he needs to know so he can ensure the place is safe during the show?"

"David?" Bree asked. "Yes, he's very conscientious, but he doesn't work just for me. He's employed to provide security for several of the businesses in the Diamond. He also does maintenance work for us. He's a busy guy."

Rylan was a native Coloradan, but he was new to Roaring Springs. Nestled within the valley, the town, with its bustling downtown area, was surrounded by the mountains, forests and a large lake.

First settled in the late 1800s because of gold mining, it grew to be a tourist destination, then blossomed further a decade ago when the Roaring Springs Film

Festival was created. Although it always had celebrity visitors, the town had become a must-see trip for A-listers and wealthy executives.

Rylan had learned that the former warehouse units on the edge of Second Street were just on the cusp of the trendy part of town. Like this gallery, the new companies were young and vibrant. Restaurants, bars, nightclubs and technology firms formed the bulk of the businesses. The area was named after the central diamond-shaped space within, where tables and chairs spilled out from the bars, coffee shops, restaurants and the Yogurt Hut.

"I hope you're taking care of yourself." Rylan kept his voice light and teasing, trying to avoid showing that he actually did care. "Getting plenty of sleep. Eating proper meals."

"I'm dyslexic." Bree said it casually, but the sidelong look she gave him told Rylan his reaction was important. "By the time I've read a recipe, the ingredients have gone stale."

"You need someone to cook for you." He tried to remember the last time he'd felt this nervous. He seriously didn't think he ever had.

Bree's smile held a trace of shyness. "Well, if you're offering…"

Aware that, if she wasn't careful, her lips had a tendency to turn up at the corners in an I-have-a date-with-a gorgeous-man smile, Bree did her best to appear brisk and levelheaded as she walked through the gallery. It wasn't easy, because Rylan really was the most handsome man she had ever seen.

He had the kind of looks that made her belly flutter,

her pulse race and her thoughts stray into dangerous territory. Her first glimpse of him had made her jaw drop, and he had only improved on closer acquaintance. His hair was light blond and slightly curly, his neatly trimmed beard just a shade darker. There was something about the strong, determined lines of his face, an alertness that became more intense when she was around. His eyes were as blue as a summer sky. When they looked her way, their expression became so hot and hard it made her skin feel too tight.

He was tall and very well built. Broad in the chest and shoulders, with long, strong legs and the thickly muscled arms of a man accustomed to physical exercise. She was used to being around tough men, her brother and most of her cousins certainly fit that description, but she had never been so aware of a man's power. Rylan's raw masculinity made her conscious of her own femininity in a way she had never experienced before.

There was something else about him as well. Something she couldn't quite put her finger on. An air of danger, mystery…and more. It felt like sorrow. He was a puzzle she couldn't quite put together. All she knew for sure was that she wanted to try.

And he was cooking her dinner later.

Reminding herself that she was a successful businesswoman, she resisted the temptation to dance the length of the gallery. Because this was more than a date. They'd both known it as they made the arrangements. He was coming to her *apartment*. He was cooking her his signature dish. The night was leading somewhere…

What if he thinks I do this all the time?

Doubt hit her like a slap in the face, and she glanced

over her shoulder. Maybe she should go back, talk to him, explain that she liked him, but she wasn't very good at this whole dating thing? She bit back a groan. *Here we go again.*

No. She gripped the handle of her office door tightly, taking a moment to get her thoughts under control. Just because she had been burned in the past didn't mean it was about to happen again. It was just dinner, for goodness' sake. They were both adults. It didn't have to lead to anything more… But she liked Rylan. A lot. What was wrong with taking a chance?

With a decisive nod, she stepped into her familiar space. She had a lot to do, starting with some calls. As she moved toward her seat, her gaze fell on the desk. There, in the center of the polished surface, was her digital recorder.

She gave an exclamation of delight and, snatching it up, hurried across the corridor to Kasey's office. "Where did you find it?"

"Find what?" Kasey looked away from her pile of papers with a frown.

"My recorder." Bree held it up to show her.

"Um… I didn't. I've been right here since we last spoke."

"Oh." Bree turned the recorder over in her hand, studying it carefully. It was definitely hers. "I wonder who found it? Did you hear anyone go into my office?"

Kasey shook her head. "Maybe it was there all the time, and you just overlooked it?"

Bree knew that wasn't the case. Yes, today had been an early start after a late night, and the caffeine had still been working its way through her system when she first reached for the recorder. But she had searched her office thoroughly. The device had not been there when she left and went to the promotions office to talk to Rylan. Which meant someone had found it and put it on her desk while she was gone.

"You could ask David to check the security cameras and see if anyone went into your office," Kasey suggested.

Was it worth that sort of effort? Bree had her recorder back, which was the important thing, and she was too busy to take any more time out of her schedule. Besides, David Swanson, the security guard and handyman, was always running here, there and everywhere as he tried to meet the competing demands of his various employers.

Ignoring a tiny lingering doubt, Bree shrugged. "Too much to do." She tried to make her next words sound casual. "And I don't want to work late tonight."

Chapter 2

Bree looked down at her empty plate with a contented sigh. After a three-course meal that would have graced the menu of the most elegant restaurants she'd visited, she regarded Rylan with newfound respect. "You are the only person I've met who has a signature dish that deserves the name. Where did you learn to cook?"

"I taught myself. I figured, as a single guy, I could live on takeout and microwave meals, or I could enjoy my food."

As a single guy. The matter-of-fact statement intrigued her, made her want to ask him more questions. Why was he single? Why did he sound so sure he would stay that way?

Instead, she tilted her wine glass toward him. "The meal was a charming gesture. Thank you."

A corner of his mouth turned upward. "I have a confession to make."

Her heart began to beat a little faster. "You do?"

The smile deepened, quickly becoming irresistible. "I hoped you'd be charmed."

This was where she should smile seductively. Maybe twirl her hair and bat her lashes. Even trail a finger down his bicep. The problem was, Bree didn't do flirting. The only times she had attempted it she'd either knocked things over or came across about as sexy as a lost puppy. Since she really liked Rylan, she wasn't going to scare him off by trying.

"Do you live in Roaring Springs?" She almost groaned out loud. Just because she didn't flirt, did she have to turn the conversation around and make it sound like a job interview?

Rylan didn't appear to notice. Leaning back in his chair, he stretched his long legs in front of him. Although he had drunk one glass of wine at the start of the meal, he'd switched to water because he was driving. He took a sip before he spoke. "Not quite. I was born near Denver, but I joined the army when I was eighteen. When I got out, I went into business and traveled around a lot. But I always planned to settle down in Colorado, and—" He broke off abruptly, making her wonder what he'd been about to say. "I had an army buddy who talked about his home here in Roaring Springs. When I sold the business, I found a ranch a few miles west of here."

"You're a rancher in your spare time?" She raised her brows at him.

He laughed. "I'm a lot of things in my spare time."

"I can see that." She started to count on her fingers. "Soldier. Chef. Rancher. Art promoter."

She wasn't sure she could pinpoint exactly what it was that changed about his manner. It was as if her words made him watchful. "I'm new to the art world. As you can probably tell."

Bree frowned, sensing that he was closing down a line of conversation that made him uncomfortable. Since she didn't know him well enough to prod further, she was forced to let it go. However, the knowledge that he could be hiding something nagged at her. What bothered her even more was the idea that, after knowing him for less than a week, she cared that this man might be keeping secrets.

"You said you went into the army at eighteen." She decided on a different approach. "Didn't you come back to visit your family between then and now?"

He hunched a shoulder. "There was no one to visit. I'm an only child. My father died when I was twelve, and cancer took my mom just before I enlisted."

Bree sensed a whole world of pain behind those words. Reaching across the table, she took his hand. "I'm sorry."

He responded with a slight smile. "I'm thirty-four. Being on my own is what I do best."

"Coming from such a large extended family, I can't imagine how that would feel."

Rylan looked around the spacious, elegantly furnished loft apartment. "I guess being a Colton has its advantages." It was the same assumption many people made, but somehow it hurt more coming from him. As Bree made a movement to withdraw her hand, Rylan tightened his grip. "Hey." His gaze scanned her face. "What did I say?"

Usually, she avoided explanations, but his opinion mattered. "Thanks to my mom's tenacity, my dyslexia was diagnosed early. I went to a public school for pupils with learning disabilities, not a private school. Our parents wanted to keep us grounded, so they made sure Trey and I had chores on the farm. I grew up loved and cherished, but I was taught that working hard, not money, is the key to success." She cleared her throat. "So when I wanted to pursue art as a career, my mom and dad were unsure if I was capable of meeting the academic demands of a college course. To show them what I could do, I paid my own way through art school with a series of side jobs."

"I didn't mean—"

"I came into my inheritance on my twenty-fifth birthday. I'm now twenty-seven." She waved a hand to indicate her surroundings. "The gallery, my business, my *reputation*, this apartment… You think I achieved all that in just over two years?"

"Bree, I'm sorry." Rylan caught hold of her free hand, stopping it from fluttering. He held both her hands in a strong, warm clasp. "I jumped to an incorrect conclusion, and I've offended you."

She exhaled slowly. "No, I'm the one who should apologize. I overreacted. Sometimes the name Colton can be a burden."

He bent his head, grazing the knuckles of her right hand lightly with his lips. The action sent pleasurable little bursts of heat shimmering along her nerve endings. "Tell me what you did."

"Hmm?" She'd been too focused on the sensation of his mouth on her flesh to concentrate on the words.

"How did you build up your business before you came into your inheritance?"

"Oh?" Were they still on that topic? "Even in art school, I was selling my own work for really good prices. I used the proceeds to buy new pieces, and before long, I was getting great returns on my investments."

He raised his brows in acknowledgment of her achievement and she allowed herself a little smile of pleasure.

"I was also making a name for myself in the art world, showcasing my own work and that of other African American artists. That was how Wise Gal was born. When it came to finding a site for the gallery, real estate in the Diamond was low in price with incentives for new businesses, so it was the obvious place."

Rylan smiled. "Wise Gal? I figured it was a joke, but I can see it has a deeper meaning for you."

Bree nodded, pleased at his understanding. "Growing up in a family of overachievers was hard. I didn't make those childhood milestones on time and, as a consequence, felt like I was always running faster than my cousins just to keep up." She gave a self-conscious laugh. "While my family was worrying about me, I was always aware that being different is an important part of who I am. I don't necessarily see my dyslexia as a gift, but I believe it is linked to my creativity. It may sound corny, but I feel my artistic vision is stronger than my ability to see characters on a page."

The way Rylan was looking at her made her breath

catch in her throat. "That's a very inspiring way to view your condition."

"You wouldn't say that if you heard my language when I try to read without text-to-speech software," she said. "But to return to your comment about the gallery name... Yes, it's a play on words. I may not be a wise gal in the traditional sense, but the little Colton cousin who couldn't speak in sentences until she was nearly five hasn't done too badly."

"I'd say you've done very well." Rylan's voice was deep and smooth, like cream poured over chocolate. It made her insides melt.

Conscious that she was gazing into his eyes and clutching his hands as if she might never let go, Bree roused herself from her trance. "Let's take the dishes through to the kitchen, and I'll load the machine." Reluctantly, she stood. "The least I can do is take charge of the clean-up operation."

She was smiling up at him as she got to her feet, but the smile faded when he rose with her. His nearness was a dangerous reminder of an attraction that could easily spin out of control. With only inches between them, desire rippled through her, driving the breath from her lungs. She saw an answering flare in the depths of Rylan's eyes.

For an instant, his gaze hooked her and held her, refusing to let her go. Then he blinked, and the spell was broken.

"I'll make coffee." His voice was slightly husky. "Point me in the direction of your machine."

"Follow me." Bree carried their plates through to the open-plan kitchen. "I was out of coffee, but I got some from the store at lunch time." She indicated a cabinet above the coffeemaker. "The new pack is in there."

As she bent to open the dishwasher, she heard Rylan searching through the shelves. After a minute or two, he closed the door. "I can't find the coffee."

Bree straightened. "Are you one of those guys like my dad?" she teased. "If it doesn't jump out at you the first time, you just give up?"

"Ahem." He crooked a finger at her. "Come and find it for me, wise gal."

Chuckling, Bree went to stand beside him. Since she knew exactly where she had placed the coffee, she suspected this was a ruse to get her close to him. If so, she was happy to play along.

Except…where *was* the coffee? She turned her head, frowning at Rylan over her shoulder. "It was right here." She indicated the empty spot on the shelf where she had placed the new pack of coffee beans earlier that day.

"Hey." He put his hands on her shoulders, turning her to face him. "It's not a problem. There's an all-night convenience store on Second Street, right? I can just—"

"It's not that." She stopped biting her lip long enough to blurt out what was bothering her. "This has happened twice today."

His grip tightened slightly. "You've already lost your coffee once before now?" Although the words were light, his gaze was intent.

"No." Quickly, Bree told him about the incident with her recorder. She brought her hands up across her body to grip her forearms. "I think of my brain as a filing cabinet. Because I'm dyslexic, the drawers weren't la-beled properly when I was born. That means I have to be extra organized. If I'm not, I can file something in the wrong drawer and lose it forever. I don't make mistakes like this."

"You're under a lot of pressure with a big show coming up," Rylan reminded her.

She tilted her chin. "I accepted what happened with the recorder as a mistake on my part for just that reason. Maybe I mislaid it, and someone found it and returned it to my office. But this?" She gestured to the empty space in the cupboard. "I *know* I bought coffee, and I know I put it right there."

"Does anyone else have a key to your apartment?" Rylan asked.

"Only my mother, but why would she come down here without telling me just to move my coffee?" The question struck her as so ridiculous that she had to bite back a laugh, even though she didn't find the situation remotely amusing. Could she actually be losing her mind?

"I don't want to alarm you, but this is classic stalking behavior."

"Is it?" Bree wrinkled her brow. "How do you know that?"

There was a momentary pause before he answered. "I must have read it somewhere. The stalker moves, damages or hides the victim's belongs. It unnerves her, making her think she's imagining things. Has anything else been happening lately that could be linked to this?"

She swayed toward him slightly, her mind on the emails. Was it possible the two things were related? She instinctively trusted Rylan, but she barely knew him. Did she really want to start sharing secrets with him?

* * *

Tell me about the emails, Bree.

For a second, Rylan thought she might be about to open up to him. Then she gave him that too-bright smile and he knew it wasn't going to happen. Had he blown it with his comment about stalking? The words had left his lips before he'd thought them through. Even though he regretted them now, the comparison was accurate. In his work as a private security consultant, Rylan had protected several celebrities who'd been threatened by obsessive fans. He knew most of the tactics.

Although he hadn't seen the emails, he was convinced this was the start of some low-level scare tactics. He was willing to bet the coffee would turn up again in a day or two, in the exact place Bree had left it. The person who was doing this would be close by, observing her confusion and distress, enjoying the impact of his actions. The biggest problem was that Rylan knew from experience that most stalkers weren't content to stick with the minor stuff. Having fixated on Bree, this guy would soon be planning something bigger and bolder.

She'd said that the only person who had access to her apartment was her mom. Although Bree might try to brush this aside as a forgetful episode, Rylan wasn't convinced. Which meant someone other than Audrey was able to get into Bree's home. He didn't want to frighten her, but the image of a shadowy figure slipping into her bedroom while she was asleep chilled his blood.

"You should change your locks."

Bree blinked. "You seriously think someone came in here?"

"You told me your family has been having a few

problems. A brick was thrown through the gallery window a week ago. Your recorder and coffee going missing may be unconnected." He became aware that his hands were still on her shoulders, and he slid them slowly down to her upper arms. "But it couldn't hurt to tighten up your personal security."

Her perfect white teeth caught briefly on the plump cushion of her lower lip, and everything Rylan knew about himself started to unravel. *Tough. Professional. In control.* In that moment, he was none of those things. All he wanted to do was wrap Bree up and protect her from anything that could cause her harm.

Could he really have developed such strong feelings for a woman he barely knew? He almost laughed out loud. There was no "could have" about it. The first time he had seen Bree, he had been rocked by an emotion so tender, wild and all-consuming, he knew his life had changed. Turning his back on her now wasn't an option, even though he was terrified by what was happening to him.

Rylan didn't do vulnerability. The son of an alcoholic, abusive father and a downtrodden mother, his early life had been about dodging the blows—physical and emotional. Although his father's death freed him from fear, the damage had been done. *Worthless. Weak. Cry baby. Mommy's boy.* He'd spent the rest of his life fighting those labels. Now he'd met Bree and, for the first time, his iron control had snapped.

Was he prepared to give his feelings a name beyond heady physical desire? After all, he had known her less than a week. As for how much he wanted her... Rylan had never known it was possible to feel this way. His whole body was humming with awareness of her. It was so intense that he was waging a constant internal fight to stop himself from saying to hell with the disguise. For once in his life, maybe he should forget he was a stand-up guy. Just follow his instincts, lean in closer and taste those pink parted lips…

With an effort, he forced his attention back to the subject at hand. "Your brother is the sheriff of Bradford County. Why not ask his advice?"

The corners of her mouth turned down. "I love Trey very much, but I don't want him marching in here in full-on overprotective-big-brother mode. Not when I don't even know if there's a problem."

Rylan shoved a hand through his hair. He could see why her parents were half-crazy with worry about her. There *was* a problem, but Bree was determined not to face it. Since he wasn't supposed to know about the emails, he couldn't use them as evidence that she was in danger. Instead, all he had was the brick through the gallery window and the possibility that someone was moving her property.

Rylan was like a man caught between two fires. His determination to protect her was stronger than ever. It was no longer a favor to Blaine. This was all about Bree. But if he was going to guard her properly, he had to stick close. And that meant enduring more of this agony.

As Bree reached up a tentative hand and stroked his cheek, her touch hit the center of his chest, making his heart beat faster. It also connected with another point, one south of his belt buckle.

Her smile was shy. "The meal was delicious."

Catching a hold of her wrist, he dropped a kiss onto her palm. "Thank you for a wonderful evening."

As she rose on the tips of her toes to move closer, Rylan sensed her nervousness. "Is it over?"

He almost groaned aloud. This was the worst kind of torture. Clasping her hands to his chest, he pressed his lips lightly to the corner of her mouth. "I have to go. I'm needed at the ranch." He didn't feel good about the lie but consoled himself that it was necessary.

"Oh." Her eyelids fluttered, long lashes shadowing her cheeks. "Of course, you have animals to care for."

She was probably picturing a traditional ranch with cattle or horses. Since she was unlikely to ever visit his home, there was no reason for Rylan to explain that the reality was very different. Even so, his lips quirked into a smile at the thought of his assortment of misfits.

Bree's golden eyes scanned his face. Apparently satisfied at what she saw—he was fairly sure there was no hiding the regret he was feeling—she gave a tiny nod. "I can't cook, but maybe I can take you out to dinner to return the favor?"

His smile widened. "I'd like that. A lot."

She reached up and hooked a hand behind his neck, pulling his face down until they were nose-to-nose. With her breath fanning his lips, her voice was barely a whisper. "So would I."

When she kissed him, she tasted of the strawberries and melon they'd eaten for dessert. Her lips were deliciously sweet, tender and warm on his, and as their mouths parted and tongues entwined, his thoughts shut down. All he could smell was Bree's light floral perfume. All he could hear was her cotton skirt rustling against his jeans. All he could feel was the heat of their bodies and how good she felt in his arms.

Breaking that kiss was like a physical pain, but he couldn't let things go any further. "I really do have to go." Bree looked slightly dazed as she walked with him to the door. "Make sure you lock this behind me."

She laughed. "You've met my mom, right?"

Where was this going? Had he given something away? Cautiously, he nodded. "Yes."

"Locking my door at night is one of her obsessions. That and eating plenty of fiber."

He grinned. "I'll settle for the door."

When it was closed, he waited until he heard the lock click into place before making his way down the stairs that led to the parking lot at the side of the Diamond. Bree might be careless with her personal security, but Rylan knew she would be safe for the rest of the night. How could he be sure? Because he would be hunkered down in his car, watching over her apartment until daybreak.

Chapter 3

Dawn was turning the summit of Pine Peak gold when Rylan eased his body into a more upright position. Although he hadn't been expecting to spend the night in his vehicle, years of conducting surveillance had taught him to be prepared for any eventuality. As well as his licensed firearm, he had an overnight bag with toiletries and a change of clothes in the trunk. He also carried bottled water and snacks. Since the temperature had dropped below freezing, the items he had been most grateful for were a warm blanket and his woolen beanie.

Turning his head from side to side, Rylan attempted to ease the tightness in his neck muscles. The view through his windshield was of the Wise Gal Gallery with Bree's apartment above it. To the rear, the mountains were slowly being revealed by the rising sun. The streetlights of Second Street curved away to his right. To his left, across the empty parking lot, the Diamond was still in darkness.

He shifted his body to face forward and a flicker caught his attention. Barely a movement, it was enough to have him diving out of the car and running toward the gallery. As he approached the entrance, he heard a soft groan from the base of the stairs that led to Bree's apartment.

Rylan bit back a curse as he measured the distance to his vehicle and weighed his options. Return to get his weapon from the trunk and risk an intruder getting up those steps? Or remain unarmed and take his chances?

Another groan, clearly the sound of someone in pain, took the decision out of his hands. Cautiously, he moved forward. As his eyes grew accustomed to the darkness, he was able to make out the shape of a person lying on the floor.

Dropping to his knees, Rylan withdrew his cell phone from his pocket and activated the flashlight. Its beam revealed a large man wearing a security guard uniform. Although he was lying on his back on the concrete, the guy raised an arm to shield his eyes from the light.

"Where are you hurt?" Rylan tried to remember what Bree had said the guard's name was. Swanick? Swinson? *Swanson.* That was it. David Swanson.

"Hit my head." David struggled into a sitting position. "Low-life pushed me as he ran past."

"Take it easy." Rylan hooked an arm under his shoulders and eased him backward until he was leaning against the wall. "I'll call 911."

"No." The other man raised a hand and felt the back of his head. "The skin isn't broken. There's hardly even a lump."

Rylan wasn't convinced. "You can't be too careful with a head injury."

"I know the drill." David gave a shaky laugh. "If I get any severe headaches, blurred vision or dizziness, I'll see a doctor."

"What happened?" Rylan asked. "Have you been on duty all night?" If so, David had been slacking. Rylan hadn't seen him patrolling the area.

David winced as he shook his head. "I start work at seven. Even though the sun doesn't come up until about six forty-five at this time of year, I always follow the same routine. My apartment is over the Yogurt Hut." He jerked a thumb in the direction of the Diamond. "When I leave home, I check the perimeter of the parking lot before I go into the gallery and sign in."

Rylan frowned. At this time of year, David would need to use a flashlight to do his first patrol. He was certain he'd have observed any signs of light or movement. "I was in my vehicle, but I didn't see you."

"You wouldn't have." There was a trace of bitterness in the security guard's voice. "As soon as I stepped out of my apartment, I saw someone heading toward the gallery."

Rylan tried to picture the scene. Was it likely that David could have noticed someone he had missed? It was a possibility. The Yogurt Hut was in the far left corner of the Diamond at a point just on the periphery of what Rylan was able to see from where he had been sitting in his car. Although he had taken time to observe each angle at regular intervals, he didn't have his surveillance equipment. Consequently, a constant 360-degree view had not been available to him.

Even though the thought chilled him, he accepted that the other man could have seen something he hadn't. "What made you suspicious?" he asked. "Couldn't it have been someone like you, just heading to work?"

"Like I said, I do this every morning. *No one* is around at this time. When I saw the guy approaching the gallery, I was even more surprised since Bree doesn't open the doors until about eight thirty most mornings. As I caught up with him, what really shook me was that he was heading for these stairs. The only place that can be accessed from here is Bree's apartment, and why would anyone be sneaking around before it's fully light?"

"Did you get a look at him?" Rylan asked.

"No. He had a hood pulled up, hiding his face. When I challenged him, and asked what he was doing here, he shoved me. That's when I fell back and hit my head," David said. "While I was lying on the ground, he ran off."

"Bree said the security systems were updated after the recent attack. Are there cameras?"

"Not here. The closed-circuit TV is focused on the front of the gallery. There won't be any footage of this incident." David sat up straighter, directing a curious look at Rylan "Why are *you* here so early?"

It was time to think fast. Rylan couldn't guarantee that he hadn't been seen during his overnight vigil. He may as well tell the truth, even if he invented a reason.

"Engine trouble." He grimaced. "Had to spend the night in my vehicle."

"That was a cruel bit of luck." Staggering slightly, David made an effort to get to his feet. Rylan gripped his elbow, supporting him until he was able to remain steady. "Couldn't you get a tow?"

Rylan ignored the question. "Let's go into the gallery. I'll make you a drink and we can call the police."

Although David took out his keys as he accompanied Rylan toward the huge glass doors, he didn't seem to think much of that suggestion. "There's nothing to tell them."

"This guy was on his way up to Bree's apartment." Once they were inside the foyer, Rylan leaned on the reception counter while David deactivated the alarm. "That needs to be logged. What if he comes back and reaches his destination next time?"

Even as he made the comment that caused his blood to run cold, his analytical brain was assessing the situation. If Bree was the intended target, the timing was odd. Why not try to get to her during the night instead of waiting until dawn? Unfortunately, the only person who could answer that question would be the stalker himself.

They went through to the staff kitchen. While Rylan fixed coffee, David went to the first-aid locker in search of painkillers.

When they were seated at a table, Rylan studied the other man thoughtfully. David was only of average height, but his physique was powerful. "Boxing? Or MMA?"

David gave an appreciative grin. "A little of both.

Although I don't have much time these days." He returned the measuring glance. "You?"

Rylan laughed. "I boxed a little when I first joined the army. Now, the only fights I get into are with a temperamental donkey." Aware of the other man's look of surprise, he shook his head. "Long story. At least we know one thing about your attacker."

David paused in the act of sipping his coffee. "We do?"

"If he knocked you over, he must be a big guy."

The security guard shrugged. "He caught me by surprise. I didn't get a sense of his size."

Frustrated by the lack of information, Rylan held up his cell phone. "You want me to call the police?"

"Please." David showed him a trembling hand. "I'm still shaken up."

It was only as he began to relay the details of the incident to a dispatcher that Rylan realized he was doing the very thing Bree didn't want. He knew enough about her to be aware of how much she valued her privacy. He could already hear her skepticism. There was no proof that the guy who pushed David had intended to harm her. Was he letting his protectiveness toward her override his common sense? Definitely. Where she was concerned, he would choose caution every time.

He only hoped she would see his point of view.

Although Bree went through her morning routine in her usual first-light daze, a new awareness forced its way through the brain fog. Her body was on high alert, moving fast instead of dawdling, conspiring to get her out of the apartment and into work faster. Why?

The answer to that was easy. Because Rylan would be at the gallery.

She had always believed there was a possibility the bad-relationship fairy had been present at her birth. A few months into her first serious relationship, she had realized that the man who had sworn undying love was actually more interested in the Colton money. That could have been bad luck. However, when it happened a second time, she started questioning her judgment and eventually came to the conclusion that dating was not for her

Being out of that whole relationship loop hadn't bothered her. Right now, she was too focused on her career. Maybe she'd feel differently in a few years when her biological clock started ticking. That was what she'd told herself. And it had been true. Until now.

Although she had initiated last night's earth-shattering kiss, Rylan had still left. It would have been easy to have woken this morning feeling dispirited and spurned. Instead, she felt curiously optimistic. She had made her feelings plain. She had suspected all along that Rylan felt the same and his response to the kiss confirmed it.

After he'd gone, she'd indulged in some lengthy analysis of his behavior, while also reliving the heady sensation of his lips on hers. By walking away instead of taking things a step further, was he saying she meant more than a quick fling? The thought made her shiver with pleasure.

I hope so. Because he already meant so much more to her. There. The thought was out there. Scary but true.

After showering, she studied her hair in the mirror. She loved her curls, but they could be rebellious. They definitely needed to be kept in their place when she was working. Giving her hair a quick all-over spritz with her favorite macadamia oil product, she pulled her wild locks back into a ruthlessly tight braid.

When Bree purchased this property, she'd had a walk-in closet built. Her father had laughed and asked how long it would be before she needed another one. As she rifled through the overflowing rails, she realized Calvin Colton had been right. She either needed more space, or she would have to part with some of her precious vintage treasures. But how would she choose which of her 1950s cocktail dresses or rock-chick biker jackets to give away?

She pulled on black leggings, a short floral dress and knee-high brown boots. Over the top, she layered a long Scandinavian knit jacket in bright geometric blocks and twisted a contrasting scarf loosely around her neck. Moisturizing sunscreen, a touch of lip gloss, a spray of perfume, and she was a splash of color dashing past the mirror next to her front door.

Two minutes later, she regarded the man seated behind her desk with a wary expression. "I'm always pleased to see you, Trey. I also know how busy you are, so I'm guessing this isn't a social call."

Her brother grinned. "Most people start with good morning. How are things with you, sis? Still struggling to decide which you hate most…morning or anchovies?"

"The answer depends on whether I'm listening to my alarm clock or ordering pizza." Bree flopped into the chair opposite him. "Seriously, why are you here?"

His expression became serious. "We got a report of

a person behaving suspiciously close to these premises just before seven a.m. A security guard…" He checked his notes. "A guy named Swanson was attacked."

Bree jerked upright. "David? Is he okay?"

"Fine. He had a fright, but he wasn't seriously injured. He's already back at work." Her brother leaned forward with his hands clasped on the desk. "What bothers me is that Swanson thought the intruder was intending to climb the steps to your apartment."

A cold trickle of fear tracked its way down Bree's spine. She pushed it aside, frowning over the vagueness of Trey's statement. "David *thought* that was his intention? A minor injury and the suspicion that a man may have been planning to climb the stairs to my apartment? Was that really the most pressing item on your schedule this morning, Trey?"

He had the grace to look sheepish. "I wanted to check and make sure you were okay. The guy who called this in—"

She held up a hand. "I thought David Swanson called you?"

"No." He consulted his notes. "The 911 dispatcher spoke to a Rylan Bennet."

Bree rubbed the bridge of her nose. It was early. She was caffeine deprived and Trey's presence had taken her by surprise. That must be why nothing was making sense. Because why would Rylan be here before the gallery opened?

"You know him?" Trey was watching her closely. Nothing escaped her brother.

"He manages a group of artists who are taking part in my next show. Mom introduced him to me."

The Audrey Colton seal of approval acted like a charm, and Trey relaxed back into his chair. "Since I'm here, help me out. It's only been a week since someone threw a brick through the gallery window. You've been getting threatening emails. So far, I don't have any leads on who is responsible. Has anything happened since to make you feel uncomfortable?"

Thoughts of her recorder and coffee being moved flashed through her mind, but she suppressed them. If Trey found out she was being harassed, she would be transported back to her childhood. He would be the big, strong brother and she would be in his shadow once again. She loved him, but she didn't want to hand control of her life over to him. Not unless she was forced to.

A tiny voice at the back of her mind asked the question, *Shouldn't Trey be the one to decide?* If the strange incidents were linked to the broken window, and now this attack on David, wasn't it time to confide in the sheriff? A second voice spoke up, drowning out the first. *What if they aren't linked?*

"Bree?" Trey's prompt brought her back down to earth. "Is there something you want to tell me?"

"No." She looked him up and down. "But there is something I need to ask you."

He raised his brows. "Ask away."

"Why am I on the wrong side of my desk?"

Laughing, Trey got to his feet. When he held out his arms, Bree rose and was enveloped in a hug that lifted her off her feet.

When he released her, Trey gave her a long look. "You'd tell me if there was a problem?"

"I'd tell you if there was something you could help me with."

He frowned. "That's not the same thing."

She patted his cheek. "It's all you're getting. Now scoot. I have work to do."

"Unfortunately, so do I." He turned reluctantly toward the door. "How about lunch next week?"

"As long as you're buying, it's a date." Bree waited for him to close the door before she sank into her chair. Almost immediately, the dance music ringtone on her cell phone signaled an incoming call. A glance at the display showed her Rylan's name.

She didn't bother with a greeting. "I need to speak to you."

"Do you like dogs?"

The question threw her off balance. "What do you mean?"

"Dogs, wise gal. You know. Four legs. Tails that wag. Make a noise called barking. Do you like them?"

"Yes, but…"

"Good. Come out to the parking lot."

She started to protest, but he'd already ended the call. *What* was going on? Feeling as if she'd entered a parallel universe, Bree left her office and walked the length of the gallery.

All this, and I still haven't had my first cup of coffee.

When she stepped outside, two things hit her. One was the chill breeze. The other was Rylan's magnetism. Dressed in jeans, boots and a worn leather jacket, he was leaning against the hood of his car. The smile that lit his eyes when he saw her did something wicked to her insides.

Bree didn't return the smile. She wasn't here to be charmed. Since the last time she'd seen him, he'd somehow gotten involved in the incident with David, and he'd just given her an order. She wasn't sure she liked either of those circumstances.

A slight frown creased her brow as she crossed the distance between them. "What do you want, Rylan? I have a lot to do today."

The blue of his eyes darkened, like clouds crossing a summer sky. "Hey. What is this?"

"My brother told me you called in the attack on David." Although she let him take her hands, she didn't return his grip. "Why were you here before the gallery opened this morning?"

He hesitated for a few seconds. "I slept in my car last night. I told David it was because I had engine trouble. That wasn't the real reason."

Bree felt as though her world was spinning further off course with every passing second. "What was the real reason?"

"I wanted to make sure you were safe."

When her family became overprotective, Bree bristled and fought back. It was a reaction to her childhood, when her parents had tried too hard to shield her from the effects of her dyslexia. However, in this instance, instead of Rylan's admission provoking a similar response in her, it made her feel warm and comforted. Swaying toward him, she rested her forehead on his chest.

After a moment or two, he ducked his head to get a look at her face. "Are we okay?"

She nodded. "But you didn't have to do that."

The look he gave her was charged with so much

electricity it almost threw her backward. Any doubts she may have had about his sincerity were gone. "Believe me, I did."

How could she begin to explain it to him? *No, Rylan, you didn't. Because you had a place to stay. In my apartment. In my bed...*

Changing the subject was probably a good idea. "Why were you in such a hurry to get me out here?"

"I wanted you to meet someone."

Bree's emotions went on a new roller coaster ride as he strode toward the passenger side of his car. *Someone?* After a minute or two, he returned with a leash attached to...a large mop.

"What is it?" She stared at the creature in fascination.

Rylan laughed. "This is Papadum. He's a komondor, a Hungarian sheepdog."

"I can't tell which end is which," Bree said.

"Well, they perform very different functions." Rylan lifted the dog's long corded bangs so Bree could see his eyes. The other end of the animal wagged. "I wouldn't recommend getting them mixed up."

Laughing, she stroked Papadum's head. The wagging increased. "Papadum? Were you craving Asian food when you named him?"

"He was abandoned. The owner of an Indian restaurant found him in a dumpster when he took the trash out one night."

"How sad." Bree stooped to hug Papadum and the dog licked her cheek.

"See, you figured out the right end," Rylan quipped. "That could have gone horribly wrong if you hadn't."

"Rylan!" Bree gave a choke of laughter. "Your dog is lovely, but why is he here?"

"Ah." He gave her a sidelong glance. "I thought you might like to borrow him."

Chapter 4

Bree was regarding Rylan as if he'd gone mad. "You thought I might like to *borrow* your dog?"

"Hear me out." From the look on her face, the outcome hung in the balance. Although she appeared bemused, there was a definite flash of something more dangerous in the golden depths of her eyes. "Papadum may look like Mother Nature's idea of a joke, but he's a great guard dog. He's calm with strong protective instincts. He would defend his family with his life."

"Apart from the fact that I don't need protection, I live in an apartment and work long hours." Bree looked at the dog, who was sitting between them, his dreadlocks stirring in the breeze. "Papadum is big. He looks like he needs plenty of exercise."

"That's where I come in. Bring him to the gallery

each day and I'll take him for walks." She was still viewing him with suspicion. "And you'll be doing me a huge favor."

"How?" The single word was hardly encouraging.

"I have a number of rescue dogs. I've just taken in a new guy, and he's unsettled the dynamics. Papadum could use some space from all the drama." It was a white lie. Papadum was the most laid-back dog in the world. He wasn't part of the problem, but Rylan figured Bree didn't need to know that. "Plus, you get to hang out with the coolest canine in town."

The dog chose that moment to wave one mop-like paw in Bree's direction. "See?" Rylan said. "Papadum thinks it's a good idea."

"Why do I feel like I'm being manipulated? By both of you?" She rolled her eyes. "I'll give it a trial. Two days. If it doesn't work out, Papadum goes home with you."

Rylan resisted the impulse to punch the air in celebration. Papadum would take better care of her than any sophisticated alarm system. "It's a deal."

"What does he eat?" Bree asked.

"That's a whole other conversation." He handed her Papadum's leash. "We can talk about it later when we decide where you're taking me for dinner."

Before she could reply, a car pulled up next to Rylan's.

"Clearly, I am not meant to get any work done today." Although the words were spoken under her breath, the smile on Bree's face was genuine as she stepped forward to greet the woman who emerged from the vehicle. "I wasn't expecting to see you this morning, Mom."

Audrey Douglas Colton was an attractive African American woman in her early sixties. She had medium brown skin, short dark brown hair with a hint of gray and glowing golden-brown eyes. It was obvious that Bree got her stunning looks from her mother.

"I had half an hour to spare before my volunteer shift at the community hub." Audrey kissed her daughter's cheek before turning to survey the dog. "Oh, my. Isn't this amazing? What is it?"

"It's a dog. His name is Papadum. He's going to be staying with me for a while."

Audrey's gaze met Rylan's for a second. He read the question in her eyes. *This is your doing?* He answered with a brief nod, and saw her features relax. Anything that kept her daughter safe was fine by her.

Bree linked her arm through her mom's and steered her toward the gallery. "Believe it or not, I haven't had coffee yet."

Audrey looked shocked. "Are you ill?"

Bree laughed. "Just busy."

Rylan held the door open for them. "I'll leave you ladies now."

"Oh, please join us." Audrey placed a hand on his arm. "I'd love to know how my student protégés are getting on."

He followed them toward Bree's office with a feeling of disquiet. He liked Audrey a lot, but he wasn't a good enough actor to sustain lengthy questioning on the subject of African American art. He hoped she'd remember he was a bodyguard playing a role and go easy on him.

Bree ducked into her assistant's office to request coffee. From the squeals of delight that ensued, Rylan figured Papadum was having an impact on Kasey.

When they went into her office, Bree released the dog from his leash. Papadum immediately commenced a detailed inspection of the room. Bree took a seat at her desk and gestured toward two other chairs before turning to her mom. "How's Dad?"

"Oh, you know. Worrying about the farm, as usual. While the rest of the Colton family is celebrating the unseasonably cold weather because it means the ski season could be extended, Calvin is concerned about the impact on his animals."

"To be fair, that is his job," Bree said.

Audrey's smile was mischievous. "I know. But when I want him to admire the winter wonderland outside the farmhouse, it ruins the effect if he says, *I wonder if I should move the calves to the south barn.*"

Kasey entered at that moment, carrying a tray laden with mugs of coffee, cream, sugar and a plate of cookies. Rylan rose to help her, and she smiled gratefully as he took her burden from her and placed it on the desk. When he returned to his seat, both Bree and Audrey were staring down at the tray. While Audrey's expression was one of surprise, Bree's was more like shock.

"Aren't those the cups Nonnie gave you?" Audrey asked. The bright hand-painted cups depicted a variety of different animals.

"Yes." There was a hollow note to Bree's voice that Rylan didn't like.

"I didn't know you'd started using them."

"I haven't. I wouldn't." Bree turned to look at Kasey. "Where did you get these from?"

"They were in the kitchen next door. I thought you must have bought them to brighten the place up." Kasey looked bewildered. "Is there something wrong?"

Even though she smiled at her assistant, Rylan could tell Bree's expression was forced. "It's not a problem. Thank you for the drinks."

When Kasey had gone, Audrey turned to Bree. "Care to share?"

In the instant before she answered, Bree flashed a glance in Rylan's direction. It was a plea. *Work with me.* In response, he pressed his knee lightly against hers beneath the desk. Her shoulders relaxed slightly.

"I know what must have happened," Bree said. "I was sorting out my own artwork for the show. At the same time, I'd been cleaning out the display shelf where I keep Nonnie's cups. Nonnie was my mom's mother," she explained to Rylan. "She was also the person from whom I inherited my artistic ability. When I was a child, she painted this set of cups for me. They're too precious to use."

"They're beautiful." Rylan admired one of the intricate hand-painted pieces.

"The box containing the pieces from the shelf in my apartment must have somehow gotten mixed up with one of the boxes containing my paintings." Bree turned to Audrey with a shrug. "It's easily done when everyone is so busy."

Audrey's shrewd gaze assessed her daughter for a moment or two. "Is that the best you've got?"

Bree gave her a look of near-perfect innocence. "What do you mean?"

Audrey pursed her lips and shook her head. Glancing at her watch, she picked up her tote. "Lucky for you, I have to go or I'll be late for my shift." She got to her feet and stooped to kiss Bree's cheek. "Work on that story before we meet again, loved one. It has more holes than a piece of Swiss cheese."

After she'd gone, Bree gave a little sigh. "I hate lying to her."

"Don't worry," Rylan said. "She didn't believe you."

Bree gave a little laugh. "I had almost convinced myself that the coffee-thing, like the recorder, was due to my own absent-mindedness. But this?" She gently touched one of the cups. "There's no mistaking this."

"Someone is sending you a message," Rylan said tersely, "and it isn't a pleasant one." When she raised her eyes to his, he could see the fear in their depths. "It's time to tell me all of it, Bree."

She nodded. "Not here. Do you like Thai food?"

He raised her hand to his lips. "You just found my weakness."

She turned to look at Papadum, who had fallen asleep and looked like a large, unusual rug. "AppeThaizer allows dogs. I'll make reservations for seven o'clock."

"Okay." Rylan got to his feet. "I'll be in the promotions office if you need me."

When he reached the door, he turned back to look at her. She was already reaching into her desk, but there was a crease between her brows that troubled him. He wanted to go to her and smooth it away. More than anything, he wanted to tell her that he was there to protect her.

Once Bree knew he was deceiving her, their closeness would be over. That scared him more than the

shadowy figure who was threatening her. He could deal
with the external danger, but he honestly didn't know
if he could cope with having to watch Bree walk away.

I should have smashed those cups and used the pieces
to slice your pretty face.

The voice Bree had chosen for her text-to-speech
software was light and female. Most of the time, she
found it soothing. Whenever she converted one of the
threatening emails to speech and listened to it, the gen-
tle tones somehow made the words even more frightening.

She gripped the edge of the desk with both hands,
feeling as though a pillow was being pressed over her
mouth and nose. Enough air was getting through to en-
able her to breathe. Just. But she was fighting to function. Each thought took a huge amount of effort.

She couldn't ignore this any longer. This time there
was a direct link between the emails and the person
moving her belongings.

Rylan. Every instinct urged her to go to him. Relief
flooded her veins at the thought of his strong, reassuring presence. She was halfway out of her seat when the
alarm on her cell phone buzzed.

"Two o'clock appointment." This voice was different. Robotic and mechanical. She'd set the reminder for
ten minutes before her meeting with Lucas Brewer, the
lighting engineer she employed for her shows.

Biting back an exclamation of annoyance, she headed
for the hall. Papadum, who had been snoring like a

freight train for most of the day, decided to accompany her.

"I guess you must be thirsty, big guy." Bree patted the end that didn't wag.

Pausing in the kitchen, she found a bowl and filled it with water. Leaving Papadum to the noisiest drinking she had ever heard, she went into the bathroom. A glance in the mirror confirmed her worst fears. She looked flustered and wan at the same time. Splashing cold water on her face helped a little. A fresh spray of perfume and a new application of lip gloss restored a little more normality. With a nod at her reflection, she returned to her office to collect the documents for her meeting.

"Oh, my goodness!" She gazed at Papadum in horror. "What happened to you?"

The dog was seated next to her desk. Long frothy strands hung from his jowls. He made a soft moaning sound.

Since Rylan was at the opposite end of the building, Bree decided to call him. "Papadum is foaming at the mouth."

"I'm on my way."

Bree ducked into Kasey's office. "Tell Lucas I've been delayed." She thrust a file at her assistant. "Here's the lighting specification. I'll be with him as soon as I can."

She returned to her office and sat on the floor next to Papadum, stroking his back. The dog hiccupped miserably. Rylan arrived a few minutes later.

"I don't know what happened," Bree told him. "I

gave him a drink and left him alone in the kitchen for a few minutes. When I got back, he was like this."

He knelt next to Papadum. To Bree's surprise, he sniffed the dog's breath. "Do you by any chance use lemon-scented soap in your kitchen?"

"Um…yes."

Rylan pried Papadum's jaws open and gently shook the dog's head. A bar of soap fell out of his mouth and onto the rug. "Yeah. That was one of the things I meant to warn you about. Papadum eats a lot of things he shouldn't. Soap, socks, coins, nails, rocks… His best so far was my phone charger. Nature takes its course with most things, but he needed surgery to remove that."

"You loaned me a broken dog?" Bree huffed.

His face was inches from hers, his blue eyes alight with laughter. "Sorry about that."

"Anything else I should know?" She edged a little closer.

"When you ask him if he's been fed, he may not always give you an honest answer."

His arms closed around her and his lips met hers. The kiss was exactly what Bree needed. She felt safe, warm and protected. Giving a little murmur of appreciation, she pressed tight against him. The embrace didn't last long. Papadum raised a paw and struck Rylan on the shoulder. The move almost sent him sprawling face first to the floor.

"I think that means he needs more water." He grinned. "Although I have no sympathy for him."

Papadum rubbed his face affectionately along Rylan's arm, leaving a trail of lemon-scented foam.

Bree laughed. "Go see to your dog. I'm late for a meeting."

He got to his feet, holding out a hand to help her up. His gaze scanned her face. "Has something happened? Other than my crazy pet eating your soap?"

"Later. I'll tell you all of it then." Just being near him had given her new strength.

He took her face in his hands and pressed a kiss on her forehead. "Okay." Stooping, he ushered Papadum toward the door.

She drew in a breath. "Rylan?" He turned to look at her, and her nerve almost faltered. "You don't have to sleep in your car tonight."

The change in his expression almost sent her running back into his arms. Somehow, she managed to get her trembling limbs under control and make her way out into the gallery for her meeting.

"No one is ever going to believe I didn't train you to do this." Kasey had provided Rylan with a roll of paper towel, which he used to dry Papadum's dreadlocks. "Although I think you could have found a smarter way of getting her attention than eating her soap." The dog held up a heavy hairy paw. "Shaking hands? Yeah, that could have worked, but it's hard to see how it would have needed my intervention. Maybe you should have tried the non-stop sneezing thing you did that time when you caught a fly."

Once Papadum was restored to normality, Rylan decided to return him to Bree. The dog's purpose was to guard her after all. He couldn't do that if they were in different rooms.

The gallery was a vast open space. Having studied a floor plan of the building, Rylan knew there was ten thousand square feet of floor space. With its high ceilings and white walls, the former warehouse provided a unique opportunity to display large sculptures and paintings, as well as smaller pieces. Bree had made it bright, open and fun, with a strong sense of diversity.

Her own paintings were glorious. Celebrating people, African American women in particular, she had a knack for capturing the perfect moment. Characterized by bold angular shapes and brilliant colors, her pictures evoked feelings of heart and home. Little girls playing, women gossiping, family gatherings—all were treated with Bree's own unique empathy and quirky humor. Her signature was a simple letter *B*.

Rylan found her in an area that had been completely cleared, ready for the Spirit show. She was so deep in conversation with a dark-haired man about her own age that she didn't notice Rylan as he approached. They were standing side by side with their heads bent over a large sheet of paper. The guy's stance caught Rylan's attention. He was just a little too close to Bree, a little too attentive.

He tried to dismiss his unease, telling himself he was letting his feelings for Bree get the better of him. When Papadum saw Bree and gave a delighted bark, interrupting their conversation, Rylan had a chance to review his first impression. Instead of changing his mind, however, his opinion was reinforced.

Over Bree's head, her companion gave Rylan a look that was so laden with suspicion and jealousy it was almost comical. Almost. With everything that was going on, it immediately sent Rylan's protective instincts into overdrive.

"Hey, Papadum." Having finally figured out the dog's anatomy, Bree found his ears and scratched between them. Since that particular caress was Papadum's favorite thing in the whole world, he promptly fell at her feet in an ecstatic canine heap.

Laughing, Bree turned to Rylan. "He seems to have recovered."

"I don't think there'll be any lasting effects. Just hide the soap—and anything else that you consider inedible but that would fit down the gullet of a large, foolish dog—and everything will be fine."

"Is that a dog?" Although it was a common reaction to Papadum, when it came from the guy who was still standing way too close to Bree, Rylan found it irritating.

"Papadum is my new guard dog," Bree explained. "Oh, sorry. I forgot you two don't know each other. Rylan Bennet… Lucas Brewer. Lucas does the lighting for all my shows. Rylan manages a group of young artists who will be showcasing their work during Spirit."

Lucas tried to get away with a curt nod, but Rylan smiled and held out his hand. "Good to meet you."

The other man was forced to return his handshake and make eye contact. Did he get the stern warning Rylan flashed his way? He certainly pulled his hand away quickly and dropped his gaze fast. One thing was for sure, Rylan didn't think Lucas would forget him… and that had been his intention.

"I'll leave you to your meeting." Ignoring Lucas, Rylan spoke directly to Bree.

She smiled, apparently oblivious to any hostile undercurrents. "Papadum and I will see you later."

Rylan walked away, convinced he could feel Lucas's stare hitting a point just between his shoulder blades. The guy clearly had a thing for Bree. Did that mean he was the person harassing her? It was a big leap from one to the other, and possibly said more about Rylan's own insecurities than anything about the other man. Even so, he would be using all his resources to find out more about Lucas Brewer.

When he reached the promotions office, he checked his cell phone. Although he employed a full-time helper, Rylan liked to maintain a hands-on approach to the welfare of his animals. The personalized app he used allowed him to monitor what was going on at the ranch while he was away.

Not for the first time, he wondered what Bree would think if she could see his mismatched collection. *Ranch* described the property he had bought. *Sanctuary* was the home he provided for his animals.

From duck pond to donkey stall, the video cameras showed him scenes that were about as tranquil as it ever got. As the number of his adopted animals had grown, he had promised he wouldn't spend much time away from home. That had been before he met Bree. She had changed everything.

Watching her with Papadum, he could see that she obviously loved animals…even quirky ones. A slight smile touched his lips as he tried to picture her among his other misfits. But what was the point? Looking into the future was a waste of time. As far as Bree was concerned, Rylan had blown it before he'd even started.

Chapter 5

Although Bree ordered her favorite Thai meal of pad gra prao goong, she barely touched the delicious stir-fried king prawns with vegetable chili and basil leaves. There were two reasons for her gastronomic indifference. One was Rylan's presence. The other was the topic of conversation.

His expression grew increasingly stony as he read through the emails on Bree's cell phone. "I had no idea."

It seemed like a strange statement. "How could you? I've only just told you about them."

He took a long slug of his beer. "What I meant was, I never would have known you were dealing with all of this." His gaze searched her face. "You said your brother knows about these emails?"

Bree shifted in her chair. "I haven't told him about

the most recent ones. The ones with the pictures and the violent threats." She speared a prawn, then dropped her fork back onto her plate. "Or the racial slurs."

"You have to tell him, Bree. And about how this creep has upped his game and is moving your personal belongings." Rylan's jaw muscles tightened. "This situation is dangerous. The guy who is threatening you has been inside your apartment. I don't understand why you are so reluctant to confront this head-on."

Bree took a moment to glance around the busy restaurant. With its cool contemporary colors and stylish decor, the owners had given the classic Thai themes of gilded lacquer work and lotus flowers a modern twist. Most tables were occupied, and the early evening atmosphere was relaxed.

Are you here? Are you watching me?

So much for the chilled vibe. It was working on everyone except Bree. Her gaze roamed around the room, lingering briefly on each of the men as she tried to assess which, if any, of them might be responsible for threatening her. *This is exactly what he wants.*

With an effort, she forced her attention back to Rylan's comment. "It all comes back to what I was telling you last night. My family is wonderful. They love me and look out for me. Sometimes they care so much they forget I'm an adult."

Rylan smiled. "You mean they get a little overprotective?"

Bree snorted. "A *little*? If they could have me wrapped me up in lambswool for my whole life that would suit them just fine." She sighed. "They—and *they* means uncles, aunts and cousins, as well as my parents and Trey—still see me as the little girl who needed extra support. If they think I'm in trouble, my life will cease to be my own."

Rylan reached across the table and took her hand in his. "Bree, you're one of the strongest people I know. I don't see why getting help from the police with this stalker means your family would need to step in and take over your life."

"That's because you don't know how being a Colton works. The combined strength of my family is a fearsome thing...especially when they're right."

"My nickname in the army was Lucky," Rylan said.

"Okay." Bree blinked at him. "Smooth subject change—"

"Let me finish, wise gal. Although I learned some tough skills in the army, I figured another tour of duty would see me coming back in a body bag. I got out of my commission, just before my unit was wiped out by a roadside ambush."

"Oh, my goodness." She squeezed his hand. "I'm sorry. I can't imagine how awful that must have been."

He lowered his gaze to their entwined fingers but not before she caught a glimpse of how much the experience had torn him apart. It was clearly something he was not comfortable talking about.

Bree decided to move the conversation on. "So Lucky comes from your knack of escaping just in time?"

"Yes, but that's not the reason for this story," Rylan said. There was a hint of gratitude in his eyes as he raised them to her face. "The skills and experience I gained in the army haven't gone away. Your family doesn't need to protect you, Bree. Not when I'm around." His eyes locked on hers. "And that will be for as long as you need me."

The people, light and noise around them faded. Heat spread throughout Bree's body. It had the power to overwhelm her, and also complete her. When she looked at Rylan, it felt as though she was standing in the center of a dangerous fire, yet she was completely safe. Her heart constricted, squeezing the air from her lungs. At the same time, she wanted to dance, run, sing, leap... anything to release the energy surging through her.

Before she could speak, Rylan's attention was diverted. "Isn't that the guy you met with earlier today?" He nodded in the direction of a nearby table.

Bree followed the direction of his gaze. Sure enough, Lucas Brewer was deep in conversation with his younger brother, Joe.

"That's strange." She allowed herself a momentary distraction. "When I told Lucas I was coming to Appe-Thaizer with you tonight, he didn't mention he would be here as well." She shrugged. "Maybe I gave him the idea."

"I'm sure that was it." Even though Rylan's expression was unreadable, there was an underlying intensity that Bree hadn't seen before. It was fleeting, and he turned back to her again, his eyes dropping to her almost untouched food. "Do you want coffee?"

She nodded. "But not here. I *definitely* got a new pack today."

He reached for Papadum's leash. "Then what are we waiting for?"

Once Bree had locked her apartment door, they removed their warm outdoor jackets, and Rylan stooped to remove Papadum's leash. As he straightened and turned toward the kitchen, Bree reached for his hand…and everything slowed. He wasn't sure who made the first move—maybe they both acted at the same time—but their lips met, and his resolve faded.

Can't do this.

The thought was a faint echo, almost drowned out by a passion that was instant and raging. Bree's fingertips traced the muscles of his back as her lips parted and her tongue caressed his. If he didn't stop this soon, he would be lost…

Breathing hard, he broke the kiss and took a step back. Bree watched him with wide-eyed wonder. The silence between them stretched, became awkward, then tipped over into uncomfortable.

Coming back here had been a bad idea. But *not* coming back here wasn't an option. How was he supposed to protect her from a distance? *Self-control.* That was the answer. All he had to do was forget how much he wanted her, get a grip on his emotions and stay professional.

"Um, coffee." He jerked a thumb in the direction of the kitchen. "Wasn't that what you wanted?"

Bree stepped up close, took ahold of his arms and drew them around her waist. Rylan resisted the temptation to groan out loud.

"That *was* what I wanted. But there's something—or someone—I want more." A little of the light faded from her eyes as she scanned his face. "Unless…?"

How much worse could this situation get? Until he met Bree, Rylan had never known there was such a thing as the woman of his dreams. Now, she was in his arms, and her beautiful lower lip was quivering because she thought he was about to turn her down. He already knew how fragile she was. How could he be the one to hurt her?

"Bree, you must know how much I want you." He tightened his arms around her. *Always a good way to keep your distance.* "I just wonder if this is the best idea. You know, with us working together..."

She gave a relieved laugh. "Is that all? Because we're not exactly employed by the same company." Rising up on her tiptoes, she whispered against his lips. "And I won't tell if you don't."

That whole self-control thing? Yeah, that wasn't working out quite the way he'd planned. Bree gave a little squeal as he swung her off her feet and marched her out of the living area.

"Other direction," she murmured into the curve of his neck. "You're heading for the guest bathroom."

Rylan turned on his heel, finding her bedroom and closing the door just before Papadum could follow them inside. When he set her on her feet, the smile in Bree's eyes nearly sent him to his knees. Desire surged through him, savage and fierce, setting his blood alight. Alongside it, there was a deeper sensation that mirrored the swelling tide of passion with a soft tenderness that astonished him.

Despite the urgency firing through his body, he wanted to savor the perfection of that moment. Of how it felt to be with her. Of how he could search his whole life and never feel this good again.

Bree gave him a quizzical look, but he smiled into her eyes before leaning down to kiss her deeply, his own need reflected in the quiver that ran through her body. He pressed his tongue against hers, feeling her, learning her, tasting her. Teasing, they drew back just enough to let the tension build, breath warm on each other's lips before drawing closer again.

The next kiss heated up. Still slow, dragging out the excitement, savoring it, building the fervor, feeling every nuance. When they broke apart once again, they were both breathing hard.

"Sure this is what you want?" Rylan managed to get the words out.

"I practically begged you." Bree slid a hand under his sweatshirt, her soft touch causing his stomach muscles to tighten.

"I need to hear you say it."

"This is what I want." She smiled into his eyes. "*You* are what I want."

Feeling as though his heart had developed an extra beat, he drew her to him, his hands sliding down to her butt. Lifting her into him, he molded her body intimately to his.

Bree's fingers moved lower, following the trail of hairs down past his navel and inside the waistband of his jeans. Her fingertips stoked the fire until it became a furnace. In a flurry of hands and lips, jeans, sweatshirts, boots and socks were flung aside. Scooping Bree up, Rylan deposited her on the bed.

Before he joined her, he reached for his jeans, snagging his wallet from the back pocket and placing it on the bedside table.

"I missed you." Bree wrapped slender arms around his neck, drawing him down next to her.

"Protection." He kissed his way along her collarbone, easing her bra strap down.

"Need you now." The words ended on a soft whimper that made his whole body tingle.

Bree hooked her fingers in the elastic of his boxer briefs, easing them down, and Rylan lifted his hips to help her. When they were off, she kissed her way slowly down his stomach until she reached his straining erection. With a scorching glance from those tawny eyes, she bent her head and gave his tip a single featherlight lick.

"Bree…" Rylan arched his back as electric shocks tingled along his nerve endings.

She smiled before continuing to lick, rubbing her tongue all over his sensitive flesh until he was ready to howl in ecstasy. Just when he thought he couldn't stand the exquisite pleasure any longer, Bree took his head into her mouth. Squeezing her lips tightly around him, she slid forward, inch by inch. Teasingly, maddeningly, wonderfully. Holding her position, she ran her tongue up and down his rock-hard length. Rylan drew in great gulps of air like a drowning man who has just broken the surface.

When she started sucking, he reluctantly cupped her face with his hands. "Too much," he gritted out, in response to her look of disappointment. "I don't want this to be over before we've even started."

Kneeling, she reached behind her to undo her bra. With her perfect breasts freed from their lacy restraint, he reached up to tweak one dark-cherry nipple. As Bree's eyelids drooped and her teeth caught her lower lip, Rylan decided he might just have found his new favorite view.

He was forced to change his mind when she shifted position to remove her white lace underwear. The neat golden globes of her ass were revealed in all their rounded beauty. The impression that her skin was like silk was confirmed when he placed a hand on her taut cheeks. Sliding a finger into the cleft between her buttocks, he moved it gently down and pressed inside her.

Bree gasped and bowed her head, tightening her muscles to let him feel how much she wanted him. Her encircling heat made Rylan's own desire burn brighter, the intensity building and flaring.

"Oh, please, Rylan."

Her sigh was the signal he needed. Tipping Bree onto her back, Rylan lay across her and reached for a condom. Moving a hand down between their bodies, he kissed her as he sheathed himself. Slowly, he eased into her welcoming warmth. With each inch, Bree contracted her muscles, gripping him tightly. Rylan's breath quickened, and his eyes closed. Was it possible to experience a feeling beyond perfection?

When he was fully inside her, he opened his eyes. She looked so beautiful that his throat tightened. Picturing the connection between them almost tipped him over the edge. His hardness throbbing inside her soft pink flesh. Stretching her as she cradled him...

He circled his pelvis. "Tell me how that feels."

"So good." Her voice was barely a whisper.

He pulled out a little, then drove back in.

"Yes. More." Bree lifted her hips to meet him.

Rylan took his cue from her. Gazing into her eyes,

he drew back again, tensing his hips this time before slamming hard and fast all the way back in. Bree cried out, gripping his shoulders and digging her nails into his flesh.

Her gasps matched his heavy breaths as they settled into a rocking motion. Wrapping her legs around his waist, Bree met his firm thrusts with upward jerks of her hips. Each movement became faster, more intense, less controlled…

Rylan could feel her thigh muscles quivering, see the look of concentration on her face coming apart. "Ah."

When she arched beneath him, he thrust hard and held still. As she tightened around him, the first pulse of his own release began. He remained in that position, looking into her eyes as they trembled uncontrollably. Rylan's own orgasm was made more intense by the glow in Bree's eyes, the sheen of sweat on her forehead and her warm breath on his cheek.

When his muscles relaxed, he slumped forward, taking his weight on his elbows, breathing into the curve of her neck.

Bree wound her arms around him. "Tell me this beats sleeping in your car?"

"This beats *everything*." He laughed huskily as he rolled to one side. "Although I have to do two things before I can sleep."

"You do?"

"The first is…uh, take care of the condom." He pointed toward the bathroom. "Then I need to call home."

Bree raised a brow. "Is this where I find out you're

married with three kids?" Although the words were light, he sensed a current of insecurity beneath them.

He swung his legs over the side of the bed. "No. This is where you find out I have a very unique collection of animals. I have to check in with Dinah, who helps me on the ranch, to make sure they're okay."

"Rylan—" Bree placed a hand on her heart "—are you…could you be…*softhearted*?"

"Yeah," he growled, as he placed a kiss on her forehead. "But don't you dare tell anyone."

Bree was fascinated by the way Rylan slept. She was a light sleeper, tossing and turning, and waking at the slightest sound. Whereas, he lay on his stomach, breathing deeply, so still and peaceful she envied him. She wondered what he was dreaming about, where his subconscious was taking him.

Was it considered creepy to watch someone sleep? Particularly when it was the first time they'd spent the night together? It didn't look as if he was likely to wake any time soon, so she figured Rylan would never know.

Bree herself was wide-awake, her thoughts flitting back and forth between the show, the stalker and the gorgeous man at her side. Focusing on Rylan made her feel safe. His presence was like a warm, cozy blanket wrapped around her. With him beside her, it would be easy to let the emails and the knowledge that a stranger had been inside her apartment fade into the background.

Unfortunately, even the delicious memory of being in Rylan's arms couldn't keep the fears at bay for long. She had to consider the truth of her situation. The person sending those emails wanted to harm her. Even if the attacks remained threats and never became physical, there was someone out there who hated her so much he was relishing causing her pain. And Bree had no idea why.

Her biggest fear, aside from the immediate risk to her personal safety, was the impact on everything she'd worked so hard to achieve. Stepping outside the Colton sphere of influence had not been easy for Bree. But breaking free to pursue her art as a career, making a success of her business, those things belonged to her. They were all Bree and, contrary to what her tormentor claimed in his emails, they owed nothing to her family name.

Whatever this person's motive was, she couldn't let him succeed in driving her away. This was her gallery, her home, her *life*. Having Rylan at her side made her feel more secure, but she needed more than protection. She wanted a resolution. Whoever was behind this had to be stopped.

She had told Rylan that her family had been having a few problems lately, but she hadn't gone into any detail. As it turned out, it wasn't a great time to be a Colton. Her cousin Wyatt had been through a tough time when a body was found on his ranch and he was briefly under investigation. He had also been dealing with a rival rancher vandalizing his stock. Another cousin, Sloane, had been the subject of a hit, when the grandparents of her young daughter took drastic steps to try and gain custody. As if that wasn't enough, Decker's wife, Kendall—the same person who had been hit in the face by glass when the gallery window was broken—had been the subject of an attempted kidnapping prior to their marriage.

Bree had been over and over it in her mind, and couldn't see any way that these things were linked to what was happening to her. It was just a family run of awful luck.

There was no doubt that the tone of the emails had changed over time. Initially, the focus had been that she was a Colton, using her wealth to take advantage of local people. Lately, the emails had become more personal. They were about Bree, how she looked, the color of her skin and, more specifically, what the sender would like to do to her.

She shivered and drew closer to Rylan, pulling the bedclothes tighter around them both. From the detail in the messages, it was obvious the author had seen her. Possibly, he was someone she knew. The thought troubled her. How could she have upset another person so much to incite such a powerful grudge?

She was still puzzling about it when Rylan turned to face her. "Can't sleep?"

"How do you do that? Comatose to wide-awake in the blink of an eye?"

"Years of practice." His gaze scanned her face. "What's troubling you?"

"Right this minute?" She snuggled closer to him. "Absolutely nothing."

Chapter 6

It was 10:00 p.m., and the Diamond was full of people who were determined to party hard despite the sub-zero temperatures. Live music poured out from various bars, along with delicious food aromas and the mingled scents of cocktails and beer.

Bree and Rylan, having bundled up warm, were content to soak up the atmosphere. Walking hand-in-hand through the crowd, pausing to sway in time to a favorite track, or try a sample from one of the street vendors, they were too focused on each other to care about much else.

"Who'd have thought a Hungarian sheepdog would be so squeamish about the cold?" Bree was referring to Papadum's reluctance to accompany them. When he realized they were going out, the dog had attempted to cram his large body under Bree's bed. Trying to get him out had turned into something resembling a scene from a slapstick comedy. In the end, they had given up and left him in the apartment.

"At least I have two hands free to do this." Rylan caught her around the waist, drawing her tight against him.

Decorative iron street lamps were set at regular intervals around the perimeter of the Diamond, and colored lightbulbs were strung between them. They had halted beneath the glow of a yellow bulb, and as Rylan bent to kiss her, golden highlights touched his hair and cheeks. Bree's eyelids fluttered closed as she clutched his lapels. The things this man could do to her…

They had been lovers for two days, and every minute had been as magical as the first. The only problem was that reality kept intruding. She wanted to spend every moment with Rylan, but she had a gallery to run and a show to prepare for.

Just as her lips touched his, the high-pitched crack of a gunshot jolted them apart. It was followed by an explosion as the glass bulb over their heads shattered.

Bree barely had time to utter a startled exclamation before Rylan moved. Grabbing her arm and pulling her down so she was hunched over next to him, he propelled her into a zigzagging run. When he dragged her into the nearest bar, Bree expected him to dive for cover in one of the booths. Instead, he kept on going, straight through the public area, into the kitchen and out through an emergency exit at the rear.

"Rylan, what…?"

They were in the parking lot. Ducking behind the

nearest car, Rylan reached inside his jacket and withdrew a gun from a shoulder holster. Still holding tight to Bree with one hand and the weapon with the other, he dodged from vehicle to vehicle, his sharp blue gaze constantly taking in his surroundings.

Releasing Bree's hand, he reached into the pocket of his jeans and withdrew his keys. A nearby vehicle beeped, and Rylan opened the passenger door before gesturing for Bree to go ahead of him. After another quick scrutiny of their surroundings, he joined her and gunned the engine.

As he maneuvered fast onto Second Street, he cast a quick glance in her direction. "Are you injured?"

She raised a hand to her forehead, feeling a thin trickle of blood. "Not seriously."

Lapsing into silence, she gazed out the window for a few minutes as the built-up area thinned and they left the center of Roaring Springs behind. Finally, when her thoughts became too much to bear, she turned to look at Rylan. At his muscular body and the strong determined lines of his profile. She thought about the speed with which he'd moved. As soon as that gunshot was fired, he'd been all action. A total professional.

"You are not an art promoter." It wasn't a question.

"No. Until recently, I was a personal security consultant. I ran my own agency."

Bree swallowed hard. She should be glad he hadn't lied, right? So why did she feel like her whole world had just come crashing down around her? The happiness she'd felt in his arms minutes earlier had been an illusion. It had shattered like the golden bulb above their heads when it had been hit by a bullet.

"I guess it was my parents who hired you." She forced the words past the choking sensation in her throat. "If you're not still in business, how did they find you?"

"I was in the army with Blaine."

Bree had always been slow to anger. Her mom used to say her daughter lived in the wrong state. She didn't see life's highs and lows. Instead, her emotional landscape was easy and even, more like rolling pastures than dramatic mountains. But Rylan's words triggered a spark unlike anything she had ever known.

"You listened to me. You let me tell you what it was like when my family takes over…and the whole time…" Her hands curled into fists. "Take me home, Rylan."

"We're going to my ranch—"

"Take. Me. Home." Although she tried to disguise it, anger, hurt and sorrow quivered in each word.

Rylan must have heard it too. After a brief sidelong glance in her direction, he checked for oncoming traffic. The road ahead was clear, and he swung the car onto the opposite side of the highway. They completed the return journey in stony silence.

When Rylan halted the vehicle in the Diamond parking lot, he turned to face Bree. "I respect what you must be feeling right now, but I can't let you risk your personal safety. Someone fired a shot directly over our heads. Because we left the scene fast, I have no way of knowing what happened next. Was that a single incident, or was it an active shooter situation? I have to find out if we were the only target, or if other shots were fired."

Through the fog of her competing emotions, Bree's

initial reaction was fear for his safety. What if the person who fired that shot had intended to kill one, or both, of them? What if he was waiting for their return?

"Can you shoot?" Rylan's question jolted her attention back to him.

"I grew up on a farm. My father insisted on teaching me how to handle a firearm."

"Good." He held out his gun. "Take this. Go up to your apartment. Don't open the door unless you're sure it's me, or the police."

Bree's feelings were in free fall. Rylan had deceived her. She wanted to cling to her anger, to wrap it around herself like a security blanket as a defense against the pain. Instead, the fear that this might be the last time she saw him pushed everything else aside

"I don't want—" *What? I don't want to lose you?* After what he'd done, her thoughts weren't making sense.

"Go." Rylan leaned across her and opened the car door. "We can talk later."

She exited the vehicle and dashed toward her apartment. It was only when she was inside, and dealing with an overenthusiastic greeting from Papadum, that she stopped to consider his words.

Rylan had destroyed her trust. What could they possibly have to talk about?

Normally, in a volatile situation, with so many unknown factors, Rylan would have been totally focused on his surroundings. Instead, as he moved from the parking lot toward the Diamond, his concentration was on the hollow ache in his chest.

These last few days with Bree had been a glimpse of everything he wanted and thought he could never have. The life he had believed was out of his reach. A woman he could love. Someone to share his hopes and dreams, to walk at his side, meeting the highs and lows with her hand in his. He had seen it all. Bright days, cozy nights. Children. Facing old age together.

He had blown it. Thrown away the future before they'd had a chance at it. The knowledge that it was all his own fault made the pain even worse.

I should have told her.

But how could he? He'd made a promise to keep his identity secret. And Rylan kept his promises.

It was at times like this that he could hear his father's slurred, sneering words. *Worthless. Weak. Never amount to anything.* All true. Now, more than ever. And despite his vow to the contrary, he'd succumbed to the intensity of the attraction he felt for Bree. He had been enchanted by her, so caught up in the magic of his emotions he'd been unable to walk away. *Weak?* He was a living, breathing example of the word.

As he stepped onto the paved surface of the Diamond, everything appeared normal. The atmosphere was vibrant, yet laid-back, with no evidence that anything had disturbed the revelry. It looked as if he and Bree were the only people who had been affected by the gunshot.

Maintaining a careful scrutiny of the area, Rylan made his way back to the point where they had been standing. Tiny shards of glass crunched beneath his feet. He couldn't find any trace of the bullet, but he figured it was probably embedded in the brickwork above his head. The sound had been unmistakable. Rylan, of all people, knew a gunshot when he heard one.

Turning back to view the Diamond, his gaze took in every detail of his surroundings. The place was crowded. If anyone standing on the cobbles had drawn a gun and fired up at the string of lights, there would have been witnesses.

He scanned the buildings. The renovated warehouses had been separated into individual units, and above each of the bars, cafés, offices and restaurants was a second floor. Rylan remembered that David Swanson had said his apartment was above the Yogurt Hut. He assumed there were similar dwellings above the other businesses. From where he was standing, he figured the shot must have come from a second-floor window on the opposite side of the Diamond.

Although it was impossible to pinpoint which window the shooter had used, Rylan studied each of them carefully. He had no intention of checking what was going on behind each window right there and then. That was a task for the police, and despite Bree's reservations, he had every intention of taking this latest incident to her brother so he could investigate what had happened.

The nearest bar was called On the Rocks. There was a security guard at the door and, although Rylan couldn't be sure the same guy had been there earlier, he was hopeful that there hadn't been time for a shift change.

"What happened there?" Rylan pointed to the string of lights. The gap where the yellow one had been was now a conspicuous dark spot in the center of the colored string.

The guard gave him a blank look. "I guess one of the bulbs blew."

"No, that's not what I meant. Twenty minutes ago, I was standing under that light with my g—with my friend and it exploded," Rylan said. "Did you see what happened?"

The guy shrugged. "If you're looking for compensation from the city council, I can't help. I've been here for the last four hours, but I haven't seen anything unusual."

Rylan thanked him and turned away. Although it was frustrating that the security guard hadn't seen the incident, he'd learned enough from the encounter. He was convinced that the shot had not been random and that he and Bree were the targets. He looked again at the buildings from which the gun must have been fired, judging the distance. The shooter had been skilled enough to single out that bulb, and confident enough to know that he could hit it without risking injury to anyone in the crowd below.

That meant the shot had been intended as a scare tactic. A proficient gun handler, with enough self-assurance to fire over a crowded area, could have killed or injured them if he'd wanted to. Instead, he'd chosen to warn them.

Even so, this was an escalation. Threatening emails and moving Bree's possessions was bad enough. A bullet took this to a whole new level. Had Bree's stalker been triggered by seeing her with Rylan? If that was the case, they could expect more. Or worse.

Which was a good reason not to leave her alone. He

wasn't looking forward to the coming confrontation, but at least he could be honest with Bree from now on. And that would include letting her know that he wasn't leaving her side until this shooter was behind bars.

Bree removed her hat, feeling the shards of glass that were buried in the wool crunch beneath her gloved fingers. She wondered if she should be clutching the gun instead of Papadum. Somehow, the dog made her feel safer…and the firearm was only inches away. Even so, when the door buzzer sounded, she jumped so much that Papadum let out a startled grunt.

"Sorry, big guy." She patted his head to reassure him.

Her security included a video camera linked to the entry system. When she pressed the button, a black-and-white image of Rylan filled the screen.

"Bree? Let me in."

She paused. Now was probably not the best time to tell him to get out of her life forever. At this moment, her feelings about his behavior took second place to that bullet. She could tell him to take a hike anytime. But right now…

I need him.

"Bree?"

She pressed the button to admit him and moved to open the door. The tension in her jaw was reflected in the set of her shoulders, and her stomach muscles tightened as though trying to disguise the fluttering sensation inside. It felt as if her brain were filled with static, firing off random thoughts. This could go one of two ways. She could greet Rylan with stony silence or wild recriminations. Until she saw him, Bree had no idea which it would be.

It didn't help that he was just so gorgeous. As he walked toward her, Bree's heart flipped over with an emotion that had nothing to do with anger. All she wanted to do was run to him and feel those strong arms close around her.

"You lied to me." Silence wasn't an option.

"If you knew how much I regret that—"

"How did you think this was going to end, Rylan? Did you think I would never find out that you'd been hired by my parents to watch over me?" She could feel her voice rising, and she forced it back under control. "Or didn't it matter? Because it was just a brief fling—"

Rylan caught hold of her upper arms. "Don't say that. Please, don't even think it."

Bree jerked out of his grip, storming into the apartment. She heard Rylan close and lock the door before he followed her. Although he was standing just behind her, she didn't turn to face him.

"This wasn't supposed to happen." The gentleness in his voice almost undid her resolve. "I promised Blaine I would look after you. One last job, as a favor to him. That's all it was. Until I met you."

"I don't want to hear it." She swung around to face him. "You and me… Whatever it was, it's over. No amount of talking can justify what you did. Now, before you go, tell me what you found out about that gunshot."

"Can I sit down?" He indicated one of the sofas in her open-plan living area.

Reluctantly, she nodded. Once Rylan was seated, Bree sat as far from him as she could. Papadum looked from one to the other. With his loyalties torn, the dog decided on a position on the rug mid-way between them.

I'm going to really miss the dog.

What sort of crazy, mixed-up thought was that with everything else that was going on?

"From what I've been able to discover, there was a single gunshot fired directly at the bulb over our heads. I spoke with a security guard at the nearest bar. He didn't notice what happened, and he didn't see anything else." Rylan kept his gaze fixed on her face. "It seems we were the only targets."

"Could the bulb simply have shattered?" Bree asked.

He shook his head. "We both know it was a shot."

"I just hoped…"

"This has gone beyond hoping, Bree." His expression was serious. "He won't stop here."

"Thank you for your professional opinion. Be sure to add it as an extra on the bill you give my parents."

There was a flash of hurt in the depths of his eyes, and his fists clenched on his thighs as he took a moment before he answered. "I'm not charging for my services. Blaine is my friend."

"How noble." Her lip curled. "Am I supposed to be grateful that you came out of retirement and made me a charity case?"

She'd said she wasn't going to talk about it. She *shouldn't* talk about it. But her hurt pride wouldn't let it go. She wanted to prod Rylan, to goad him, to wound him. To make him feel a fraction of the pain he'd caused her.

"What about the artists you are representing?" Rylan was looking down, and she flung the angry words at the top of his head. "Don't they deserve to know you are a fraud?"

He reached into the pocket of his jeans and withdrew his cell phone. "From the day I took this job, I made it clear to your mom that I wasn't going to waste my cover role. I promised I would help these young artists." Flicking through web pages, he held up the screen. "I've made sure they all have websites, that they promote their work on social media, each of them now has a blog, and they share each other's posts. We've been involved in charitable and community events, some of the group have been into schools to help the children with art lessons, we're publishing an ebook of African American art—" He drew in a breath. "I've been coming into your gallery every day to watch over you, but I've also been keeping my promise to them."

Bree felt a flicker of guilt. She quickly buried it. This wasn't how it worked. She wasn't the bad guy. She hadn't told lies or deceived anyone. There was no point at which she deserved to have him walk into her life and make her fall for him.

"I'm glad something good has come of this." Did she succeed in keeping the bitter note out of her voice? She wasn't sure. "I'll get Papadum's things."

"Don't bother." Blue eyes caught and held hers. "He's not going anywhere...and neither am I."

Bree blinked at him. "Pardon?"

"You are in danger. I made a promise to Blaine, and to your parents, that I'd protect you." He sat back. "It's going to be a lot easier now that you know about it."

For an instant, she wanted to laugh. The temptation soon disappeared. Because just who did he think he was? Sitting there with a smug half smile on his face, on *her* sofa, in *her* apartment, telling *her* what was going to happen…

"Get out." She managed to utter the words despite the rising tide of her anger.

"No." He started to unlace his boots.

Unsure which of them was crazy, Bree stomped toward the door. "You have two minutes before I call the police."

"Call them." Rylan smiled. "I was planning to wait until morning to contact your brother, but I'm sure he'll come straight over once he knows what's happened."

She sucked in a breath. *Trey? Now?* On top of everything that had happened? She didn't think she could handle that.

She tried a different approach. "I don't want you here."

It was true. She was sure of it. Hurt and humiliation burned through her every time she looked at him, every time she thought of them together and knew their closeness had been based on a lie. But she'd grown used to the comfort that came with his presence. Without him, she wouldn't feel safe. That was a long way from letting him stay.

"Right now, I have to place your personal safety above your wishes." There was nothing of Rylan, her lover, in that statement. The man uttering those words was a stranger. A trained, emotionally detached, bodyguard. And maybe that was exactly what she needed when there was a violent stalker on her tail.

She drew herself up to her full height. "I can't forgive what you did."

He bowed his head, the stiffness gone from his manner. "Until this guy is caught, or unless you tell me otherwise, ours will be a professional arrangement. Nothing more."

She regarded him for a moment or two, unsure whether to keep fighting, or be relieved that she wouldn't have to spend the night with his gun under her pillow.

"You know where the guest room is." She turned and headed to her own bedroom.

Chapter 7

"I can't believe Mom and Dad hired a bodyguard without consulting me." Trey Colton looked like he couldn't decide whether to be angry or shocked.

Rylan had driven Bree to the sheriff's headquarters immediately after breakfast. It had been a frosty journey. Now, they were seated in Trey's office, and Bree had shifted her chair as far from Rylan as she could get.

"They didn't consult *me*," Bree reminded her brother. "Kind of more important, don't you think?"

For the time being, Rylan was content to observe the dynamics between brother and sister. He could see how physically alike they were. With his light brown skin and golden-brown eyes, Trey's coloring was similar to Bree's. When he removed his cowboy hat, his hair was close cropped, but it was the same dark brown shade as his sister's. Although Trey was tall and broad-shouldered, the siblings also shared the same strong runner's physique.

There was more to it than a physical likeness. Even though they were clearly in the habit of sparring verbally, he could feel the fondness between them. And it reminded him all over again of what he didn't have. This was normality. Family. Affection. Caring. The things that would always remain out of his reach.

Worthless. Yeah, like I needed a reminder.

"Yes." When Trey smiled, he and Bree appeared even more alike. "I suppose you were more closely involved." His manner became serious again. Rylan thought of what he'd heard of Trey Colton. The Bradford County Sheriff had a reputation for playing by the rules and getting the job done. "Tell me about this gunshot."

Rylan quickly filled him in on what he knew about the ambush. "Bree needs to tell you the rest."

"There's more?" Trey raised a brow as he looked up from the notes he was making.

"I've been getting more emails. They've been getting more threatening." Bree held up a hand. "I know what you're going to say. I should have come to you sooner."

"Damn straight." Trey frowned. "I'll need copies of the emails. Anything else?"

"Other things have been happening." Bree shot a glance in Rylan's direction. He couldn't tell if she was annoyed at him for forcing her to tell all or including him as a coconspirator in her silence. "Someone has been moving my property." She told him about the digital recorder, the coffee and the teacups.

Trey was silent for several seconds after she finished

speaking, his eyes fixed on his notes. When he looked up, Rylan wasn't looking at the by-the-book sheriff. He was seeing Bree's brother.

"I don't suppose you'd consider going to stay at the farm until we catch this guy?" Trey didn't sound particularly hopeful.

"No."

Trey turned to Rylan. "Then I guess Mom and Dad did the right thing after all."

"I'll keep her safe."

Bree made a sound like an enraged kitten. "Uh... still here, guys. Still not happy."

Trey rubbed a thumb along his jaw. "Bree, if I had the resources to assign an officer to watch over you 24/7, I would. Since I don't have that sort of manpower at my disposal, I'm glad to know Rylan is doing the job instead."

"I don't want preferential treatment because I'm the sheriff's sister," Bree said. "And especially not because I'm a Colton."

Trey flicked a look in Rylan's direction. It was a silent plea for help that, in other circumstances, would have made him smile. In that moment, he was too focused on Bree's well-being to share a male bonding moment with her brother.

"Just for a second, stop trying to take stubborn to a whole new level. If someone stalking you wasn't serious enough, think about the bigger picture. What if this is linked to the other problems the family has been experiencing?"

Bree's trim frame stiffened at Trey's chastising tone. Rylan might have only known her for a short time, but he knew her brother was going the wrong way about this. Bree might be quiet and reserved, but she'd spent too much of her life being told what to do by her family. When she'd broken free, she had vowed to stand on her own two feet.

"What family problems?" Rylan asked. "Both Blaine and Bree have hinted that there's something going on. If I'm responsible for guarding Bree, I need to know if there is anything that could affect her safety."

"We're a big family with a lot of business interests, as well as individual personal issues. Inevitably, things go wrong sometimes. We've had a bad few months, and most of the things that have happened are unrelated." Trey tented his fingers beneath his chin. "What I'm about to tell you is confidential. The body found on Wyatt's ranch may not be the only murder victim."

"*What*?" Bree sat up straighter, her antagonism forgotten. "I didn't know about this."

"That's because it's not public knowledge," Trey said. "I recused myself from the investigation because Wyatt is my cousin, but obviously I'm aware of what is happening. The body found on the Crooked C was that of a high-class call girl named Bianca Rouge. Initially, Wyatt came under suspicion because she was found on his land and he didn't have an alibi for the time of her death. He was cleared when another man killed himself and took the blame for Bianca's death in his suicide note."

"You said she may not have been the only one," Rylan said. "That sounds like it's not conclusive."

"That's the difficulty my deputy, who took over the investigation, is facing. Shortly after Bianca was found, a woman called Ruth Thomas arrived in Roaring Springs looking for her missing daughter, April, who left Denver and came looking for work in Roaring Springs. She looks almost exactly like Bianca Rouge."

Rylan frowned. "That's a mighty big assumption. April looked like Bianca, so you think she might also have been killed here?"

Trey shot him an impatient glance. "The link is not that tenuous. The last time April spoke to her mom, she told her she had a job interview. Staff at The Lodge confirm it's possible she applied for a post there. The point is that we are dealing with one confirmed murder, possibly more. I've no wish to sound alarmist, but the killer may be determined to hurt our family. Bianca was definitely on Colton property at one time, and April may also have been."

"You're saying it's possible there's a serial killer targeting women and, through them, getting at Coltons?" Bree's voice was quiet.

"I can't rule it out." Trey gave her hand a squeeze. "I wish I could. At the same time, I don't have anything that ties what happened to Bianca—and may have happened to April—to the person who is threatening you. Which is what I meant when I said I can't justify allocating any of my officers to your protection."

"We can't take a risk that there isn't a connection." As Rylan reinforced what Trey was saying, Bree turned her head in his direction. He hated the knowledge that he was responsible for the hurt in her eyes. Hated even more that there was nothing he could do to take it away.

"Okay. I accept that I need a bodyguard." Rylan anticipated what was coming next. "I just don't want it to be you."

The coldness of her tone was like a knife slicing his skin. She spoke to him as if he were a stranger when, for those few magical nights, they had been as close as it was possible for two people to get. *It's what I deserve.* Although he knew he was to blame for them reaching this point, it didn't take the pain away.

Trey appeared unaware of any hostile undercurrents. "I'm not sure changing the arrangement now would be such a good idea, Bree. Particularly as Rylan comes recommended by Blaine."

"We can ask Blaine to suggest someone else," Bree said.

"He won't." Rylan managed to keep his voice calm.

"How can you be so sure?" Her eyes were somber as they scanned his face. Would she ever smile at him again? It was probably too much to hope for.

"Because I'm the best." It wasn't arrogant or boastful. It was honest.

"That must be true." Trey nodded.

"Just like that?" Bree's tone was scornful. "He tells you he's the best, and you take his word for it?"

"Think about it," Trey said. "Mom and Dad asked Blaine to recommend someone to protect you. Where you are concerned, Blaine wouldn't settle for anything less than first-class."

Before Bree could respond, her cell phone buzzed. She scanned the message quickly. When she looked up, her expression was a mix of confusion and despair.

"That was Kasey. She's been unpacking the Spirit artwork ready for the show. Some of the exhibits have been damaged."

* * *

The lump in Bree's chest alternated between red-hot coal and solid ice. Even though the heating system in the gallery kept the temperature at a comfortable level, the chill mountain wind seemed to be blowing straight out of the mountains and through her skin, leaving her insides raw.

Kasey was on her knees with the ruined paintings fanned out around her. Tears streamed down her cheeks.

"Who would do this?" Her expression was broken as she looked up at Bree and Rylan. "And why only *your* pictures, Bree? Every one of them has been slashed."

Bree couldn't answer. She wished she could speak, or cry, but nothing would come. No tears, no words. Not a sound. All she could do was stare at her precious pieces—the paintings she had so lovingly created—and scream inside.

Someone had taken a blade and repeatedly sliced through each canvas until it hung in shreds from its frame. It wasn't about the hours of work she'd put into each one, or even about her artistic vision, or the senseless waste. Bree could feel the anger and hatred that had gone into the attack. It was directed at *her* artwork. The pieces by other artists were untouched. This was *personal*.

She was conscious of Rylan's gaze on her profile. A day ago, she'd have taken comfort in his arms. And even though she would never admit it, his presence was reassuring. He was calm and focused. With the sensation that her world was crashing down around her, she still needed him to be that strong, stalwart figure keeping her thoughts on track.

Trey was right. Blaine had chosen Rylan because he was the best. From now on, she would keep her distance, but she would depend on him to do his job.

"Who had access to these pictures?" Rylan asked.

"Um…" Kasey got to her feet, dabbing at her eyes with a Kleenex. "They were in boxes in the basement storeroom. It's not locked, but it's not easily accessible to the public, and there's no reason for anyone to go in there unless they need to."

"But technically anyone who entered the gallery could have gotten into the room where the pictures were stored?"

"I guess so." Kasey nodded. "Even so, they would have to know what they were looking for. And the gallery is busy during the day, so whoever did this was taking a chance if they took a knife into the storeroom to damage the paintings while the building was open."

"You mean he risked discovery?" Rylan squatted to look at the pictures.

"Yes," Kasey said. "A member of the gallery staff could have walked in and disturbed him at any time."

"Specifically, who from the staff goes in there?" Rylan asked.

"Most of us do at different times." Bree was glad to find her voice sounded normal. "We exhibit artwork here, but our main purpose is to sell it. Once a piece is purchased and removed from display, we have to replace it. That's when we take new stock from the storeroom. The craft and coffee shops also keep their supplies in there. And, of course, we often have items like these—" her hand shook slightly as she indicated her wrecked pictures "—ready for the next show."

"David goes into the basement fairly regularly as well," Kasey added. "His main job is security, but he sometimes does maintenance. He keeps his tools and ladders down there. Oh, and if there's a show coming up, Lucas Brewer stores his lighting equipment in the basement."

Rylan straightened. "Are the boxes clearly labeled?"

"Yes." Bree turned to Kasey. "Can you bring one of the boxes that contained these paintings, please?"

As Kasey went to a corner of the room where she had stacked a pile of cardboard boxes, Rylan spoke quietly to Bree. "Stupid question, but are you okay?"

She didn't want him to care about her. It was easier to think of him as the man who had abused her trust because he wanted to have sex with her. If she tried to step past that, to analyze his motives, she would get lost in a world of what-ifs.

She tilted her chin. "I'm not going to fall in a heap on the floor. But..." Her eyes went to the paintings. "These were *mine*."

"I'm going to find out who did this, Bree." His gaze snagged hers and held it. She read anger and determination in his eyes, and despite what had transpired between them, she believed he would see this through.

Kasey returned with the box. "This is the label we use for shows." She pointed it out to Rylan. "It's a different color to our standard stock items. It has the show details, the date and the name of the artist."

Rylan nodded. "So anyone who wanted to access Bree's paintings for the Spirit show would be able to find them without any problem."

As her assistant's face crumpled and more tears began to fall, Bree placed an arm around her shoulders. "No one could have predicted this would happen, Kasey."

"Of course not," Rylan said. "I'm just pointing out how easy it would have been. Even so, whoever did it must have had some idea of how Wise Gal works."

Kasey gulped back a sob. "What makes you so sure?"

"You said yourself that the gallery is busy during the day. While anyone can come in here, the person who did this was clearly looking for Bree's paintings. He had to know where the boxes would be stored and how they'd be labeled. It had to be someone who was familiar enough with your basement to know how you store your artwork."

Rylan's eyes met Bree's over Kasey's head, and she knew what he was thinking. The person who had done this wasn't a random visitor. He had sent threatening emails and delighted in scaring her by entering her apartment and moving her property. He had also fired a bullet into a light over her head just the previous night. Rylan had warned her things would escalate. She just never would have foreseen *this*.

"Your show is in two days. Can it go ahead?" Rylan asked.

Bree squared her shoulders. "It has to."

Kasey gave a forlorn cry. "Without *your* work?"

"I won't let the other artists down, so if that's what it takes, yes." She hooked her arm through her assistant's. "We have our work cut out for us, so let's get started." She walked toward the door, turning to look back at Rylan. "What will you do now?"

His expression was grim. "Talk to your brother, then do some background checks on the people who have access to your basement."

* * *

Trey was furious to learn the details of what had happened to his sister's paintings and promised to send a deputy over to the gallery to investigate. Rylan ended the call, secure in the knowledge that the sheriff would play it by the book. Luckily, he wasn't bound by the same constraints.

Although he'd sold his private security consultancy—and made a hefty profit from the proceeds—Rylan still had friends in the business. He knew they would come through for him whenever he needed a favor. Police background checks were bound by strict legalities and took time. Rylan's former colleagues could cross lines that law enforcement didn't even know existed.

A few calls later and he sank back into his seat, feeling some of the tension in his limbs ease. If anyone connected to this gallery had secrets, his PI friends would find them. He was sure of that. In the meantime, his mind returned to the information Bree and Kasey had revealed. He couldn't criticize the security of the gallery, since there had been no reason in the past for it to be tight. There was no doubt, however, that a number of people had access to the basement.

"Maybe a visit to the coffee shop is in order?" He addressed the words in the general direction of his feet. "Seems as good a place as any to start."

Papadum, who had been doing his usual impression of a large corded rug, grunted and shook himself.

As Rylan got to his feet, the dog bounced ahead of him toward the door.

"I can see what you're thinking." Papadum tilted his head at the words. "It would be easy to focus on Lucas

Brewer as our chief suspect. Let's not get ahead of our-selves. Until we find out otherwise, we treat him the same as everyone else. Okay?" Clearly deciding some-thing more was required of him, the canine gave a soft woof. "Yeah, I know. We don't like the guy, so it won't be easy. But let's try."

The coffee shop, Arty Sans, was located at the rear of the main gallery. It was a bright square space with eight tables inside and doors leading into a courtyard with a further six tables and a children's play area. The walls were decorated with paintings bearing discreet price labels. Shelves and boxes of tastefully displayed goods invited patrons to browse at their leisure.

The place was half full, with a small queue at the counter. Even so, as soon as Rylan entered, a middle-aged woman behind the counter pointed at Papadum. "Courtyard."

"Can I get a smoked turkey panini and an espresso?" Rylan asked.

He wasn't sure if the disapproving look she sent over the top of her glasses was meant for him or the dog. "I'll bring it out to you."

Once outside, Papadum was on the receiving end of a rock-star welcome from a group of little girls. Swings and slide were forgotten as they rushed over to him.

"Is it real?" one girl asked, as she reached out a hand to touch him.

Children were one of Papadum's favorite things. He panted happily as Rylan lifted up his bangs to show that yes, he really did have a face.

"Does he do tricks?"

"Can I sit on his back?"

"Can Poppy-dum share my ice cream?"

Rylan answered the high-pitched questions until his order arrived, at which point Papadum's fans were removed by their parents. The woman from the coffee shop placed his food on the table. Papadum, still high on little-girl adulation, offered her his paw.

"It's a sign that he likes you." Rylan checked her name badge. "Judith."

"I've lived around here a long time, and seen many things, but a dog like that?" She shook her head. "That's a new one."

Rylan took his time counting out the cash to pay her. "If you've lived here for some time, you must have seen a lot of changes in the area."

"Tell me about it. Not so long ago, the makeup of this place was very different." Although her gesture took in the small courtyard, she looked upward at the redbrick facade of the gallery and beyond to the rooftops of the other units within the Diamond.

"This was a warehouse, right?" Rylan asked.

"Most of these buildings were originally used for that purpose," Judith said. "There was an iron foundry and feed and grain mill nearby, so these warehouses were needed to store their products. The foundry closed first, but the area retained its industrial identity. This building housed a construction company."

"You talk like someone who knows a lot about it."

She looked self-conscious. "You got me started on my favorite subject. Local history, especially the Second Street area, is a real hobby of mine."

"It's fascinating." It was true, possibly because she was so enthusiastic about it. "What happened?"

Judith shrugged. "The recession hit. Businesses closed one by one. These buildings started to fall into disrepair and there was talk of pulling them down. A foundation was set up to try and save them from demolition and preserve their identity. Some people were very passionate, talking about how it felt to have their future ripped away, but they just couldn't raise the funds. Then a development company bought them up and renovated the buildings. With support from the city council, they sold them on with business incentives for the new owners. The Diamond is the result. Tourists come for the skiing, and this is an additional attraction."

"Was there any bad feeling about the change in the area?" Rylan asked.

Judith pursed her lips. "Not that I'm aware. I run an online local history forum. The comments there were all positive. The developer bought these buildings about five years ago and, at that time, they were a real scar on the Roaring Springs landscape. I don't think anyone would view the way they look now as a bad thing. The Diamond has breathed new life into this area."

She took the money for his meal, together with the tip Rylan gave her, and went back inside. Judith's brief history had given him a new perspective on the Diamond, but he wasn't sure it helped him in any way. It sounded as if the area had been dead, and the new businesses had revived it. Was there a grudge buried in there somewhere? If so, it wasn't immediately obvious.

Although Judith had firmly banished Papadum from the interior of Arty Sans, Rylan was able to view the setup from his position outside. There were three members of staff, including Judith, all of them female. Two worked behind the serving counter while their colleague manned the cash desk. Every now and then, one person would step out from behind the counter to clear tables.

None of the three women looked like crazy stalkers. But that was the problem. Crazy stalkers didn't usually advertise the fact.

Judith had admitted her devotion to local history. Was her positive attitude to the changes sincere, or did she wish the area's true past had been preserved? Even if she hadn't been truthful with him, was it a motive for harassment? And why target Bree? If this was about the Diamond, surely the other businesses would also come under attack? Maybe they had…

He sent a quick text message to Trey, asking him to check. It occurred to Rylan that the sheriff might not like taking orders from the hired help. He shrugged. *Tough.* They were in this together, and he would do whatever it took to protect Bree. If that included ruffling a few Colton feathers, he'd live with the consequences.

He finished his coffee. "Where next?" he asked. Papadum snorted. "Craft shop? Good idea. Maybe we should get you a beret. It would give you a creative air. And let people know where your head is."

Chapter 8

Everything had been gearing up to this day. The gallery show would take place later that evening, and Bree was working with Kasey to make sure the final arrangements were in place. The excitement was like a buzz of electricity in the air and, even though her own paintings weren't on display, she knew this would be one of the best shows Wise Gal had put on.

It was almost noon when she became aware of raised voices coming from the lobby. Frowning, she headed in that direction. The last thing they needed was more trouble.

"I demand to see Ms. Colton." As David tried to reason with him, a man was shouting and waving a booklet in the security guard's face.

Before Bree could step forward from the gallery and

into the lobby, Rylan came out of the promotions office with Papadum at his side. Taking in the scene at a
glance, he gestured for her to stay where she was. Although she had a clear view of what was happening,
she remained out of sight.

"Why do you want to see Ms. Colton?" Rylan asked.

"I need to talk to her about *this*." The man threw
the booklet down onto the reception desk. From where
she was standing, Bree could see that it was the program Kasey had recently sent out containing details of
the Spirit show. It had been mailed to all the gallery's
newsletter subscribers.

As the irate visitor strained to get past David, Rylan
stepped closer. His muscular build and air of authority
worked in a way that David's uniform hadn't. The man
sucked in an audible breath and took a half step back.

"Right now, your body language and tone of voice
aren't going to get you anywhere near Ms. Colton." Although Rylan spoke quietly, it was clear he meant business. "Now, how about you wind your temper back, then
tell me what this is all about?"

For a few seconds, the outcome hung in the balance
as the guy looked like he couldn't decide whether to
swing a punch or walk out. After clenching and un-
clenching his fists at his side a few times, he pointed
to the program he'd thrown down.

"That…*filth* was in my mailbox. I have two young
daughters who regularly collect my letters. They could
have found this."

Filth? Bree was stunned. Wise Gal was family
friendly. The gallery held art classes for kids, and every
exhibit was carefully checked to ensure it met her high

standards. There had been nothing offensive in that program.

"Can you show me what you're talking about?" Rylan asked.

His cool manner appeared to be having an effect on the visitor. Calmer now, he reached for the program. From her vantage point, Bree saw him flick through booklet until he reached the middle pages. Holding it open, he drew out a loose piece of paper and handed it to Rylan. Bree could see it had color pictures printed on both sides, but she couldn't make out the detail.

Rylan studied both sides of the paper in silence. "And this was definitely inside the program you received from the gallery?"

"Didn't I just say that?"

"I just needed to get the facts straight," Rylan said. To anyone else, he was still in complete control. However, Bree, who was in tune with his reactions, could tell he was thinking fast. "One thing I'm certain about is that this—" he tapped a finger on the separate sheet of paper "—was not sent out by the Wise Gal Gallery."

The visitor was unconvinced. "It was inside the program. They were in the same envelope. The gallery stamp was on the back."

"I'm aware that you're upset and, having seen these images, I can understand why. I know Ms. Colton will share my concern." Rylan tucked the paper back into the program. "If you will leave this with me—"

"Not a chance." There was a pronounced sneer on the guy's face. "I see what you're trying to do. You take this away and I don't hear from you again."

"Not at all." Rylan leaned over the reception desk

to get a pen and a piece of paper. "Write down your name and number and I'll be in touch as soon as I've spoken to Ms. Colton. I know she'll want to do something to apologize for the distress this has caused you and your family. Maybe a visit to The Chateau? A ski day for your kids?"

After a few minutes, Rylan was shaking the guy's hand and escorting him out of the building. As he left the lobby and came toward Bree, he was frowning.

"What's going on?" she asked.

"Not here."

He kept on walking, and she matched his long strides, with Papadum trotting beside them. When they reached her office, he held open the door so that she could step inside before him.

"This isn't good."

"I figured that from what I overheard." She held out a hand. "Can I see what was inside the program?"

His lips twisted slightly. "It's not pleasant."

She gave him a cold stare. "I have enough of this from my family. Don't try and sugarcoat real life for me, Rylan. I'm a grown-up. I can deal with it."

"Sorry." He handed over the program.

Even though she'd given him the tough talk, Bree opened it tentatively. He was right. The insert had been cut to the same size and shape as the pages of the program. It even had the Wise Gal logo across the top. But the pictures it included were unlike anything Bree had ever exhibited. They were the worst kind of pornography, depicting a range of unsavory acts.

"How…?" She looked up at Rylan in confusion.

"How did that get inside your promotional program?" he asked. "That's what I was going to ask you."

A tap on the door made them both turn in that direction. When Kasey stepped inside, her face was ashen. "Bree, I don't know what's been going on, but my phone has been ringing nonstop."

"Could it have anything to do with this?" Bree held up the insert.

Kasey gasped as she looked at the images. "When the first few calls came in, I didn't know what was going on. I've had sponsors calling to withdraw their support, customers canceling orders... Even the mayor has been on the phone." She raised tear-filled eyes to Bree's face. "I swear to you...those pictures were not in the programs when they came from the printer. I checked them myself."

"Did you check the programs again before you sent them out?" Bree asked.

"No, I didn't see any reason to do that..." Kasey looked from Bree to Rylan. "Why would someone do this? How did they do it?"

"You forgot the key question," Rylan said. "Who did this?"

By working nonstop for the next three hours, Bree, Kasey and the two receptionists had managed to contact most of the people on the gallery's mailing list. It was a relief to learn that not all of the programs that had been sent out had contained the ghastly insert. Most of those they had spoken to had calmed down once the situation had been explained.

Afterward, Bree put a call into the mayor. Like most

local politicians, he was a little in awe of the Colton name, and it hadn't taken her long to pacify him as well. The local newspaper and radio station had asked for comments. Both had run with a one-sentence statement about a mix-up. So far, it looked like the damage had been contained.

"But it still means someone got into Kasey's office and put those things inside the programs before she mailed them." Rylan called Trey and relayed the details of the incident to him. "That took time and planning."

"It also took audacity," the sheriff said. "Whoever did it could have been interrupted at any time."

"Unless it was done at night, or when the gallery was closed." Rylan had given it some thought. "If that's the case, the person who did this overrode the security system. David thought the person who attacked him that morning was heading for Bree's apartment. What if that was a cover? What if the guy had actually just left the gallery?"

"It's a possibility," Trey conceded.

"There are two lines of inquiry here," Rylan said. "Someone had those pornographic leaflets printed. And he also entered this gallery at some point."

"I'm on it," Trey assured him. "What's the motive here? Damage Bree's business so she's forced out of the Diamond? Wasn't that the message in the original emails?"

"It's a two-pronged attack. It's personal because he's attempting to destroy her reputation with these vile pictures, but he's also hitting the gallery. After the guy who came in here today to complain gave us a heads-up, we've been able to calm things down," Rylan said.

"Nevertheless, it's the last thing Bree needed to deal with right now."

Frustration was building like a bubble in his chest. How was he supposed to endure this? Wanting to care for Bree, yet being forced to keep his distance? He could be her bodyguard, but he wanted to be more than that. He wanted to hold her, to shoulder her troubles and shut out the world. But it was his own damned fault that he couldn't do those things. He had told her lies, broken her trust and hurt her beyond repair. And the worst part? He'd known all along what would happen once she knew the truth, but had not done anything to stop it.

"I'll be there later," Trey said. "I just hope Bree has some beer, as well as the usual champagne."

After ending the call, Rylan went in search of David. He found the security guard studying the alarm panel that was situated in the staff kitchen.

"Someone must have gotten in here and tampered with those programs while they were in Kasey's office." David echoed Rylan's own thoughts. "But I can't find any disruption to the alarm system."

Rylan looked at the display. He had a good understanding of security systems, having devised a few himself. This was one of the most expensive on the market, and it had all the features he would recommend. The problem was, no matter how supposedly foolproof the technology, there would always be someone who could get around it.

David was looking for signs that someone had switched off the alarms. If the person they were looking for was clever enough to do that, it was possible he was also smart enough to cover up what he'd done.

"What about the cameras?" he asked.

"It'll take time, but I can start looking through the images," David said.

"No. The sheriff's office will do that. Just make sure everything is preserved for him."

Rylan left him and went to Bree's office. The door was open, and he paused before going in. She was seated at her desk with her chin resting on her hand as she gazed into space. Papadum had his head on her feet. Rylan took a moment to just drink her in.

"Don't you have a show to prepare for?"

Bree turned her head, blinking slowly as though his words had roused her from a trance. As he gazed at her, tenderness was like a sugar rush directly into his bloodstream.

"Oh." She looked at her cell phone. "I didn't realize the time."

She looked so forlorn it took every ounce of strength he possessed to stop from crossing the room and wrapping his arms around her. "You've worked hard for this, Bree."

"And he's managed to take it from me." Her lip trembled.

"He can only do that if you let him." He snapped his fingers to Papadum, and the dog ambled to his side. "Don't let him."

Bree remained in her seat for a moment, then she gave a decisive nod. "You're right. I need to get ready."

Kasey was arranging the refreshment table, where champagne and canapés awaited the guests. The artists stood around, either alone or in small groups, looking nervous, proud or both. David waited by the doors, decked out in his security guard uniform, checking his watch.

Rylan, who looked better in a suit than any man had a right to, strode the length of the gallery with Papadum at his side. As he approached her, Bree smoothed the skirts of her coffee-colored vintage lace cocktail gown over her hips.

"You okay?" He raised a brow in her direction.

I am now. How did he do that? Reassure her just by being there? More importantly, why did she still let him?

She nodded. "Let's do this thing."

Together, they headed toward the entrance. At a signal from Bree, David unlocked the doors and stepped back as though expecting a crowd to pour through. Nothing happened.

"No one is here," Rylan said.

"This is normal." Bree tried to reassure herself with the words. To convince herself it wasn't because of those awful images that had been sent out with the programs. "People generally arrive later than the time on the invitation." The doors swung open. "Except my mother…"

Audrey was elegant in cream satin, her smile wide and proud. Bree gave an exclamation of delight when she saw the man at her side. "Dad!"

Calvin Colton was the middle son of ninety-four-year-old Earl, the founder of The Colton Empire. The shortest, thinnest and quietest of the three brothers, Calvin had dark brown hair that was graying and receding and kind brown eyes. Since marrying Audrey, he had embraced her commitment to noble causes.

"You didn't think I'd stay away?" Calvin kissed Bree on both cheeks. "Let me look at you." Although his smile was as wide as ever, she could see the concern on his face. "I wish you'd come home, sweetheart. Let us keep you safe."

Audrey drew Rylan forward. "Calvin, you remember Rylan. The *art promoter*."

Bree rolled her eyes. "You can drop the act, Mom. Rylan has told me the truth about why he's here. And Trey knows all about it now as well."

"Well, that's a relief." Audrey tucked one hand into Bree's arm and the other into Rylan's. "I can stop worrying and relax, knowing that Rylan will be at your side the whole time."

Bree cast a sidelong glance in Rylan's direction. Did his lips just twitch? When he looked her way, his expression was all boyish innocence.

"Do you really think *he* will come here tonight?" Bree asked, as her parents moved away to view the exhibits. The idea that the stalker might be at the show, moving among the guests, bothered her more than she cared to admit. "Hasn't he scored one victory already with the programs?"

"It wouldn't surprise me," Rylan bit out. "Where's the fun for him if he doesn't get to observe the impact of all his hard work?"

"Fun?" Bree shivered slightly, wrapping her arms around herself.

His expression softened. "Sorry. Wrong choice of word. But, in my experience, stalkers like to get up close to their victims as often as they can."

"*Is* he a stalker?" Her brow furrowed. "He wanted me

to leave because he said the Coltons took advantage of people who were less fortunate. I thought stalking was more about an attraction that had become obsessive."

"There isn't a stereotypical stalker," Rylan said. "Just as there isn't one type of victim. However his campaign against you may have started out, there is no doubt it has become personal. And what he's doing is in fact classic stalking."

They were interrupted by more arrivals. As Bree went to greet them, she tried to push aside the thought that any one of them could be the perpetrator who was targeting her. Even so, as the gallery began to fill with invited guests, there was a constant prickle of electricity down her spine. The sensation of someone watching her refused to go away and, despite everything she said to the contrary, she was glad to have Rylan close by.

Together, they spoke to the group of young artists Rylan had been promoting. Bree was reassured by their obvious gratitude to him for all his hard work on their behalf.

"I may have a proposition for you," she told the group of six women and four men. "It's still early days, but I'm in talks with the city council about producing some Banksy-style street art here in the Diamond. If any of you are interested—" She laughed as her words were drowned out by the excited clamor. "Okay. Let's leave the liaison to Rylan."

After an hour or two, Bree could officially claim that the show was a success. The gallery was crowded with collectors, critics, artists, students, journalists, Bree's friends and a few members of her family. She had enlisted the help of a local non-profit African choir and drumming group to add color to the event. Their contribution had been so popular that they were continuing to perform, with some of the guests joining them and dancing to the irresistible beat.

"You think he's here?" Trey had managed to snag two beers from somewhere, and he handed one to Rylan.

Rylan had been watching Lucas Brewer, who was checking the uplighters at the base of one of the sculptures. He turned his attention to Trey. "Don't you?"

With their superior height, the two men were able to easily scan the crowd. "It would help if we had a clue—any clue—to his identity," Trey said.

"Nothing on the email address?" Rylan asked.

"You know how it works. If, while using my usual laptop, in my own home, I open my main email account and send a message to you, the police will be able to determine where it came from with only minimal effort. If, on the other hand, I buy a cheap electronic tablet for cash, take it to a bar, log into their guest Wi-Fi, create a new email account and send the message from that…it's a different story."

"Either way, you also have to prove whose fingers were on the keyboard at the time the message was typed," Rylan said.

"It's a whole lot easier with the first scenario." Trey drained his beer. "I'm going to mingle, chat to a few people. You?"

Rylan shook his head. "Staying with Bree."

"Good answer."

"I need to thank everyone for coming," Bree said. "The proceeds from this show are going to charity, and the total amount raised will be posted on the gallery website in the morning."

She could see Rylan assessing the situation. Although the choir and drummers were in position at the far end of the gallery, there was a small stage near the entrance to Arty Sans. A microphone and overhead spotlight had been set up there, together with a podium. Since Bree never used written notes, the podium remained empty.

"Okay." He nodded. "I'll stand to one side of you."

"He wouldn't make a public move." She turned worried eyes to his face. "Would he?"

"I don't think so." He placed a hand on her arm, sending electric shocks along her nerve endings. "It's not his style." Looking down at where his fingers connected with her bare flesh, he quickly withdrew his touch. "Sorry."

Bree knew his intention had been to comfort her, but she didn't know how they would get past this. Because even though they were no longer together, their need to touch each other was instinctual, as simple and as primal as breathing. And she didn't believe it would fade with time.

She sighed. This was not the place for an in-depth analysis of her feelings toward Rylan. She spoke to Kasey, who organized for the choir to take a break while the guests gathered around the stage.

Holding up her long skirts, Bree gripped the microphone and stepped under the glare of the single spotlight. She had done this several times now and, although she was naturally a reserved person, she found it got easier each time.

Smiling at her mom and dad, who were looking at her with a glow of pride, she started with a simple thank-you. "To all of the artists who have made this such a stunning visual celebration. We have so much talent in the African American community, and it is my pleasure and honor to be able to share it with you."

As she spoke, she felt something drop onto the top of her head. It could have been an insect, or a small piece of plaster from the ceiling. Possibly a spot of water. Bree shook her head slightly and continued, listing the people who had helped make the show a success.

The next time it happened—a definite *plop* onto her hair—she shifted position, trying to avoid the irritation that was distracting her. Even so, if she moved too far from the spotlight, she wouldn't be visible to the people at the back of the room.

"...and, of course, my amazing assistant, Kasey Spencer, without whom I would not be able to function..."

This time it was three heavy droplets in quick succession, one of which ran down from her hair and onto the back of her neck. Bree raised a hand to brush the liquid away, looking up at the ceiling at the same time to see if she could locate the source of the nuisance. As she did, everything slowed.

Because her face was tilted up, she saw the ceiling tile above the spotlight move, then fall away. The liquid that poured like a river out of the gap was thick and dark, its smell sickly and overpowering. It covered her head and shoulders, running down her arms and dripping into a puddle at her feet. She must look like something from a horror movie.

Bree froze, unable to move or even breathe. She was vaguely aware of the shocked faces of the guests, of her mom's mouth opening, ready to scream, of Trey charging toward her. But it was Rylan who reached her first. It was only when he wrapped his jacket around her and pulled his shirt over his head to wipe the sticky mess from her face that the trembling started. She staggered into his arms, her mind whirling, her heart beating a new, uneven rhythm.

"It's chocolate." He scooped her into his arms and carried her from the stage. "Just chocolate."

Chapter 9

Just chocolate.

Rylan's fists clenched every time he thought of it. He saw the thick dark liquid pouring through the opening in the ceiling onto Bree's upturned face. Until the sweet, sickly smell had hit him, he'd thought it was worse. He'd believed for an instant that his beautiful Bree was being doused in blood.

He shook his head, clearing it of the fury that threatened to consume him. What was the point of wanting to rush out and take a swing at an invisible opponent? He had to stay calm and confront this rationally. Bree needed his skill and experience on her side. His emotions would have to stay locked away.

It hadn't been blood, but did that make it any better? Her show, everything she loved and worked so hard for had been ruined. It was bad enough when her paintings had been destroyed. But this?

No one would remember the artwork, the money she had raised for charity, the choir, the celebratory atmosphere or the prestigious guests. They would remember Bree, standing on that stage, humiliated, covered from head to foot in chocolate. Of course, the journalists who had been there would be only too eager to report on it. Because she was a Colton, there would be those who would be equally happy to learn of her mortification.

His tumultuous thoughts were interrupted by the security buzzer, and Rylan was glad of it. It was Trey, and he pressed the button to admit him.

"Where is she?" Trey looked all around as soon as he strode through the door.

"In the shower." Rylan checked his watch. "It's been an hour."

"You're sure she's okay?"

"She answers me when I speak to her through the door, which I've been doing every five minutes," Rylan said. "Her response started out as a request to leave her alone. It's been getting steadily less polite."

"Sorry." Trey rubbed a hand over his face. "I know you're not an amateur. How did you get Mom and Dad to leave?"

"Bree told them she was fine and that she'd call them later. They didn't want to go, but they knew I'd be here." Rylan led the way through to the kitchen and pointed to the coffeemaker. "What did you find in the gallery?"

"David Swanson helped me to get rid of the guests. Most people were keen to leave. They were in shock and just wanted to give Bree their best wishes. The press—" Trey's lips tightened. "Yeah, a few of them needed more persuasion."

"I don't suppose you can stop the story from getting out?" Rylan already knew the answer even as he asked the question.

Trey choked back a laugh. "About as much chance of that as an overnight thaw on Pine Peak."

Rylan handed him a cup of coffee. "And the chocolate? How was that rigged up?"

"A basic electronic device with a remote control. The chocolate was in a tub. It was set up so that when the button was pressed on the remote control, the ceiling tile would drop away and the tub would tilt forward at the same time," Trey said. "We found the remote control in a trash can in the lobby."

"Fingerprints?" Rylan asked.

"I've sent it for testing, but I'm not hopeful. Anyone who goes to these lengths is likely to have taken the precaution of wearing gloves."

A sound made them turn. Bree was dressed in gray sweatpants and a blue sweater. She wore thick socks and a towel was wound around her head like a turban. Rylan thought she looked small, fragile and so lovely it made his heart hurt to look at her.

"Hey." He tried for a bright tone that didn't work. "Do you want coffee? Anything to eat?"

"I'll get some water." She went to the refrigerator, pausing to pat Papadum as he shoved his nose into her hand.

Me and the dog. We both have it bad.

When she returned, Trey told her what he'd found out about the setup with the chocolate.

Bree paused with her water bottle part way to her mouth. "Wouldn't that take time to organize?"

Trey shrugged. "The actual electronics might take some putting together, but I don't think it would have been done in the gallery. I'm picturing our guy making the device and then putting it in place as a complete unit. That would only take minutes."

"But it was in full view of the gallery," Rylan pointed out. "Anyone carrying a tub of chocolate and an electronic device would have stood out. Plus, he must have had to climb a stepladder to booby trap the ceiling tile. Just like the stunt with the programs, it must have been done when the gallery was closed."

"I hadn't thought of that," Trey admitted. "But there haven't been any break-ins, right?"

Bree shook her head. "With everything that's been going on, I would have told you."

"Even so, someone must have overridden your security system." Trey headed toward the door. "I'll check with David before I head home."

When he'd gone, Rylan watched Bree's face as she picked at the label on her water bottle. It took every ounce of willpower he had not to go to her and take her into his arms.

"He's winning, isn't he?" Her eyes, when she lifted them to his face, were swimming with tears.

"While I have breath in my body, he won't hurt you, Bree."

"Even though I've washed myself over and over, I can still smell the chocolate." As she choked back a sob, her cell phone pinged. Reaching into the pocket of her sweatpants, she pulled it out. "It's an email."

Her fingers trembled slightly as she highlighted the text and swiped the speak button on her cell phone screen. The serene voice read the email out loud.

Sweet like chocolate. Is that how your blood tastes? Guess there's only one way to find out.

Bree hadn't expected to sleep, and she'd been right. Every time she closed her eyes, her mind insisted on replaying the awful incident.

She had fought to overcome the shyness that had characterized her childhood, but it was still there in the background. The fear of humiliation, of pointing fingers, of being the center of attention for all the wrong reasons...

Today, her worst nightmare had become reality. She still couldn't believe it had happened, and in front of everybody who mattered in her chosen sphere. It was as if the stalker knew and had chosen the perfect way to shame her. The chocolate had washed off, but the trauma went pore deep. She would never live this down. People would make jokes about chocolate when she was in a nursing home.

If he lets me live that long.

Abandoning any pretense at sleep, she sat up in bed, hugging her knees beneath her chin.

No. She wasn't going to think that way. *He* was a coward, tormenting her from afar. Bree was determined to survive this. The question was...would Wise Gal?

She bit her lower lip. Her beautiful gallery, her pride and joy, the symbol of her independence... The stalker was getting at her through her work, trying to drive her out. She couldn't let him win. But how could she fight a faceless enemy?

Her thoughts jumped a step, reaching Rylan of their own accord. She had never felt so conflicted. He had betrayed her. It sounded dramatic, but it was true. Bree, who didn't give her trust lightly, had opened up to Rylan, giving him a glimpse inside her heart. When she found out he'd been lying to her, he'd taken that priceless gift and made it worthless. The pain of what he'd done didn't recede. Somehow, it kept multiplying.

Once she'd discovered the truth, all she wanted was to walk away from him. Figuring the hurt would be wiped out if she never had to look into those smiling blue eyes. That this desperate longing to touch him would fade if he weren't around.

But fate had other plans for them.

With a stalker on her tail and Rylan the best man to protect her, showing him the door was going to have to wait. Which meant they had been thrown closer together than ever. The attraction hadn't gone away—it was as strong as ever—but it no longer had a release valve. Wanting him, while not *wanting* to want him… It was a special kind of hell. On top of everything else that was going on, it was driving her crazy.

At the same time, she was glad of his presence. If she had to face this nightmare, there was no one she would rather have at her side. Not only did Rylan know what needed to be done to defeat the person who was harassing her, he also understood how she was feeling about the long-term damage this could do to her life.

Bree had confided in him enough that he knew how hard it had been for her to break free of the Colton chains. No matter how much she loved her family, Bree had to cling to her independence. Rylan was the only person who appreciated that. He hadn't judged or questioned her. He just got it, without the need for lengthy explanations.

Maybe his empathy had something to do with the undercurrent of sadness she sensed within him. In the short time they'd been lovers, they had been too busy enjoying being together for any lengthy soul searching. She had assumed they would get there eventually.

Bree sighed. *I thought we had time to get to know each other. Back when I didn't know it was a farce.*

A snuffling sound drew her attention to the bedroom door. There were only two other occupants of the apartment, and she didn't imagine Rylan would try to get her attention in quite such an unusual way. When the snorting was followed by a scratch and a whine, she slid from the bed and opened the door.

"What's up, Papadum? Can't sleep either?"

The dog nudged her thigh with his nose, then dashed down the hall to where his leash was hanging by the front door.

Bree followed him. "Oh. Call of nature?"

She cast a look over her shoulder in the direction of the guest bedroom. Papadum was a bright dog. He knew who would wake up easily, and it wasn't his master. A glance out the window showed her that dawn was lighting the sky.

She hesitated only briefly. Rylan would tell her not to go without him, but how much harm could she come to if she had Papadum with her? The poor dog couldn't wait for his comfort break, and there was no point in disturbing Rylan for a five-minute walk to the waste ground on Second Street. Since she was already awake, there was only one sensible solution.

After pulling on her padded coat and sheepskin boots, she stuffed doggie waste bags into her pockets. Papadum was almost dancing with excitement, or possibly desperation, as she attached his leash. Bree barely had to time to snatch up her keys before he hauled her out through the door.

She savored the silence as she walked from the Diamond along Second Street. This was a time of day she rarely saw and it was indeed a sight to behold. The pink, purple and orange hues of morning dripped from the sky and onto the dark shapes of the mountains. Colorado sunrise. It made her long for her paintbrushes.

Once Papadum had taken care of business, and Bree had cleaned up after him, she let the dog investigate for a few minutes. He charged through the grass, nose down, chasing different scents like an oversized mop swishing over the ground. When the cold made her start to lose all feeling in her hands and feet, even Papadum's antics couldn't subdue the coffee cravings. Convincing the dog that he needed to accompany her took all her powers of persuasion, together with most of her strength.

As she neared the Diamond, Bree's thoughts were on the gallery. How would she approach today? She couldn't just shrug off what had happened at the show, but how much was she prepared to tell other people? Was talking openly about the stalker the right way to deal with the situation? Rylan was probably the best person to answer that question.

A sound close by made her heartbeat quicken, and the sensation annoyed her. This was what *he* had done to her. The stalker's threats had made her nervous to be around other people. When she realized that someone was approaching her from behind, her self-preservation instincts kicked in a fraction too late.

Bree swung around at the same time that Papadum growled. The man, who was inches behind them, wore a black ski mask covering his face. Grabbing her roughly by one arm, he covered her mouth with his other hand. As Bree struggled to break free of his hold, Papadum jumped up, throwing his full weight onto the attacker.

The dog had taken her assailant by surprise, and Bree followed up, twisting around and kicking him hard on the ankle. He jerked away, muttering a curse. As he released his grip on her mouth, she seized her opportunity, and let out a few piercing screams.

Shouts and footsteps came from the direction of the Diamond. Flinging Bree to the ground, her attacker ran off. Moments later, two men in delivery uniforms came dashing over and helped her to her feet.

"We saw everything. Are you hurt?"

She shook her head, drawing in a deep breath of cold air. "Thank you for coming to my rescue."

Her fingers shook as she reached into her pocket for her cell phone. There was only one voice she needed to hear. In that instant, it didn't matter why.

"Rylan…"

"People will think I'm running away." Bree didn't look like a woman who was considering his suggestion.

"Who the hell cares what people think? All that matters is that you'll be safe." Rylan's blood ran cold at the thought of what had happened to her less than an hour ago. He was assuming that the assailant was her stalker. It was too coincidental for it to be some random mugger. Either way, the attack was a stark reminder of her vulnerability.

From the sound of it, only a combination of Papadum and luck had saved her. Anything could have happened. The guy had upped his game, and Rylan wasn't prepared to take any more risks.

But just when he had come up with the perfect solution, Bree's stubborn streak had kicked in. *Again.*

"I don't even know where your ranch is." They were seated at her table, and she was hunched over her third cup of coffee.

"You want me to show you on a map?"

She sighed, pushing curls back from her face. Rylan was momentarily distracted. Most days, Bree ruthlessly pulled her hair back into a braid, but he preferred to see it loose like this. Every kink, twist and coil fascinated him, and he loved to run his fingers through them. Since the opportunity wasn't likely to come his way again, he should probably put it from his mind and concentrate on the more immediate issue.

"That's not what I meant," Bree said. "It's just…if I leave my apartment and come to stay at your place, it will feel like he's winning."

It was time for a cold dose of reality. "If you stay here and he gets his hands on you again, he *will* have won. It will be game over." She shivered, and he softened his tone. "Why didn't you wake me?"

She raised troubled eyes to his face. "Papadum

needed some potty time. You were asleep. It didn't seem like a big deal."

"Bree, until this guy is caught, *everything* is a big deal."

She rubbed her upper arm. "Why will things be better if I stay at your ranch?"

"Firstly, only Trey and your parents will know you are there. I bought it very recently, so it's not like anyone locally knows who I am or is aware of any connection to you. But, since it's so isolated, there isn't another occupied property for miles anyway." He smiled. "And the security system is second to none."

Unexpectedly, she returned the smile. He'd missed that. "I'd expect nothing less from you."

"Is there anything at the gallery that can't wait a few days?" He saw the frown start to pull her brows together and knew what she was thinking. "This is not about letting him push you out, Bree. This is about giving my contacts time to complete their background checks, while getting you away from his clutches. Tell Kasey you're taking a few days off to focus on your painting. She can still call you, or email, if she needs anything."

"A few days off to paint." Her expression changed, became dreamy. "Wow."

"Tempting, huh?"

Bree nodded. "I just realized I haven't done that since Wise Gal opened. But it's not that easy—"

"Bree, it's as easy, or as difficult, as you make it." Rylan could see her wavering. "But I'm not offering you a vacation. I'm trying to save your life."

She placed her coffee cup on the counter. "Could I come back to the gallery if I'm needed?"

"Of course. I'd be right at your side." He nodded toward Papadum, who was finishing his breakfast. "Me and the big guy."

"One more question." Bree looked embarrassed. "How many bedrooms does your place have?"

"Four." His heart twisted slightly that she needed to ask. "You can have your choice of the guest bedrooms. Dinah, who helps me out with the animals, has her own cabin on the edge of the property."

She got to her feet. "I'll pack some stuff."

When she'd gone, Rylan breathed a sigh of relief. He checked his messages, but there was nothing new from his PI colleagues. Although he'd stressed the urgency of the background checks he wanted, he knew they would have cases of their own to investigate. These things took time, and the stalker's connection to Bree might not be immediately apparent. Or it could be glaringly obvious. His thoughts returned to Lucas Brewer.

He should just ask Bree straight out about Lucas. The guy was clearly attracted to her. If they'd dated, or he'd tried anything, and she'd given him the brush off, it made Lucas's motive stronger. *Just ask her.* It wasn't that easy. There were some questions to which he didn't want answers. Bree and Lucas? That was an image he didn't want inside his head.

Papadum came over and leaned against his leg. "Is this male sympathy or a request for more breakfast?" The dog sighed heavily. "I know. I made this mess. I have to live with it." Papadum placed his paws on Rylan's knees and peeped through his fringe of hair into his master's eyes. "You think I'm an idiot? You could be right, but at least I'm not the one who has my breakfast on my ears."

Chapter 10

About a half hour outside Roaring Springs, Rylan left the main highway and followed increasingly remote winding roads. Bree was content to take in the beauty of the surrounding scenery. They were heading away from Colton country, leaving Pine Peak and its skiing and tourist attractions behind, and this wasn't an area she knew well.

All around them, the aspen wore their bright green spring leaves, standing out in contrast to the darker pine forests. She glimpsed shimmering lakes and swooping waterfalls, with wildflowers beginning to peek through the remaining patches of snow on the lower ground. The views were gentler here than those of her high-altitude home. Still amazing, just less gasp-inducing.

Rylan's focus was on the road, and Bree found her

own attention straying occasionally to his handsome profile. She missed their closeness. Missed being able to touch him whenever she wanted to. Missed him teasing her and calling her "wise gal" in that half-flirty, half-affectionate way. Missed falling asleep in his arms.

As if he could sense her thoughts, his eyes flickered her way. "Did you speak to your parents?"

"Yes. After the incident at the gallery, they are relieved that I am finally taking steps to put my safety first. Although they did remind me about a gala at The Chateau tomorrow night. It's for one of mom's favorite charities, the Second Street Intercultural Center. The whole Colton family will be there."

"So you have to go?" Rylan asked.

"It's sort of expected." She didn't know how to explain it to him. It wasn't just a fancy party. It was about giving something back to the Roaring Springs community. Some people were quick to criticize the Coltons for their wealth and elite lifestyle, but those people never saw how much her family did for good causes.

"We can go." He looked away from the road briefly again, a smile lifting one corner of his mouth. "I have a tux."

Bree turned to look out the window, picturing the scene. Little Bree on the arm of a handsome man. Wouldn't *that* raise a few well-groomed eyebrows? And in a week or two, when the Colton cousins and their exclusive friends found out that Rylan had been hired to look after her?

Hey, I survived being publicly coated in chocolate. What's one more humiliation?

"It'll be a fun night." Her voice reflected her lack of

enthusiasm. Papadum, who was reclining on the back-seat, gave a soft grunt, and Bree turned to look at him. "Sorry, no dogs allowed, but you won't be missing anything."

They continued driving in silence for a few more minutes before Rylan turned onto a dirt track. After bumping along for about a hundred yards, he slowed as he approached high double gates bearing the sign Mountain View Ranch. The gates opened, and Rylan drove through.

"Electronic signal." He pointed to a small disk on his windshield.

Bree looked back to see the gates closing behind them. "Couldn't an intruder just climb the gates, or the fence?"

"Not without triggering an alarm. And security cameras cover the whole perimeter." He turned to smile at her. "What's the point of devising a state-of-the-art system if you're not going to try it out on your own home?"

The track continued beyond the gates, and Bree's eyes widened as she took in the vista. They were in a vast hollow, with distant mountains encircling them. "I guess this place was aptly named."

"I never get tired of waking up and seeing these views." Rylan slowed the car and pointed as he drove. "My ranch is a little under a thousand acres. There's parkland on one side, a Bureau of Land Management preservation area on another, then over there is wilderness. Finally, in that direction, there's an old ranch. It's fallen into disuse and is neglected. If I could just get my hands on that—" He shrugged. "But I can't."

Bree was intrigued by the comment, but she didn't

have time to ask for clarification. The track was rising, and they were approaching a house that had been built on a ridge, overlooking a small creek. It was a long, low wooden building with a wraparound porch. Behind it, the lower slopes of the mountains rose in a patchwork of different greens and browns with the clear blue sky and fluffy clouds stretching endlessly beyond.

Nearby, there was a stable block, paddock and a number of outbuildings. Rylan halted the car and turned to face her. "Home."

"It's…" There didn't seem to be a suitable word. "Incredible."

She sensed him relax slightly at her reaction. "I think so."

As they exited the car, there was a flurry of noise. It was a scrabbling of claws with an accompaniment of yelping, barking and whining. There was also another noise that she couldn't quite place. "I should have warned you—"

They were the only words Rylan managed to get out before an assorted pack of dogs came hurtling into view. Bree counted to six before they were too close, and she became confused. Big, small, hairy, smooth… and woolly. They threw themselves on Rylan as if they were being pursued by demons and he was their only hope of salvation.

"Get down, you lunatics." Laughing, he managed to restore something close to sanity. "We have company."

It was a mistake. Sensing fresh blood, the dogs hurled themselves on Bree and attempted to kiss her into submission. Staying upright with difficulty, she tried to fend them off with pats.

"Sorry." Rylan came to her rescue. With a dog under each arm, he pushed some of the others out of the way. "You may not believe this now, but they will calm down once they get used to you. And some of this is because they haven't seen me for a few days."

A deep bark drew their attention to the car. Papadum clawed at the window, demanding his freedom. Once he was released, the focus of the dogs' energy changed. The pack became a whirling mass of tails and limbs as they greeted their friend. After a few seconds, the whole group darted off across the grass.

Bree watched them as they disappeared out of sight. "I know you said you have a unique collection, but one of those dogs is not a dog."

"That's Merry. We do have other sheep here, but for some reason, she prefers to hang out with the dogs. She even eats dog biscuits and sleeps in the kennels." Rylan opened the trunk and lifted out her bags. "Did I mention that I rescue animals?"

"No, but I figured from some of the things you said that you had an unusual setup here."

He grinned. "Let me show you the house, then I'll introduce you to some of the other residents."

The interior of the house was as natural and beautiful as the outside. Light wood, neutral walls and local stone complemented the warm hues of the furnishings. Bree's artistic eye approved of the open fireplace, the scrubbed kitchen table, the patchwork throws and the windows with their sweeping views. If the pristine walls might benefit from one or two carefully placed landscape paintings… Well, she could always make that suggestion in a day or two.

"This is wonderful, Rylan."

He seemed relieved by her approval. "Let me show you the bedrooms."

"I really don't mind which room you give me," Bree said. "Although that view over the creek is stunning."

"That means you need this room." Rylan carried her bags along the hall and pushed open a door with his knee. Their entrance into the room was greeted with an outraged wail.

"Oh, goodness." Bree took a step back. "I didn't mean to disturb anyone."

"It's Cindy from Finance."

Confused, Bree peeped around the broad expanse of his shoulders, only to discover there was just one occupant of the room. A black-and-white feline, who was curled up on a large floor cushion giving her a measured stare.

She turned to face Rylan. "You have a cat called Cindy from Finance?"

"I was at the veterinarian's office one day and a woman brought her in. She said someone she worked with had suffered a stroke. The cat was in a bad way. Malnourished and frightened. She'd brought it in to be euthanized because the owner couldn't look after it anymore. Cindy from Finance…that was the name of the cat's owner," Rylan said.

The only thing to do with this sort of conversation was go along with it. "Do you call her Cindy for short?"

His expression remained neutral, but laughter danced in his eyes. "No. I call her Nance."

Bree regarded him thoughtfully. "Do you ever turn an animal away?"

He looked shocked. "Why would I do that when I can help them?"

Bree mentally adjusted her perception of Rylan from strong, hard security professional to compassionate animal rescuer. But hadn't she always known there was this other side to him? The one that would never leave a fellow creature in distress? Underneath all those muscles was a huge heart. She just wasn't sure Rylan understood why that made him special.

She stepped into the room. It was bright and sunny, with a huge wood-framed bed, matching closet and chest, and an adjoining shower room.

"This is perfect," she told Rylan. "As long as Nance doesn't mind?"

As Rylan stooped to lift Nance up, the cat meowed and shifted position. A different noise from the cushion drew Bree's attention.

"Oh, my stars. Does she have kittens?" she asked.

"No." Rylan rolled his eyes. "She has ducklings."

He raised the cat slightly to reveal a group of five fluffy yellow ducklings clustered together beneath her. After giving him an offended look, Nance stretched, then flounced from the room. The ducklings waddled after her in a little line.

Bree sat on the bed and, placing her head in her hands, gave way to the laughter that had been threatening to overwhelm her. When she sat up, Rylan was watching her with a bemused smile.

"Their mother abandoned them when they were a few days old. Dinah has been hand-rearing them, but, when they saw Nance, they decided she was their new mama. She doesn't seem to mind." He jerked a thumb in the direction the cat and the ducklings had taken. "In fact, I think she likes it."

"You didn't tell me I would be walking away from a crazy stalker and onto the set of a feel-good movie," Bree said. "What next? Dancing ponies?"

He grinned. "Nothing so attractive, I'm afraid. The best I can offer you is a donkey with attitude."

"Let me guess. His name is Peter from Admin?"

"Of course not. That would be silly." He waited for a moment or two, keeping her in suspense. "*Her* name is Wonkey. She's lame."

"Wonkey the Donkey." Bree shook her head. "This day keeps getting better."

"Wait until you meet Wonkey before you say that. She's a shaggy, bad-tempered rescue ass with one ear so bent out of shape it looks like a crowbar." He reached out a hand, and Bree took it without thinking. "Ready for the rest of the tour?"

"Why not?"

It was hard to explain the difference just being there had already made. From the moment Rylan had driven through those gates, Bree's heart felt lighter. It was as if she didn't have to hide behind a mask of tightly controlled efficiency. She could be honest here at the Mountain View Ranch. And honesty meant admitting she was scared. She needed this beautiful, peaceful, *safe* place with its assortment of funny characters to lift her out of the darkness that had been dragging her down.

Her gaze went to the man at her side. Did that mean admitting that she needed more from *him*? She looked down at her hand in his. Carefully, she eased her fingers away, noticing the way his features tensed as she did.

Let's not get ahead of ourselves. It would take a lot more than kindness to animals to mend the trust he had shattered.

Rylan had known Dinah Murphy for a few years. Her ex-husband had worked for his security firm. When they split up, and Dinah was down on her luck, Rylan had given her some office work. It had soon become clear that they shared a love of animals, and when he bought the ranch, he'd offered her a place to live and her dream job.

Dinah's cabin was in a private location, close to the boundary of Rylan's land and the abandoned ranch, but he found her cleaning out the kennels. She was short, plump and freckled, with a smile as big as the Colorado mountains and an even bigger heart.

"Hey." She held out her hand in greeting to Bree, then thought better of it. "Um…you know." She indicated the scrubbing brush she'd just been using.

Bree laughed. "Do you need some help?"

Rylan could almost read Dinah's mind. *Didn't you say your name was Colton?* Bree's family didn't have a reputation for rolling up their sleeves and lending a hand with the dirty chores. From what he'd seen, it was unfair, but perceptions still lingered.

"I'm almost done here," Dinah said. "Maybe another time?"

"How have things been?" Rylan asked.

"Oh, you know. The usual chaos." Dinah smiled at Bree. "I wouldn't change a thing."

"What about Boo?"

She shook her head. "Not good."

"Who's Boo?" Bree staggered slightly as she spoke. The reason turned out to be Papadum, who, having discovered one of his best friends was nearby, had barged his way into the kennels and straight into the back of her knees.

"Boo is a goose," Rylan explained.

"Is he ill?" As Bree stooped to pet Papadum, the other dogs charged through the gap he'd made in the barrier. Dinah calmly shooed them outside, so she could finish her cleaning.

"No, he's in mourning." Bree gave him a look that said she wasn't quite sure whether to believe him. "Seriously. Geese mate for life, but Boo's partner, Lucy— they are wild geese and Dinah chose the names—was struck and killed by a car a few weeks ago. Boo was devastated. When the rest of the flock moved on, Boo stayed at the very spot where Lucy died."

"That's so sad." Bree looked from Rylan to Dinah. "So you rescued him?"

"We did. Although it wasn't easy," Rylan said. "In fact, it was one of the hardest things we've done. We couldn't leave him where he was, right at the side of a busy road...but Boo didn't want to come with us."

"I still have the bruises." Dinah rubbed her thighs reminiscently. "He was one unhappy gander."

"The problem is that Boo is still pining for Lucy. He doesn't want to eat or drink. He spends most of his time huddled in a corner," Rylan said. "We're worried that he could die of a broken heart."

"Can I see him?" There was a sheen of tears in Bree's beautiful amber eyes.

"Sure. I was planning to check on him." Rylan turned back to Dinah. "Anything you need?"

"Nothing I can think of." She paused before returning to her work. "Nice to meet you, Bree."

They left the kennels and headed toward the creek. April weather could be unpredictable but, although there was a light breeze, the sun was shining and the sky was cloud free. Since it could be snowing heavily three hours from now, Rylan and Bree had both dressed in layers. As they walked, she removed her hooded sweatshirt and tied it around her waist.

"Kasey said everything is fine at the gallery," she said.

"You sound like you don't know whether to be pleased or disappointed about that."

She smiled. "It's nice to at least be able to pretend I'm indispensable to the firm I created."

"Take it as a compliment. You've built up systems where everyone knows what they're doing. You can take a break without it all falling apart." They walked on in silence for a minute or two. "Does that feel strange?"

"It's probably the circumstances," Bree said. "It's not like this break was planned."

They reached an area of the creek with a high bank. Rylan jumped down and held out a hand to help Bree. Boo was a Canada goose, a large wild bird with a black head and neck, white cheeks and a brown body. He was hunkered in close to an overhanging rock and didn't respond when they approached him.

"Can I touch him?" Bree asked.

"He'll let you stroke his head." Rylan demonstrated by gently running a finger over the gander's feathers.

She knelt on the stony ground, silently stroking the sorrowful bird. Boo's long neck drooped under her touch.

"Imagine how it would feel—" there was a catch in Bree's voice "—if everything you believed about your future was suddenly snatched away from you."

Where had Rylan heard something like that just recently? He frowned in an effort to remember. Oh, that's right. It was when Judith, the server at Arty Sans, had talked about a conservation group who had tried to preserve the original buildings that had become the Diamond.

"Boo should have a friend," Bree said.

Her understanding of the bird's plight felt like cold fingertips touching Rylan's heart. He knew what loneliness felt like. How it could eat you alive and spit out the pieces. How it left you aching to feel warm hands embracing you, or a sympathetic shoulder to cry on.

The difference between him and Boo? Rylan wasn't going there. Not know. But, unlike him, the poor bird hadn't done anything to deserve this.

"You're right. Even if he never finds another love interest, he needs company." He knelt next to Bree. "I'll call the local rescue center and see if they have a lonely female goose they can send us."

"Also, maybe the creek is too much for him right now. He's weak and depressed." She kissed the top of Boo's head. "Why don't we move him close to the house and get him a kiddie pool? It'll be more interesting for him there."

"Good thinking," Rylan said. "Looks like you're going to be an asset around here."

She turned to look at him over her shoulder. "Don't get used to it. I'm not planning on sticking around."

Chapter 11

Bree had called Trey and given him detailed instructions for where to find the gown she wanted for the charity gala. When she ended the call to her brother, Rylan had quirked a brow at her.

"Did I just hear you give the sheriff *coordinates*?"

"Not quite." She had squirmed slightly under his amused stare. "I have a lot of dresses in my closet."

True to his word, Trey had dropped off her gown earlier that day, staying only to let them know—in a frustrated tone—that he had no more leads on the case. He had said he would see them both later.

Now, as Bree stepped into the family room, dressed for the swanky function, Rylan sucked in a breath. "Those numbers you gave Trey?"

Her fingers plucked at her skirt as she returned his gaze. "Yes?"

"Totally worth every digit."

Her shoulders lowered as some of the tension went out of her frame. The full-length evening gown was a deep rose pink, a shade that complemented her tawny coloring. High-necked in front, the back swooped low. The bodice was tightly fitted, the skirt flowing out from the waist in an A-shape. Her curls were piled on top of her head, and she wore diamond drops in her ears.

The whole effect took his breath away. Even more than usual.

"You don't look so bad yourself." She indicated his designer tux.

He gripped his lapels. "Standard item in any bodyguard's wardrobe."

Bree picked up her purse and wrap. "Have you worked for many famous people?"

"Yeah. But it's confidential." He tapped the side of his nose, then mentioned a couple of names.

"Really?" Bree turned to look at him as they walked out to the car. "Wow. Is he as handsome as he appears on screen? And what about her? There are rumors that she can be difficult. Are they true?"

He spent the journey recounting stories of his celebrity clients and answering Bree's questions. "This is all top secret, you understand."

"Of course." She was half turned in her seat to face him, delicious wafts of her floral perfume tantalizing his senses. "Besides, I'm not sure I believe any of it."

Rylan placed a hand over his heart. "You wound me, Bree." He laughed. "Especially because some of it is true."

"Like the story about the famous actress who made

you cook her dinner with your eyes closed because she was having a bad hair day?"

"That may have been an exaggeration." He took his eyes off the road for a second, catching a glimpse of her smile. It warmed him all over. "She made me wear shades."

Bree gave a gurgle of laughter. "Admit it. You just can't be trusted to tell the truth."

As soon as she said the words, the atmosphere changed. The easy, companionable mood they had been enjoying was gone. In its place, tension rose between them like a brick wall. Would it always be that way? Given what had happened, it was hard to see how it could be otherwise.

Rylan drove past the edge of Roaring Springs, taking the secluded valley road that led to The Chateau. Although he had never been there, he had heard of its history. Once known as the Gilford Springs Hotel, it had been renovated and expanded into a world-class hotel. A well-known spring ran through the back of the property, and an old 1920s bathhouse had been fully converted into a five-star spa. Marketed by the Colton family as a "little piece of France," it was a haven for the rich and famous, a place to get away from the paparazzi.

Even so, he wasn't prepared for the magnificence of the property that came into view at the end of the sweeping drive. Whoever designed The Chateau had achieved the remarkable. A mix of authenticity and fairytale, The Chateau combined the luxury, splendor and comfort of the great French mansions.

As Rylan halted the car, two uniformed parking attendants sprang to attention. One opened the passenger door for Bree, while the other took Rylan's keys and arranged to take care of his vehicle.

Rylan offered Bree his arm. When she took it, relief flooded through him. If she could still bear to touch him… But no, letting himself hope would be a special kind of madness.

As they mounted the steps, porters held open the doors.

"A pleasure as always, Ms. Colton." The concierge bowed low. "Your parents are already here."

The interior of the building was as seductive as its facade, with marble columns, light wood paneling, parquet inlaid floors and richly decorated ceilings. The focal point of the lobby was a central fountain, with a grand staircase sweeping down in two wings at either side. On one side of the reception area, a large hearth fireplace provided a warm welcome.

As they ascended the staircase, a young red-haired woman aimed a cell phone at them. Rylan stepped in front of Bree. "No photographs."

"What is this?" As they drew level with the woman, she pulled Bree into a hug. "You look so gorgeous I *have* to share a picture on Instagram."

"This is my cousin Skye," Bree explained to Rylan. "She's the marketing director for The Colton Empire."

Skye held out a hand to Rylan. "And you are?"

"Rylan Bennet." He could see her storing up his name, while hoping for more information.

"Please, Skye. It's a long story, and I don't want to go into it here," Bree said. "But don't share any photos of me on social media, okay?"

Skye's animated features became serious. "Of course

not." She looked Rylan up and down before her gaze returned to her cousin's face. "Is there anything I can do?"

Bree placed a hand on her arm. "I'm fine. Honestly. But thank you."

Although Skye appeared unconvinced, her attention was claimed by a group of new arrivals. Murmuring something about the two of them doing lunch *soon*, she turned away.

Bree took Rylan's arm again, and they continued up the stairs and into the ballroom. It was a glorious cream and gold space, with twelve full-length arched windows on each side. Six huge chandeliers were suspended from the ceiling, and fresh flowers in shades of white, pale blue and lilac were artfully placed at regular intervals. The whole effect was light, bright and elegant.

Rylan's first glance around the room revealed that the wise, wealthy and politically motivated of Roaring Springs were already gathered. It also honed in on Skye...wearing a different dress.

"Whoa." He jerked a thumb over his shoulder. "Didn't we just...?"

Bree laughed. "Skye is an identical twin. Come and meet my *other* cousin Phoebe."

Although Skye and Phoebe were identical in looks, it was immediately obvious that their personalities were very different. Skye was the outgoing, bubbly twin, while Phoebe was quieter and more thoughtful.

"Everything looks wonderful," Bree assured her, after she had completed the introductions.

"Do you think so? It's so hard keeping track of every detail." Phoebe's eyes darted around the room as she spoke.

"Phoebe is the manager here at The Chateau," Bree explained to Rylan. "She's my aunt Mara's right-hand woman."

"I'm not sure Mom would agree with you if you'd seen the fiasco we had earlier with the napkins. Oh, my goodness, what is going on over there?" She gave Rylan and Bree an apologetic smile. "Please excuse me. I distinctly told the serving staff to move *clockwise* with the champagne..."

"How will we survive?" Rylan deadpanned as they watched her cousin hurry off in the opposite direction.

"Stop it." Bree's lips twitched. "Phoebe is the most conscientious person I know. Events like this are very important to her."

For a few minutes, they stood to one side of the crowd. A quartet of violin, harp, cello and flute played on a stage at the far end of the room, their haunting melodies just audible above the conversations. One of the errant servers paused beside them with a tray of champagne.

Bree took a glass, but Rylan shook his head. "Water, please."

"I'm sorry," Bree said, when the waiter went away to fulfill his request. "Most people will spend the night here in The Chateau, so driving won't be a problem."

"It's not just driving. I'm working, remember?"

"Oh." Her teeth caught her lower lip. "Of course, you are."

He frowned. She appeared to be upset, but he couldn't understand why. He had been hired to protect her. If he could turn the clock back to the moment when he'd agreed to do it, would he change things? His gaze lingered on Bree's profile. That would mean he never would have met her. He couldn't wish for that. Even though his heart had taken a beating from which it might never recover, Bree had brought a new perspective into his life.

And let's not forget...she didn't hurt me. I hurt us.

"Guys." Bree's dad smiled as he approached their position at the side of the ballroom. "Why are you hiding over there? Come and say hi."

Although Audrey greeted them with delight, she quickly returned to a nose-to-nose conversation with the director of her favorite non-profit organization. The next fifteen minutes passed in a blur of introductions, during which Rylan tried to keep track of the Colton family. He already knew that he wouldn't meet Earl, Bree's ninety-four-year-old grandfather. Earl was not in the best of health, and dementia had slowly eroded his memories. Bree had explained that he needed to spend most of his time in his own home, with his team of caregivers close by.

They finally drew breath and stopped to talk to Russ Colton, who was Earl's oldest son, and the man who ran The Colton Empire. Now in his mid-sixties, he was tall and broad-shouldered, but getting a little heavier around the middle. His wife, Mara, was director of operations at The Chateau. She was stylishly groomed, and rail thin, with not a single short dark blond hair out of place. Rylan, who was used to reading people, got the impression he was looking at a woman who wasn't happy. He also noticed that, although she and her husband barely spoke to each other, there was clearly some tension between them.

"Congratulations, Aunt Mara," Bree said. "Mom told me that Wyatt and Bailey are expecting a baby."

For the first time, Mara's dark blue eyes sparkled with genuine pleasure. "I'm so excited. Being a grandmother is such a joy."

The man who came up behind her laughed. "And we're excited that you're excited, Mom. Seriously." He winked at Rylan and Bree. "We already have Grandma Mara lined up for babysitting duty."

"And you know I'll be delighted to do it, Wyatt." Mara tapped him on the arm before turning to the woman at his side. "How are you, Bailey, dear?"

"Fine." Bailey held up her glass of water in a salute to Rylan. "Just glad I'm not the only one who can't touch the champagne."

"Rylan is driving," Bree explained, in response to Mara's raised eyebrows.

"You should have stayed here at The Chateau," Mara said. "Most other people are."

"Work commitments." He gave an apologetic shrug.

"Yeah, Cindy from Finance can't keep things running all by herself." Bree hid a smile as she snagged another glass of champagne. "What about you, Uncle Russ, are you ready for babysitting duty?"

Russ smiled, but before he could speak, Mara cut in. "Oh, Russ doesn't do children, do you, darling?" There was a definite lack of warmth in the endearment.

There was no ignoring the provocation in her words. Rylan waited for the storm to break around him. It didn't. Instead, Russ gave Mara a bleak look and returned to his conversation with Calvin. No one else seemed to notice anything unusual.

"What was *that*?" he said in a quiet tone, making sure Bree was the only person who could hear.

"What was what?" She frowned.

"The way Mara spoke to Russ. She may as well have taken a knife and cut him open."

"I didn't notice," Bree admitted. "They're not a very warm couple. It's just their way."

Rylan always felt like families were a mystery to which he didn't have the key. Maybe that was because his early life had been so unhappy. Looking at Russ and Mara, he could almost feel the friction between them. Yet he only had to turn his head to see an example of a loving couple. Bree's parents had their heads together as they laughed at a private joke. Audrey had her hand on Calvin's arm, and he tenderly brushed her hair back from her cheek.

Rylan had believed family life was not for him. After his mom died, he had been at a crossroads. The trauma of his early life could easily have led him into a dysfunctional adult life. Luckily, he had chosen the army, and found the sense of belonging that had been missing from his childhood.

But lately… Well, it was possible his view of himself as a family man could have changed.

"I need to find Kendall," Bree said, as she drained her champagne glass. "She's my cousin Decker's wife, the one who was injured when the gallery was vandalized."

In the time they'd spent meeting members of the Colton family, the ballroom had filled up. As a bodyguard, this would normally be Rylan's nightmare scenario. There were too many unknowns. But he had already assessed the dark-suited men standing close to the windows. The Colton security guards looked like they knew what they were doing. Although he wouldn't relax, it was good to know he wasn't alone.

Finding Decker and Kendall proved difficult among the crush of designer-clad bodies, but Bree managed it eventually. Kendall still wore a patch covering the gauze pad over her eye, but she was in good spirits and assured them that her doctors had said her sight would be fine.

"Ahem." She waved her hand at Bree and the stones in her ring caught the light from the chandeliers.

"Oh, my goodness! That's gorgeous." Bree hugged first Kendall, then Decker. "I'm so happy for you both."

As Kendall looked up at Decker, happiness shone on both their faces. "The engagement ring is beautiful but the wedding ring means even more."

A buffet dinner was served soon after, and speeches followed. Remy Colton, The Chateau's director of public relations, joked about the unseasonably cold weather. Since that meant the ski season could be extended— which would be good for business—he asked everyone to raise their glasses in a toast. As he left the podium, Rylan heard Remy take a different tone as he confided to Mara that he feared the upcoming Film Festival might not have the same attendance as usual.

It was a brief glimpse inside the well-oiled Colton machine. Rylan guessed Remy's words related to the issues the family was experiencing. Bad publicity was the last thing the Coltons needed with a prestigious event like the Film Festival on the horizon. It raised the question in his mind yet again. Was the person who was targeting Bree the same one who was going after her family?

Speaking of Bree…

He leaned in close. "What's troubling you?"

She straightened her shoulders and tilted her chin. "Why do you ask?"

"Because I can see you're not happy."

"Oh, that. Nothing like a stalker to deflate a girl's mood." She waved her empty glass at him.

Rylan shook his head. "Something has changed since we arrived here."

She shrugged, her skirts swishing as one elegant shoe traced the pattern on the floor tiles. "Wyatt and Bailey are having a baby. Decker and Kendall are married. I should be pleased. I *am* pleased—"

Before she could finish, a band started playing a hit from the latest Hollywood musical. Rylan held out his hand. "Dance with me, Bree."

"I thought you were working?" She let him lead her onto the dance floor.

He drew her into his arms, resting his cheek against her hair. "Best job I ever had."

"I see what you're doing." She draped her arms around his neck. "I'm sad and you're trying to cheer me up."

He frowned down at her. "You're sad because your cousins are happy?" She nodded, her cheek rubbing against his chest. "I don't understand."

She lifted her head to look at him, and the temptation to kiss her right there on that dance floor in front of her whole family was almost overwhelming. *Just one problem. She hates me.* "I guess you wouldn't."

A suspicion entered his head. "Are you drunk, Bree?"

Her smile was dreamy. "Might be."

"How much champagne have you had?" He hadn't been counting, but now that he thought about it, she *had* drained quite a few glasses.

"A lot." She put her finger on his lips. "Don't tell my mom, 'kay?"

"Okay." He held on to her as she slumped against him. "Maybe we should leave now?"

"Nice idea. Take me home, Rylan." She chuckled. "Just you, me and the crazy animals."

He beckoned to Phoebe, who was close by. "I need to get Bree out of here."

"I see what you mean." Phoebe cast an experienced eye over her cousin. "Don't worry, I'll tell my aunt Audrey that Bree has a slight headache."

"Thanks." He slid an arm around Bree's waist and walked with her to the door.

"Bye, Phoebe. Love you." Bree waggled her fingers over her shoulder.

When they stepped outside to wait for the car, the air was biting. A few flakes of snow drifted down and landed in Bree's hair. Ahead of them, the lights of the gondola that carried Colton guests between The Chateau and The Lodge glowed gold against the white tip of Pine Peak.

"Weren't we dancing?" Bree swayed as she hummed a few bars of the song.

The parking attendant brought Rylan's vehicle to the front of the building. He had already turned the heater up full blast. After tipping him, Rylan reached into the trunk to retrieve the blanket he always carried.

Once Bree was settled in the passenger seat, he tucked it around her.

By the time he'd driven a few miles, Bree was asleep. Rylan smiled. If she could see herself now, she'd be mortified. Her mouth was open, her hair was springing loose from its restraints and she was snoring. Not pretty dainty snores either. Oh, no. Bree Colton sounded like a wounded warthog.

She was the most beautiful sight he had ever seen.

Bree woke to the sensation of a rock being repeatedly hammered against her skull. Groaning, she rolled onto her back. It was a mistake. The room began to spin, and her stomach rebelled. Cautiously, she returned to her side and groped for her cell phone.

Deciding there must be something wrong with the display, she placed the cell back on the table at the side of the bed. It couldn't possibly be nearly noon. Even Bree, with her morning aversion, never slept that late.

Lying as still as possible, she tried to piece together the events of the previous night, but it remained stubbornly incomplete. The gala, particularly the last part, was like a puzzle with missing pieces.

And why can't I remember anything about getting back here?

She sat up slowly, reaching for the glass of water that had somehow appeared beside the bed. Even if the pounding headache and nausea weren't enough of a clue, the sandpaper tongue and dry throat completed the picture. Bree wasn't much of a drinker, but she knew a hangover when she was in the grip of one.

Ugh. Why had she drunk so much champagne? She

knew the answer to that question and it didn't make her feel good about herself. Beneath her congratulations for the cousins who had found happiness, she had experienced a profound sadness. Just a short time ago, she had been wrapped in a similar haze. Okay, so it had been early days for her and Rylan. Had she truly believed he was "the one"?

She sighed. Everything had pointed that way. He'd been perfect… Determinedly, she forced her thoughts off the self-pity carousel and in a different direction.

Seeing other family members settling into their new lives had reminded her of what she'd lost. Which was silly, because how could she lose an illusion? It didn't matter. She'd gone ahead and drowned the hurt in champagne.

Such a good look.

And now, she was paying the price. Her gaze took in the dress she'd been wearing. It had been placed on a hanger and suspended on the outside of the closet door. Her shoes were neatly placed together beneath it. She lifted a hand to hair and found the pins had been removed.

A suspicion occurred to her, and she lifted the bed covers. Sure enough, she was naked except for her white lace panties.

I never go to bed in just my underwear.

While she was considering the implications of this, there was a knock on the door.

"Come in." That was what she intended to say. What emerged was more of a feeble croak.

In just a pair of cut-off jeans, Rylan appeared too healthy and energetic to be real. For a moment, Bree's gaze refused to move from his tanned muscular torso. With an effort, she dragged it away and focused on his face.

"What time is it?" Her throat felt like she'd been gargling with sand.

"I'm not sure. I've been up for about five hours, so probably about twelve."

Bree was startled into an exclamation. The throbbing in her head intensified, and she pressed her knuckles to her temples with a moan.

"Bad, huh?" Although Rylan's tone was sympathetic, his grin was mischievous.

"I think it's probably best if you just leave me here to die. Tell my family I love them."

To Bree, his laughter sounded faintly demonic. "I have just the thing for that. Back in a minute."

While he was gone, she dredged her memory for some clue about undressing the previous night. Her mind refused to give her any hints.

When Rylan returned, he was carrying a tall glass of green sludge. Bree eyed it suspiciously. "Did Wonkey chew that up and spit it out?"

"An army buddy used to swear by this…literally. It always does the trick." He handed her the glass. "It's aloe juice, ginger, milk thistle, peppermint and willow bark. Just drink it fast."

"Nothing ventured." Bree followed his instructions and slugged the unappetizing mixture down. For a moment or two, her stomach rebelled, then her body calmed down. After a few minutes, she could almost feel the herbs cleansing her system.

"Better?" Rylan looked down at her with a smile.

She tilted her head from side to side. "Put the funeral arrangements on hold."

"Lunch will be served on the porch in twenty minutes."

Bree was about to protest that she would never be able to eat again, when her stomach gave an enormous rumble.

"Um, Rylan." He paused with his hand on the door handle and turned to look at her. She pointed at her dress. "Did you…?"

"Yeah. You couldn't manage the zipper."

"Oh." She bit her lip. "Did we…?"

His lips thinned into a line, all trace of humor dying from his expression. "You were drunk, Bree. Almost unconscious." He shook his head. "Your opinion of me must be even lower than I thought."

Bree watched him stalk from the room, all muscle and masculine indignation. The image of Rylan caring for her when she was drunk, undressing her, putting her to bed, leaving her a glass of water, then going off to his own room… It reinforced her belief that he was a good guy after all.

She was about to head for the shower when the thought hit her. Rylan had cherished her the way he looked after his animals. He collected strays and misfits. Had she just been added to the menagerie?

Chapter 12

Bree shielded her eyes as she stepped out onto the porch. "Can you turn down the sunlight?"

"You have your shades on top of your head," Rylan pointed out.

"Oh." She lowered them and slumped into the seat opposite him. Clearly, the hangover still had a hold on her. He poured her a glass of water and handed her a plate of chicken salad.

"No more messages?" Rylan asked. The last time Bree had heard from the stalker had been the disturbing email about the taste of her blood.

"Nothing." She sipped her water. "I suppose it's too much to hope that he's given up?"

"Unfortunately, yes. I imagine he's exerting all his energy trying to find out where you are." In Rylan's ex-

Dear Reader,

IT'S A FACT: if you answer 4 quick questions, we'll send you **4 FREE REWARDS!**

I'm not kidding you. As a leading publisher of women's fiction, we value your opinions… and your time. That's why we are prepared to **reward** you handsomely for completing our mini-survey. In fact, we have 4 Free Rewards for you, including 2 free books and 2 free gifts.

As you may have guessed, that's why our mini-survey is called **"4 for 4".** Answer 4 questions and get 4 Free Rewards. It's that simple!

Thank you for participating in our survey,

Pam Powers

To get your 4 FREE REWARDS:
Complete the survey below and return the insert today to receive 2 FREE BOOKS and 2 FREE GIFTS guaranteed!

"4 for 4" MINI-SURVEY

1 Is reading one of your favorite hobbies?
☐ YES ☐ NO

2 Do you prefer to read instead of watch TV?
☐ YES ☐ NO

3 Do you read newspapers and magazines?
☐ YES ☐ NO

4 Do you enjoy trying new book series with FREE BOOKS?
☐ YES ☐ NO

YES! I have completed the above Mini-Survey. Please send me my 4 FREE REWARDS (worth over $20 retail). I understand that I am under no obligation to buy anything, as explained on the back of this card.

240/340 HDL GNTV

FIRST NAME

LAST NAME

ADDRESS

APT.#

CITY

STATE/PROV.

ZIP/POSTAL CODE

READER SERVICE—Here's how it works:

▼ If offer card is missing write to: Reader Service, P.O. Box 1341, Buffalo, NY 14240-8531 or visit www.ReaderService.com ▼

BUSINESS REPLY MAIL
FIRST-CLASS MAIL   PERMIT NO. 717   BUFFALO, NY
POSTAGE WILL BE PAID BY ADDRESSEE

READER SERVICE
PO BOX 1341
BUFFALO NY 14240-8571

NO POSTAGE
NECESSARY
IF MAILED
IN THE
UNITED STATES

perience, stalkers might change tactics, but they didn't give up.

"What about your sources?" she asked. "Have they come up with any information?"

Rylan huffed out a breath. To his intense frustration, none of his former colleagues had discovered so much as a whisper about any of the people who had access to the Wise Gal basement. "Not yet. They'll keep digging."

They ate in silence for a few minutes.

"Do you have any thoughts about who it could be?" Bree asked.

It felt like a now-or-never situation. "I don't have any suspicions, but I wanted to ask you about Lucas Brewer. Has he ever shown an interest in you? Romantically, I mean."

Bree sat back in her chair, lifting her shades as she watched Nance taking her duckling brood for a stroll across the grass. She appeared to be surprised by the question. "Lucas? No, I can't say... I mean, he's suggested going for coffee once or twice, but just in a friendly way. You can't think it's him?"

"I'm not ruling anyone out." He kept his voice casual. "Did you take him up on his offer?"

"For coffee? No." She brought her gaze back to Rylan's face. He could see her struggling to find the right words. "I've only had two relationships and both times I found out they were more interested in the fact that I'm a Colton than in me as a person. It's made me careful."

Rylan wanted to close his eyes and shut out the pain he could see in her face. It was obvious how hard it was for her to talk about this, and he knew that telling him, of all people, was even worse. Because she hadn't been careful with him. She had tumbled into his arms, giving herself to him freely and happily. She had trusted him. And she'd been wrong to do so.

"Even though I didn't think there was any romantic intention behind Lucas's offer, I decided it was better to be cautious."

"That's no way to live your life." Rylan didn't want to be Lucas Brewer's advocate. He just couldn't bear the thought of Bree—beautiful, vibrant Bree—weighing every situation and deciding it wasn't worth taking a chance.

Then I came along and made it worse.

Rylan hadn't been with her because of her money, but he'd taken a hammer to her already fragile self-esteem and smashed it into tiny pieces. Bree didn't answer, but her steady gaze told him she knew what he was thinking. That look, together with her question about whether they'd had sex while she was drunk, was like holding up a mirror to his already shattered self-belief.

Worthless? Meet the poster boy.

Her answer to his question hadn't ruled Lucas out. It was impossible to know what the other man's feelings were. Bree's impression was that his offers of coffee were not leading up to anything romantic, but was that how Lucas saw it? What if the reality was that he was trying to find a way to get to know the woman he had secretly been admiring from afar? Certainly, his body language when he was around Bree revealed an interest that went beyond friendship. By turning him down, could Bree have triggered his anger?

Rylan didn't like it as a solution. *You Coltons are only good for using and taking advantage of those who are less fortunate.* That was what the first email had said. He couldn't see any link between Bree turning down an offer of coffee from Lucas and that sentence.

"Do you ride?" Bree looked surprised at the abrupt change of subject. "You're a farm girl, of course you do. What I should have said was... Will your hangover cope with a ride this afternoon?"

She pulled a face at him. "Me and my hangover will outride you any day."

"That sounds like fighting talk, wise gal." The endearment slipped out, and he waited for the storm to break over his head. It didn't. Instead, he caught a gleam in Bree's eye that might almost have been one of pleasure.

She got to her feet. "I want to check on Boo before I do anything else. He's started eating some grain, and he let Golly share his kiddie pool yesterday."

Her smile was radiant as she talked about the gander who seemed to have turned a corner now that he had a new friend. Bree had brought him back to life.

The way she did with me.

The thought jolted him as he watched her walk away. Because, one day soon, he would have to watch her leave for good. And, just like Boo when he lost Lucy, he didn't know how he was going to cope with the pain.

"My dad always says the only way to connect with the land is from the back of a horse," Bree said. It was months since she'd last been on a ride, and it felt good to be in the saddle once more.

They had been riding for an hour, passing close to the edge of the pine forest, glimpsing small waterfalls and climbing a steep elevation that gave sweeping views of Rylan's land. The flora and rock formations were constantly changing, and they had seen deer, elk and squirrels. It was wilder and more rugged than the farmland of her childhood home, but with a beauty all its own.

Now, as they dipped back down, they drew close to the border with the disused ranch. Bree was reminded of Rylan's comment when she first arrived here.

"What did you mean when you said if you could just get your hands on this land?"

Rylan reined his horse in. "I made a good profit from the sale of my business. Enough to buy this place and not have to worry about money. I planned on maybe getting a few horses, doing some traveling, even writing a security manual. That all changed around the time I was eating an Indian meal and the owner found Papadum in a dumpster."

He shifted in his saddle, turning to look at her. "Don't get me wrong. As soon as I started taking in wounded and troubled animals, everything made sense. I knew *exactly* what I wanted to do with this place. I contacted Dinah, asked her if she wanted a job and we took it from there."

He rarely opened up, and Bree was content to remain quiet, watching his changing expressions. All she really knew about his formative years was that his dad had died when he was a child, and his mom had succumbed to cancer just before he joined the army. She realized now that he never made passing references to his childhood. Those stories and memories that had shaped her, and were so much a part of her own life, didn't seem to feature in Rylan's consciousness. Or maybe he deliberately suppressed them.

"But I want to do more." He pointed to the abandoned ranch. "If I could buy that land as well, then I could really make a difference. I'd open a non-profit sanctuary for abused animals, employ my own live-in staff, including veterinarians and nutritionists, build state-of-the-art therapy facilities—" He broke off, lifting his cowboy hat and scratching his head. "Sorry, I can get carried away about all of this."

"It sounds wonderful." The enthusiasm in his face and voice when he talked about his vision was infectious. It touched something deep inside her. "You said you can't do it. Why not?"

"When I approached the owner of the land, his starting price was at least three times what it's worth." Rylan's shoulders sagged as he turned his horse around. "I have money, but not enough that I can start throwing any of it away. When I tried negotiating, his response was… Well, it wasn't the sort of thing I'd repeat in your company."

Although they rode on, Bree cast several glances over her shoulder at the land Rylan wanted. He had been so eloquent; she could almost picture the sanctuary he described. Audrey Colton's daughter understood the importance of developing noble causes. She also believed in the power of dreams and good people who made them come true.

What would her mom's advice be? She smiled. Audrey wouldn't waste time talking; she would be too busy making things happen.

"When you first brought Papadum to the gallery, you

said you'd taken in a new arrival who had unsettled the dynamics," Bree said. "I haven't noticed a problem dog."

"Jekyll has been hospitalized for a few days," Rylan explained. He checked his watch. "He should be returning anytime now."

"Jekyll? As in...?"

He laughed. "Yeah. Jekyll and Hyde. But don't be misled. We don't see much of mild-mannered Hyde."

They reached the kennels and dismounted. Inside, Dinah was sitting on the floor next to a dog bed that contained a tiny black and brown dog, whose ears appeared to take up two-thirds of his body. Jekyll was wearing a medical cone collar and looking sorry for himself.

"Is this the one you were talking about?" Bree asked. Surely, something this small couldn't cause trouble among Rylan's confident, tight-knit dog pack?

"Don't be deceived," Dinah said. "This little guy is bad to the bone."

Jekyll gave Bree puppy-dog eyes and sighed heavily.

"How did he hurt himself?" she asked.

"We took in a couple of porcupines before passing them on to a specialist rescue center," Rylan explained. "Jekyll got into an argument with one of them."

"Will he let me pet him?" Bree asked Dinah.

"Oh, yes. He loves people. Just hates other animals, especially dogs."

"He has small-dog syndrome," Rylan said. "His life would be a lot easier if he just got along with the other canines."

"Poor little guy." Bree tickled Jekyll's ears. The dog,

clearly sensing sympathy, shuffled forward until he could rest his chin on her knee.

"I have no sympathy for anyone who thinks they can win a fight with a porcupine by sitting on it," Rylan told Jekyll in a scolding tone. "It took the veterinary nurse an hour to pull all the quills out of his butt."

"It's dinner time." Dinah got to her feet. "The mob are in the exercise yard, but they'll be getting hungry."

Bree helped Dinah fill bowls with dried food, then went with her to the area behind the kennels. Although the dogs were allowed to roam free at various times of the day, Rylan had created a space to encourage socialization and problem-solving skills. With ramps, hoops, tunnels, steps and mounds, it provided the dogs with a different environment, and prevented them from becoming bored.

When they saw the two women, most of the dogs— and Merry the sheep—charged toward the gate. Rylan's prediction was proved correct. Although they remained boisterous, the dogs were generally well behaved and responded to commands.

"Let's do this nicely, shall we?" Dinah opened the gate and, to Bree's surprise, the pack left the exercise yard in an orderly line.

As they reached the kennels, she sensed a change in their manner. A few of the leaders sniffed the air and started to hang back. When they got inside, the reason for their reluctance became obvious. Each of the dogs glanced in Jekyll's direction, before skirting cautiously around his bed. They were definitely subdued as they headed toward their dinner.

"Wow." Bree shook her head. "They really don't like him, do they?"

"He doesn't make it easy for them." Rylan sighed as he stooped to stroke Jekyll. "Each one of them has been on the receiving end of his bullying tactics."

"Why don't we take Jekyll to the house to recover?" Bree asked.

"He has a self-inflicted sore butt," Rylan said. "He's not dying."

"I know. But that way, the others will get a break from him. Maybe we could reintroduce him gradually and teach him some manners at the same time."

He looked at the pitiful little dog. "I thought I was supposed to be the soft touch where animals are concerned?"

She grinned. "You just met your match."

"Thanks for the warning." He scooped up the dog bed with Jekyll inside it. "But I already knew."

The following evening, Rylan was sitting on the porch, trying to complete some paperwork. Far too much of his attention was taken up with pausing to watch Bree as she fussed over Jekyll. The dog seemed much happier now that he was being treated like a royal baby instead of an ornery canine.

All three of them looked up in surprise when Rylan's cell phone buzzed.

"It's the app I use for the gate security." He checked the image on the screen. "Hey, Trey."

Rylan typed in the code to release the gates, watching on the screen of his cell as Bree's brother drove through them. Since Trey had visited them once before to deliver Bree's dress for the gala, he didn't need directions to the house, and his car came into view a minute or two later.

The sheriff exited his vehicle and came to join them, sinking gratefully into one of the comfortable chairs.

"You sure have some weird pets." He nodded toward Jekyll.

"Don't be mean." Bree covered the dog's ears. "How are Mom and Dad?"

"Fine. They said hi."

"Coffee or a cold drink?" Rylan asked.

"Just soda," Trey said. He took off his Stetson and rubbed a hand over the top of his head. "I just stopped by for a chat, but I really need to get home and catch up on some sleep."

Rylan went inside. When he returned with the drinks, they sat together around the porch table.

"Do you have any news on the case?" Bree asked.

"Not really." Trey sounded frustrated. "Nothing that leads directly to the guy who's been targeting you. The only thing I've heard—and this was from an informant who was speaking about an unrelated matter—is that there's been some talk about sabotage of more Colton events. Specifically, at The Lodge and The Chateau."

"By the person who threw the brick through the gallery window?" Rylan asked.

"My source didn't have that information," Trey said. "It's possible it was a different group, or an individual, but is that likely?"

Rylan looked from him to Bree. "The Colton clan isn't popular with some folks. There could be several people who are gunning for your family."

It pained him to say it because he liked them both, but they needed to consider all possibilities.

Bree was obviously thinking it through. "I don't see how that fits with someone threatening me personally. Yes, the first emails were about me as a member of the Colton family. But the tone changed and became a personal attack. You've both seen them. They were about what the person sending them wanted to do to hurt me."

"It could still be the same person," Rylan insisted. "You're a Colton, Bree. Threatening you and sabotaging the family are not mutually exclusive. From a starting point of resentment, this guy's tactics could have changed and become obsession."

"True." Trey drained his drink. "But I think we have to keep an open mind. We could be dealing with a stalker who is fixated with Bree *and* someone else who has a grudge against the family. Or they could be the same person." He cleared his throat. "By the way, I stopped by the gallery this morning to follow up on a few interviews. David, your security guard, said he needs to speak to you. After the damage to your pictures, he's come up with a plan for improving the storage systems, including access to the exhibits. He was keen to run it by you."

"You didn't tell him where she is, did you?" Rylan asked.

"Yeah, of course I did. I posted a notice on the gallery door with a map showing where your ranch is." Trey's tone dripped sarcasm. "Come on, Rylan, *obviously* I have no intention of telling anyone where Bree is. You are not the only one around here who has my sister's welfare at heart. Although David Swanson isn't a suspect, is he? He was attacked as he tried to stop the stalker getting to Bree."

"I know, but the fewer people who have the details of her whereabouts, the better. Anyone can slip up and give information away."

Trey nodded his agreement. "By the way, you caused quite a stir at the gala."

Rylan's attention was focused on Bree, as she shifted uncomfortably in her seat. "What do you mean?"

"I've had a few calls and messages from different family members asking me about Bree's new guy."

"I hope you told them to mind their own business." Bree sank back in her chair with her arms folded over her chest.

Before Trey could say anything more, Bree's cell phone, which was on the table, vibrated and lit up. She glanced at Rylan as she reached for it, and he could tell what she was thinking. *Him.*

Sure enough, she scanned the screen quickly, then looked up. "It's an email." He could see the nerves kicking in as she converted the text to speech.

Your skin looks like silk. So delicate. A blade will tear right through it. Take care. Even Colton cash can't hide you forever.

"He's right, isn't he?" Bree crossed her arms over her body, gripping her upper arms as she tried to still the trembling. "I can't hide forever."

She had held it together while Trey was there, sitting quietly and listening as the two men furiously dissected the latest message for clues. Now, her brother had left, and her control had gone with him. Thoughts whirled wildly inside her head, and she had trouble holding on to them. Her breath came in gasps, and dark spots danced at the edges of her vision. Inside her chest, her heart took on its own life, leaping like a wild animal trying to escape from a prey.

The porch began to spin, and she sank into a squat, trying to slow her brain and body. Before she reached the floor, Rylan's strong arms were around her. "Shhh… it's okay. I got you."

With one hand under her knees and the other supporting her waist, he carried her into the house. Lowering her gently onto a sofa, he knelt on the floor at her side. Jekyll followed them and lay on the rug nearby, his gaze fixed worriedly on Bree's face.

"Do you want some water?"

Bree shook her head, clutching his hand. "Stay with me. Please."

Moving to sit on the sofa, he drew her close, cushioning her head on his thighs. "Better?"

The warmth of his body was exactly what she needed. "Yes…much."

She closed her eyes. After a moment or two, he began to gently stroke her hair.

"I wish we could stay like this. Just shut everything else out." She didn't care what had happened in the past, didn't care if she was making herself vulnerable again. There was that moment, and the comfort only he could give her.

"My mom used to say, when you stop wishing you may as well be dead." Rylan's voice was soft and soothing.

"That's the first time you've mentioned your mom."

His hand paused for a second before resuming its caressing motion. "She was a nice lady who got dealt a bad hand in life."

"Was the bad hand your dad?" Bree opened her eyes. Her position, with her head in his lap, gave her a distorted view, but she saw his jaw muscles tense. "I'm sorry. If you don't want to talk about it—"

"I've spent my whole life *not* talking about it. Maybe it's time to start." He tilted his head so he could look at her. "My dad was an alcoholic. Mom would never use that word. She'd say he liked a drink, or he had a drink problem. After his death, she admitted he had an addiction. But the stigma of the word *alcoholic* was too strong for her. My mom told me that my father grew up incredibly poor. He was badly bullied at school because he wore used clothes and never had any money. His father, my grandfather, was physically abusive to his wife and kids. I guess that's where my dad learned his ways."

"He struck you?" Bree was shocked.

"Sober, he was the most mild-mannered man you could wish to meet. But when he hit the bottle? He was a nasty drunk. I was a sensitive kid, and my mom would try to protect me, but he loved to torment me. While I dodged the blows, he'd call me weak, a wimp, mommy's boy…anything to make me feel worthless."

Tears stung Bree's eyes as she listened to him calmly recount the story of his nightmarish childhood. She thought of her own dad. Of his steady presence, his calm patience, his warm protection. All the things she'd had that Rylan hadn't. It was so clear to her now. Rylan's whole life had been about proving his cruel father wrong, showing he was stronger, harder and better than those around him. Underneath the tough guy exterior, the sweet, sensitive person was still there. That was the man she had fallen for.

"When I was twelve, he had a heart attack and died in his sleep. Isn't that known as a millionaire's death? Ironic, because he never had a cent to his name while he was alive. After he passed, Mom juggled a series of jobs to keep a roof over our heads. When she fell ill, I took over and cared for her. She died when I was eighteen and... Well, I guess you know the rest."

She turned, wrapping her arms around his waist and pressing her face against his torso. They stayed that way for a long time.

"Hey." When Bree lifted her head, Rylan ran his thumb down her cheek, brushing away the wetness. "What's this?"

"I'm so sorry for everything you went through."

"It's in the past." His tone was gruff.

"Are you sure?" She sat up, but didn't move away, remaining half reclined in his lap. It didn't feel wrong. They were sharing the role of comforter. "Don't you ever think about it?"

He was silent for so long she thought he wasn't going to answer. When he did speak, his voice was low. "I try not to, but the memories intrude every now and then. When my dad started shouting, my mom used to send me to my room. I knew it was because he was getting close to hitting one of us, and she wanted to make sure it was her. Sometimes, I'd hear her cries and I'd—" he dug his knuckles into his eyes "—I'd pee my pants. Brave, huh?"

"You were a *child.*"

"This one time—I must have been about eight—I decided I'd had enough. When I heard my dad beating my mom, I left my room and tried to drag him off her. I was yelling at him, punching him as hard as I could. He knocked me across the room. I blacked out." He gave a shaky laugh. "I remember coming to and hearing him telling my mom she'd have to say I fell. I still dream about that punch."

He drew her tight against him again, holding on to her as if he would never let go. After a few minutes, Jekyll jumped onto the sofa, his cone making him clumsy. Determinedly, the little dog pushed his way between them and settled on Bree's knee. With a heavy sigh, he shoved his head under her hand.

Rylan laughed. "I think that message is fairly clear."

"Yes. Let's not get things out of proportion by letting our human problems intrude on the important dog stuff."

Bree felt unaccountably cold as she shifted position to sit at Rylan's side. Their embrace had been about consoling each other, nothing more. She was still wildly attracted to him, but the days of anything else between them were over. That was what she kept telling herself. Although, at times like this, when he was up close, with that smile in his eyes, she had a hard time believing it.

It was getting late, but a glance at the darkness beyond the window brought her fears crashing back down. It wasn't the full-on panic attack of earlier. Just a shivery reminder that *he* was out there, somewhere, thinking about her.

"Will you be okay?" Rylan followed the direction of her gaze. "I could bring Papadum in to sleep in your room." He nodded at Jekyll, who was sprawled on his back across Bree's legs. "But I don't think that would be a popular move."

"I don't want to be alone." Her gaze caught on his and held. "I'm not ready to go back to where we were, but…"

His smile was sad and charming in equal measures. "I will never stop wanting you, Bree." She opened her mouth to speak, and he held up his hand. "But I can sleep in your room without spontaneously bursting into flames." The smile deepened. "I think."

What about me? For an instant, the words hovered on her lips. She wondered if they showed in her eyes. Fear. It could make you think the strangest things.

"Thank you." It seemed the safest thing to say.

Chapter 13

"Um, so how do you want to do this?" Bree looked utterly adorable in pale blue pajamas, with her hair tumbling loose about her shoulders.

Rylan almost groaned aloud. How did he want to do this? What sort of question was that? If she was offering him a genuine choice, he would start by kissing her until she was weak at the knees...

Focus.

"There's a folding bed in one of the other rooms. I could bring it in here."

She smiled. "That's a big bed. We're both grown-ups. I'll keep to my side if you stay on yours."

He held out his hand. "Deal."

Since just touching her fingertips sent flames scorching through him, he wasn't overly optimistic about his ability to get a good night's sleep. His hopes sank even further when a pitiful howl echoed through the house.

"What the actual…?" Rylan scratched his head. "He was fine on his own last night."

"I think he can sense we're both in here together. He must be feeling left out." As Bree clasped her hands under her chin, another volley of canine cries reached them.

"Left out?" Rylan growled. "He's spent his whole life feeling left out, the little—" He caught her eye. "You want me to see if I can settle him?"

"Thank you." The glowing smile she gave him didn't quite compensate for having to dog-sit tonight, but it did put a spring in his step.

Ten minutes later, Jekyll and his dog-bed had been transported into Bree's bedroom. Jekyll, having barked with delight when he saw Bree, developed an overwhelming desire to curl up on the mattress next to her. His tiny legs, coupled with the cone around his neck, meant jumping wasn't easy for him. Not one to be deterred, he persisted.

"No, darling." Bree lifted him from his chosen position on her legs for the fifth time and placed him in his own bed.

"I could take him back to the kennels," Rylan said tersely.

Something in his tone must have gotten through to the dog because, after leveling him with a resentful look, Jekyll finally curled up in his dog-bed.

"At last." Rylan, who preferred to sleep in the minimum amount of clothing, had decided to respect the situation and wear shorts and a T-shirt. Sliding under the bed covers, he switched off the light on his bed-side table.

"Good night, Bree."

Before she could answer, a sound like a metal roll shutter being pulled down filled the room. Jekyll was snoring.

Rylan groaned. "No wonder the other dogs hate him."

Bree laughed so hard, the bed shook. "This is a sanctuary for all animals, remember? Even the troublesome ones."

"That little stinker takes troublesome to a whole new level," he grumbled.

The snoring subsided slightly, and he felt the bed shift as Bree turned to face him. "Rylan?"

"Hmm?"

"Am I one of your misfits?"

He choked back a laugh. "Is this a joke?" Could she seriously believe he saw her as another rescue project?

"No. It's a genuine question." He could tell from her voice how important it was to her. "I've spent my whole life not fitting in. I need to know that you don't see me as another Wonkey or Boo."

Rylan thought of some of the things she'd told him about her childhood. She had grown up in a family of high-achievers while battling a condition that limited her ability to be judged successful by conventional means. It had affected how she saw herself and how she believed others viewed her. He was aware, all over again, of a responsibility to her that went beyond the physical need to protect her.

"Bree, you are the strongest, bravest, most beautiful person I know. I can't think of anyone less like one of my crazy oddball animals." He couldn't quite believe he was having to say those words to the woman who could juggle his heart with a mere look.

"Oh." He heard the smile in her voice. "Thank you."

"For that answer, or for not throttling Jekyll?"

She chuckled. "For everything. You didn't have to do this…any of it. I appreciate it."

His throat tightened. "I wish I hadn't screwed up."

She turned away from him again. "So do I."

He lay on his back with his hands beneath his head. He *had* screwed up, and he couldn't regret it enough. Even so, he had sensed a few times lately that Bree's attitude toward him was softening. Could that really be the case, or was it a combination of their close proximity and the circumstances?

There was no getting around the fact that Bree was in danger, and he was her protector. Which meant, even without their existing attraction, it was a recipe for romance. And before Bree had discovered that he'd been lying about his identity, they'd had an instant fiery passion that was so damn combustible the very air around them sizzled. That hadn't gone away. He didn't think it ever would.

He turned his head, unable to see her in the darkness, but acutely aware of her. For the first time, he considered what he'd previously believed to be impossible. Was Bree prepared to overlook his deception? A few days ago, he'd have said her forgiveness was the only thing he wanted. Now, he knew that was wrong.

She was what he wanted.

He loved her. If he were honest, he had loved her from the moment he first saw her. *Love at first sight.*

Who knew it was really a thing? Especially for the ultimate tough guy. His life choices were a declaration. Soldier, bodyguard and security expert. *Keep back. I don't do feelings.* But Bree had broken down his hard shell and found the part of himself he tried to keep hidden.

And that was the problem. If she forgave him, he would be overwhelmed with gratitude. If she wanted to resume their former relationship... Well, that was another matter. Because, even though that would be a dream come true, Rylan wanted more. He wanted *everything*.

He almost laughed. Why was he even thinking this way? Just supposing he was right and, by some remote chance, Bree did forgive him. It was a big leap from there to a return to what they'd had. It was an even bigger jump to anything long term.

Getting ahead of yourself, Bennet.

Why would Bree, who could have any man she wanted, choose the one who had already *proven* himself unworthy of her? The answer was simple. She wouldn't.

When Bree opened her eyes, it was light. *Morning.* She knew it happened every day, but she couldn't help wishing it wouldn't.

As she came fully awake, she became aware of something hard jammed into the small of her back. It felt a lot like a dog's neck cone. Turning slowly, she discovered that both Rylan and Jekyll were still sound asleep. One of them was stretched diagonally across the middle of the bed, while the other was clinging precariously to one edge.

Biting back a smile, she returned the dog to his bed,

then slipped back beneath the warm bed covers. As she did, Rylan murmured contentedly, and rolled over.

Now that *was a view that could make a night owl start liking mornings.*

Wishing she could reach out a hand and touch him, she studied the planes and angles of his face. There were times when his features could appear harsh, but that, like the serious look in his eyes, was an expression he'd cultivated. When he was relaxed, as he was now, the perfection of his face shone through.

Sitting up, she reached into the drawer of the bedside table and withdrew her artist's pad and pencils.

Before long, she was lost in her sketch, following the river of her creativity from the initial line through to the finished picture. Nothing quite matched the joy she got from the interaction with a piece of art. It was like a magic trick. Just her and the sketch. The details, the flourishes, the emphases… They belonged to her. No one else would capture it in the same way.

The image was influenced by what she knew of Rylan. The *real* Rylan. She didn't draw the man the world saw. She drew the man who rescued troubled and injured animals. The one who offered to protect a woman he didn't know pro bono because she was his friend's cousin. The one who slept in her bed because she was afraid to be alone.

When she'd finished, she viewed the picture with a critical eye. It wasn't perfect. Because his face was squished into the pillow, some of the perspective was wrong. But she liked it. It was *him*. The Rylan she knew.

As she returned the pad to the drawer, she noticed

a text message lighting up the screen of her cell. If she converted it to speech, she'd risk waking Rylan.

Sliding from the bed, she pulled on a sweater and warm socks before taking her cell phone through to the kitchen. Jekyll opened one eye, yawned, stretched and followed her.

The message was from Kasey.

Can you call me? Not urgent. Not really. Only a little bit. Nothing to worry about.

Bree checked the time. Almost seven thirty in the morning. She knew Kasey left for the gallery most mornings at eight o'clock.

Kasey answered the call almost immediately. "Hey, boss lady. How are you? I've been worried about you after what happened at the show."

"I'm fine." Bree switched on the coffee machine. "It just seemed like a good time to take a break and do some painting. Is everything okay at the gallery?"

"Everything has been great, but the reason I got in touch was that there was a problem yesterday with water leaking from your apartment. It was dripping through the ceiling of the corridor between our offices. David went up to your apartment and found out the problem was a pipe under the sink in your kitchen—"

"David went up to my apartment?" Bree interjected, her voice high-pitched with surprise. "How did he do that?"

"He used the keys you gave me." Kasey sounded worried. "I hope that was okay?"

Of course. How could she have forgotten about the

spare set of keys she'd given Kasey a few months ago? Audrey had booked herself and Bree into the spa at The Chateau for an overnight stay, but Bree had been expecting a furniture delivery. The following day, when Kasey had offered to give the keys back, Bree had suggested it might be a good idea for her assistant to keep them in a safe place in her office.

How safe was safe?

"Anyway... David stopped the leak temporarily, but he thinks the pipe needs to be replaced by a professional. I wanted to check with you and see if you want me to call a plumber?"

"Uh, yes. Of course."

"The problem is that the water coming through to the gallery brought down part of the ceiling in the corridor," Kasey continued. "I can get someone out to do the work, but I'm going to need your signature to authorize it."

When Bree had set up the gallery, she had taken advice from her uncle Russ about her business systems. He had imposed on her the need to ensure that the financial controls, even in a small business, must be tightly regulated. Kasey could order goods and services, but they had to be authorized by Bree. It was a simple, clear separation of their duties.

"I asked David if it could wait a few days, but he thinks more of the ceiling could fall if it isn't dealt with right away," Kasey added. "He even tried to tell me it was a hazard and that, technically, we should close the gallery until it was fixed. I said that you and I are the only ones who use that corridor and, since you aren't here right now, I was willing to take a chance."

Bree sighed. "He was probably only thinking of your safety. A chunk of ceiling hitting you on the head wouldn't be much fun."

"David worries too much." Kasey's tone was dismissive. "But there is another thing. Lucas Brewer has lost the check I gave him as payment for the lighting work he did on the show. I don't know how many times I've told Lucas to switch to electronic transfer, but he insists on doing all his business by cash or check. Anyway, he stopped by and said money is tight, and could I issue him another check as soon as possible. I've canceled the original payment, but—"

"You need my signature on the new check." Bree poured herself a cup of coffee and gazed out the window at the view she had grown to love. This was her safe place, but the gallery was her dream. She had built it up from nothing and made it a success. The feeling that she was being pulled back there against her will saddened her. It was one more example of the damage *he* had done.

"I wish I didn't have to disturb your break," Kasey said.

"It's not your fault. I'll see if I can stop by this afternoon."

As Bree ended the call, she became aware that Jekyll was running back and forth between the kitchen and the front door. "Ah. Sorry about that."

After unlocking and opening the door to release the dog, she took her coffee outside and sat on the porch step. Jekyll, having taken care of his physical needs, returned to sit beside her.

"I suppose we could try removing the cone," Bree

said. "But as soon as you start biting your butt, it goes back on."

Jekyll regarded her with an expression of adoration as she cast the cone aside and scratched his neck. A few minutes later, Rylan came to sit beside her.

"What happened?" He quirked a brow at her. "You don't do early mornings."

It was a brief reminder of the intimacy they'd lost, and, for a moment, regret surged through her. She saw an answering flicker in his eyes.

"I got a message from Kasey." She told him the details of her conversation with her assistant.

He pursed his lips in a silent whistle. "So Kasey had a set of keys to your apartment all this time?"

"Yes, but you can't seriously think…?" She shook her head. "Not Kasey."

"Why not?" His expression was thoughtful. "Serious question. She doesn't need to override the security system because she's in the gallery anyway. Access to those programs advertising the show wasn't a problem for her. They were right there in her office. She knew where to find your paintings in the basement. And she could have stayed late to rig up the chocolate."

"I understand that it *could* have been her, but I can't believe that she would do those things." Bree picked up Jekyll and hugged him close. "I've always believed the person who sends those emails is a man. I know there is no clue to the author's identity, it's just a feeling."

"Maybe that's what the sender wants you to think," Rylan said.

"Your sources didn't find anything on Kasey," Bree reminded him.

"They haven't found anything on *anyone*. Yet." He stretched his long legs in front of him. "That doesn't mean there's nothing to find. Someone has a reason to target you, Bree. To an outsider, it may appear trivial. For instance, it could be something as minor as you forgot to leave a tip, or you didn't say hi when you passed him—or her—in the street. But to your perpetrator, it has become the focus of that person's whole life."

She shivered. "That makes it even more scary."

"Broken pipe. Ceiling coming down. Lucas's lost check. Sounds like they've been having quite the run of bad luck at Wise Gal."

"That's all it is." She kept her eyes on his profile. "Surely?"

He turned to face her, his eyes endlessly blue. "It all adds up to a lot of reasons why you have to go back."

Bree nodded. "I don't have much choice. I still have a business to run."

"Then let's do it." His voice was determined. "I promised I wouldn't let this stalker hurt you, Bree. And I meant it."

Rylan could see why Roaring Springs was a popular playground for the rich and famous.

There was an eighteen-hole golf course west of town, one of the few venues not owned by the Coltons. The caverns that housed the underground springs were open to the public and proved quite a draw, especially in the summer heat. Horse and cattle ranches were plentiful in the surrounding valleys.

But, as he took the route toward the trendy Second Street area, it was the gondola that caught his eye. The link between The Lodge and The Chateau was a visible reminder of the domination of the Colton family over the area.

"How did your family make its money?" he asked Bree.

"A Colton was one of the founding fathers of Roaring Springs, back when it was still a gold mining community of tents," she said. "The Colton name is known across the United States. You know we're related to former President Joe Colton?"

"I'd heard that."

She smiled. "Uncle Joe. Now, *there's* a character. Not a real uncle, of course. More a distant cousin of my dad's. My grandfather is a third-generation Coloradoan. When he married my grandmother, he bought up a lot of land in the mountains and opened a lodge on Pine Peak with ski slopes that became hugely popular. In the valley, the Gilfords were the biggest property owners. Price Gilford needed capital, and my grandfather needed land. They both won. The Colton Empire was formed when my uncle Russ married my aunt Mara. She was Price Gilford's daughter."

"No mention of the Gilford name in the brand?" Rylan asked.

"It was before my time, so I don't know the details. When it came to business, my grandfather was always rather slick. I guess he made sure the Coltons came out on top."

They reached the Diamond, and Rylan pulled into a space in the parking lot. It was only a few days since they had last been here, and his ranch was less than an hour away, but this felt like a different lifetime.

He cast a glance in Bree's direction, wondering if she felt the same way. But why would she? This was her territory. She'd warned him not to get used to having her around at the ranch. She belonged here, in this quirky, artsy community.

She was gazing up at the facade of Wise Gal, with intense concentration on her face. "If any of this is a plan to get me back here, then he's going to be around somewhere. Waiting for me."

"I'm here." He leaned across and gripped her hand. "For you."

"I needed to hear that." She returned the pressure of his fingers.

Releasing Papadum, who was back on guard dog duty, they left the car and crossed to the gallery entrance. Once inside the lobby, Bree paused to exchange a few words with the staff on the reception desk. Everything seemed normal as they went through to the main gallery. The place was busy, with a number of people viewing the exhibits and a group of schoolchildren taking a painting class near the craft shop.

Bree led the way into Kasey's office. Her assistant was in the middle of eating lunch but placed her sandwich down when she saw them. Rylan considered himself a good judge of character. From the smile in her eyes, he decided Kasey was either a skilled actress or she was genuinely pleased to see Bree.

"You look like your break has already done you good," Kasey said, as she studied Bree with her head on one side. "Have you done much painting?"

"Not much." Bree cast a sidelong glance in Rylan's direction.

He hadn't given it much thought until now, but he realized that, instead of painting, she'd been spending her time around the ranch with him and the animals. Had he kept her from her art? He dismissed the thought. Bree had a mind of her own. If her preference had been for painting, she'd have taken her brushes and palette out.

"Shall we take a look at the damage to the ceiling?" Bree asked.

They went out into the corridor. There were water stains on the wall near Bree's office and a large chunk of plaster had fallen from the ceiling. Although someone had clearly swept the floor, Rylan could see marks on the tiles beneath the gaping hole. Tape had been placed across the corridor, with a sign warning of the danger.

"David was being safety conscious as usual," Kasey said.

"Just as well." Rylan studied the damage. "That's definitely unsafe."

"It is." David approached them from the direction of the gallery. He nodded a greeting to Rylan and Bree. "I explained to Kasey that this needs to be fixed as soon as possible. I'd have done it myself, but it needs a professional builder."

"That's okay. It looks like you had your work cut out cleaning up the mess," Bree said. "And in my apartment, from what Kasey tells me. Thank you for all your hard work."

"All part of the job." He appeared embarrassed at her thanks. "I hope you didn't mind me going up there?"

"Goodness, no. If you hadn't, things would have been so much worse." Bree turned to Kasey. "Shall we get on with this paperwork?"

Rylan accompanied the two women into Kasey's office while David went back to his own duties. Bree and Kasey began talking business, and now that he was reassured that Bree was not in any danger from her assistant, Rylan was starting to feel antsy. What he *really* wanted to do was to speak to Judith at Arty Sans.

His restlessness must have been apparent because Bree looked up from her task. "Is there a problem?"

"No."

He loved the way her eyes crinkled at the corners when she smiled. "Not fooling anyone, Rylan."

"I could make myself useful and get us some coffee." He jerked a thumb in the direction of the door.

"You can't use the kitchen because that would mean going past the damaged section of the corridor," Kasey said. "If you want coffee, you'll have to go to Arty Sans."

Rylan cast a longing look over his shoulder. Going to the coffee shop was exactly what he wanted. But that would mean leaving Bree.

She appeared to understand his thought process. "I'll be fine. Papadum is here."

Kasey was watching them. From her expression, she clearly thought *he* might be the one who was obsessed with Bree. It was true, of course. The difference was Rylan's fixation involved wanting to spend the rest of his life in a normal relationship with her. Unlike the stalker, who wanted to harm her.

"Five minutes." He headed for the door. "If you need me, call me. Scream. Set off the fire alarms. Whatever it takes."

"Is he always this overprotective?" Kasey's bemused question followed him.

When Rylan reached Arty Sans, there were only a few customers at the counter. A quick glance around revealed that Judith was clearing tables.

"Oh, it's you." Her brow cleared as she recognized him. "Where's your funny looking dog?"

"I only have a few minutes, but I need to ask you a couple of more questions about Roaring Springs' local history. Is that okay?"

She glanced at her watch. "Sure. I'm just about to take my break."

They went out into the courtyard and sat at one of the wooden bench tables.

"You said that a conservation group was formed to preserve the original function of these buildings. Can you remember the name of the group, or who was running it?" Rylan asked.

Judith shook her head. "It wasn't very successful. As I told you, the buildings had fallen into disrepair. To be honest, preserving them so that they could continue to serve their original purposes would have been an impossible task. The only future was demolition or giving the area a new focus, which is what happened with the redevelopment."

It wasn't the answer he wanted, but it was what he'd expected. "The online forum you run, does it have old photographs of this area?"

"Yes." Judith nodded. "There's a whole section dedicated to pictures."

Rylan took out his cell phone. "What's the link?"

She gave him the details as he logged on to the internet. When he found the picture gallery, Rylan almost groaned out loud. There were hundreds of old photographs. They were split into sections. Some showed the area in its industrial heyday, others documented its decline, and recent pictures highlighted its change into a thriving new hub.

He glanced at his watch, conscious of the time he'd already spent away from Bree. "I'm interested in old pictures of this building."

Judith held out her hand for his cell phone. "Because it's on the outer edge of the area, I don't think there are many, not of the entire building." She scrolled quickly through. "There's this one."

She held up the screen. The building in the picture was unmistakably the gallery because of its shape. Part of the roof had fallen in, and plants were poking their leaves through the opening. Unfortunately, it didn't give Rylan the information he needed. But to be fair, he wasn't even sure he knew exactly what he was looking for.

"Any others?" He tried to keep the impatience out of his voice.

Judith continued scrolling. "Ah. This is a better one. It shows the front entrance of the building when it was a construction company."

Rylan took the cell from her. Although the picture was clear, the photographer had only captured half of the sign over the front door. The letters he could see were enough to make his heart beat faster. Was this it? Was he looking at the link to the stalker?

He enlarged the image and turned it to face Judith. "What was the name of this company?"

"It was an old well-respected building firm. Now, what was its name?" She frowned at the screen, focusing on the four letters that could be seen in the picture. "S-W-A-N. Oh, I remember. It was Swanson Construction."

She gave a little cry of surprise as Rylan snatched his phone back. He was on his feet as he scrolled through until he found the number he wanted. "Trey? I need you at the gallery right now."

Chapter 14

"Do you think Rylan went to Brazil to get the coffee beans?" Kasey joked.

"Let's hope the delay is because he is also getting cake." Bree laughed. She became serious again as a thought occurred to her. "By the way, where do you keep the keys to my apartment?"

Kasey gave her a long serious look. "Bree, I know there's something going on. After what happened with the programs and at the show, I know it's bad. You don't have to confide in me, if you don't want to, but I'd never do anything to hurt you." She pointed to a locked drawer in her desk. "Your keys stay in there. I'm the only person who goes in there. No one has tampered with it."

Bree sighed. "I'm sorry. I'll tell you when it's all over, I promise."

The information that her keys were kept locked away wasn't as reassuring as Kasey clearly hoped it would be. Instead, it only deepened the mystery. How had the stalker known the keys were there, and how had he gained access to them? *Had* he gained access to them, or had he found another way into her apartment?

Both women looked around hopefully as the door opened, but it wasn't Rylan bearing the longed-for coffee. David paused before he entered. "Am I interrupting you ladies?"

Bree shook her head. "I think we're done here?"

Kasey flipped through the papers in front of her. "Yes. All finished."

"Is everything okay?" Bree asked.

"I wanted to talk to you about the water stains on the corridor wall," David said. "I found some paint in the basement storage area that looks like a match. I can easily repaint that area."

"That's really kind, but I know how busy you are—"

David waved aside her protest. "It won't take me long, but I'll need you to come down to the basement with me. Just to double check that I'm right and the paint really will be okay." He glanced at his watch. "We could do that now."

Bree hesitated. "I'm waiting for Rylan to get back."

The look he gave her was one of mild surprise. "You'll only be downstairs."

That was true, and she could send Rylan a message to let him know where she would be. But she knew what he would say. Until this was over, she should trust no one. His caution was right, of course. But this was *David*. The gentle-giant security guard had helped her time after time. Carrying her bags, moving her car, running errands… He had always been such a sweet, kind man. She couldn't imagine him swatting a fly, let alone sending a threatening email.

Even so, Rylan's warning stayed with her. *And by the way, where* was *he?*

"How about you come with us?" Bree looked at Kasey, holding her gaze to let her assistant know this was important. "You have an eye for that sort of thing."

David snorted. "I thought you were an artist, Bree?"

"That's the problem," she replied airily. "I'm too focused on the fine details. Kasey is better at the bigger picture."

If Kasey was surprised to learn that she had become an interior design expert, she didn't show it. Bree prodded the snoozing Papadum into life, and they headed as a group out through the gallery. The group of school kids paused in their painting to giggle and point at Papadum as he passed.

Although she glanced toward Arty Sans, Bree couldn't see any sign of Rylan. The coffee shop didn't look busy and, for the first time, she experienced a nagging doubt. Rylan was totally focused on her safety. If he hadn't come back to Kasey's office, there must be a reason. She suspected it wasn't a good one.

When they reached the door to the basement, Bree pointed to the digital door lock. "This is new."

"After your paintings were damaged, I decided it would be useful," David said. "I spoke to the sheriff about it, and he thought it would be a good idea."

Bree remembered Trey had said something about David wanting to speak with her about a new system.

The security guard had a small maintenance budget with which they had agreed he could go ahead and make minor security improvements without requiring Bree's consent.

"It's a great idea." Kasey nodded her approval. "But I don't have the code."

"No one does yet." David pressed the numbers on the keypad. "I only finished installing it today. I'm planning to distribute the code later to those members of the gallery staff who need it."

David reached inside to switch on the light, and held the door open for Bree and Kasey to go ahead of him. Since Papadum wasn't happy with the steep steps, Kasey went first while Bree held the dog's collar. This was starting to feel like a waste of time. Her thoughts were on Rylan. She should have told David to paint the whole corridor white.

She turned her head at the sudden noise of the door. Why would David need to shut them in down here? He wouldn't...and everything clicked into place.

Bree barely had time utter a protest before David was already at the bottom of the stairs with a gun in his hand.

"What—?" Kasey didn't have time to finish her question.

David raised the weapon, with the butt end turned toward Kasey. Bree cried out as he delivered a swift blow under her assistant's chin. Blood spurted from Kasey's mouth. She spun around and fell back, banging her head on the bottom step. She lay still on the floor—her body slumped and twisted.

Bree dropped to her knees at Kasey's side. She was

breathing, but the injury to her jaw was bad. Bree was scared that she might choke on her own blood. Tilting Kasey's head up and back, she ensured her airways were open.

"I don't know what's going on here, David..." It wasn't true. She knew. Of course she did. But maybe she could salvage this if she acted dumb. Right now, it was all she had. Fighting to keep the panic out of her voice, she continued. "But Kasey needs medical attention. Urgently."

"It was your idea to bring her with us. For once in your privileged Colton life, own what you've done."

The venom in his voice shook her. It also attracted Papadum's attention. Growling long and low, the dog moved closer to Bree. In response, David raised his gun.

"No." Shaking all over, Bree wrapped her arms around Papadum's neck. "You'll have to kill me first."

Since he was probably planning to murder her anyway, she wasn't sure the words would be a deterrent. In that instant, she didn't care. There was no way she was going to watch him shoot a defenseless dog.

"Very touching." She looked up to see David sneering at her with such contempt that she hardly recognized him. "Keep that thing quiet and I'll let it live. I don't really want to fire a shot down here and risk anyone hearing. Not unless Rylan finds out where we are and decides to play hero. There's nothing I'd like more than to put a bullet between your boyfriend's eyes."

"I don't understand this. You were attacked by the person who is threatening me."

"Are you really that stupid? You still don't get it? There was no attacker. The mystery man who pushed me down? He never existed. You are not the only one with a creative streak." He barked out a laugh in response to her look of confusion. "It was my way of making sure I wouldn't be a suspect. I wasn't sure Rylan would fall for it, but it apparently worked like a charm."

Bree shivered, and clutched Papadum tighter. David had said he wasn't going to shoot her, so what *was* he planning? She wasn't sure she wanted to find out.

"What have I done to make you hate me, David?" She may as well find out what had brought them to this point.

"I don't hate you." He sank into a crouch with his back against the wall. "That's the problem."

"I don't understand." She repeated the words. If she said them often enough, maybe she would have a breakthrough and this nightmare would start to make sense.

He gave a short, harsh laugh. "You stole everything from me. My name, my future, my profession, my dignity…"

Bree couldn't process what he was saying. She wasn't a thief. How had he convinced himself that she'd stolen from him? "I don't know what you're talking about."

"This!" The word was almost a scream. He waved a hand around him. "This building. Three generations of my family. Swansons was the best construction company in Roaring Springs. Then things got tough. Money was tight, debts piled up and I had to lay most of the workforce off. Selling the building, closing the business… It was never meant to be permanent. I was getting the money together to buy this place back again, but you got there first. An *art gallery.* Can you imagine how that felt?"

"I'm sorry. I didn't know."

"You're a Colton. You don't care about the little people." The sneer was back. "Trampling on us when we're down is what you do best."

He was being unfair, but Bree wasn't going to point that out. When the developer had stepped in and bought the buildings around the Diamond, the city council had been about to sign an order for their demolition. It had represented a last-minute reprieve. She, like the other new business owners in the area, had gotten her building at a good price. But that was because they had breathed new life into a dead part of town.

When she'd met with the developers about buying the building, Bree had been the only interested purchaser. Which meant that, no matter what he said, David didn't have the money to buy the place. She suspected he was talking about his hopes rather than the reality. It was sad that his dreams had been crushed, but it hadn't been her fault.

What worried her most was the bitter way he spoke about her family. There was no doubt that The Colton Empire had created a split in Roaring Springs. The Lodge and The Chateau appealed to an elite that left other hotels and restaurants in the town green with jealousy. But other businesses had learned how to cash in. The influx of wealthy visitors, particularly during the annual film festival, meant that everyone's profits soared, and shops with an eclectic flair always did well. Even so, there were always people who delighted in the Coltons' misfortunes.

But what she heard in David's voice went beyond the usual haves-and-have-nots divide. It was hatred. Deep, feral and terrifying. She remembered what Trey had said. His informant had heard a whisper about possible attacks on The Lodge and The Chateau. Could David be behind those as well?

"I don't know where this impression of my family has come from—"

"From someone who knows." He spat the words out. "But your time's up. We're going to stop you. The original plan was to start with you and the gallery. Scare you. Drive you out of town."

Bree's mind was racing. The original emails, the attack on the gallery, they had all been about forcing her to leave. What had changed?

David's face twisted in anguish. "But *you*..." He used the gun to point at her, and she flinched. "You messed it all up. You got inside here." He pressed his knuckles to his temple. "So I couldn't stop thinking about you. Couldn't stop wanting you."

Wanting you. Just the way he said the words, his voice thickening, gave the situation a whole new meaning. Bree could hear his internal struggle. Wanting a woman he should hate. A Colton. No wonder the emails were filled with threats of violence. In his head, hurting her would be preferable to liking her.

She tried to hide the shudder that ran through her. Rylan had been right when he talked about classic stalking behavior. David's plan to drive her out had changed focus and become an obsession with her personally. Which made it much more dangerous...

"A *Colton*. What kind of idiot does that make me?" David was looking down at the floor. He almost seemed to be talking to himself or repeating something he'd been told. "Get back to the plan. Too much invested in this to waste it."

He raised his head and looked directly at Bree. "Get rid of the problem."

Rylan broke into a run as he ended his call to Trey. The sheriff was close by and would be there in minutes. If David was in the Wise Gal building, the lobby was where he was most likely to find him.

This was the breakthrough they'd been looking for. It was also the reason David had slipped through the net when Rylan's colleagues were doing background checks. He didn't have anything to hide. No criminal record, no sinister past, no previous history of obsessive behavior toward women. His only connection to Bree was that she had bought the property that had been in his family for generations. It had been enough to trigger a resentment that had flared into fixation.

When he discovered David wasn't in the foyer, Rylan headed back in the direction of Kasey's office. The most important thing now was to keep Bree safe until Trey could get David behind bars.

"I don't have the coffee, but I do have a good reason—" He stopped just inside the door. He was talking to an empty room.

Okay. There could have been any number of reasons why two women and a dog had left the room. There was no reason to panic. Even so, his imagination went into overdrive, his concentration splintering.

I left her.

Alarm became a physical presence, wrapping powerful arms around his chest and pulling him down. Pressure built in his lungs, driving his heart rate up too hard, too fast.

"Rylan?" Trey's voice pulled him back from the edge. Like a drowning man breaking through the surface, Rylan pulled in a huge breath of air.

He swung around. "She was here, with Kasey."

"You think he could have them?" Trey asked.

"I don't want to take that chance." Rylan tried to keep his thoughts on track. "Papadum. Of course." He headed toward the door.

"Pardon?" Although Trey followed him, his expression was bemused.

"My dog. You've seen him. He's unmistakable. Bree had him with her. Someone will have seen him and noticed where they went."

When they reached the gallery, Rylan headed toward the group of school kids, who were just packing up. He approached the teacher. "Is it okay if I ask a quick question?"

Her eyes flicked to Trey, taking in the uniform and badge. "I guess so."

Rylan took up a position where he could be seen by all the kids. "Guys, did any of you just see a dog that looks like a giant mop?" There was a ripple of laughter and a chorus of shouts. Since the little girl nearest to him was jumping up and down on the spot, trying to get his attention, Rylan turned to her. "Where'd he go?"

"He was with two ladies and a man in uniform." She pointed to the door that led to the basement. "They went through there."

"Thank you, sweetheart."

Rylan drew Trey toward the entrance to the basement. "This didn't have a lock last time I was here. Why would David close this door and lock himself in with Bree and Kasey?"

Trey stood back, eying the door. "It looks strong, but between the two of us we could kick it down."

"And let him know we're coming so he has time to kill them both?" Rylan shook his head. "I don't think so."

He'd been in enough hostage situations to appreciate the need for caution. They didn't know for sure what they were dealing with. Didn't even know that David had the two women in the basement, or that he was holding them against their will.

He dismissed the idea of calling Bree. If she was in the clutches of her stalker, the situation was volatile. He didn't want to risk startling or antagonizing a dangerous man who had repeatedly threatened to harm her.

"Is there another way in?" Trey asked.

"I don't know. But I know how to find out," Rylan said. "I have a plan of the building on my laptop. You stay here while I check it out."

"Okay." Trey's face was grim. "But I'm calling for backup, and if I hear a sound that leads me to believe that my sister is in danger, that door is firewood."

"Goes without saying."

Rylan sprinted through to the promotions office. Through the glass facade, he could see the school kids getting onto their bus. Evacuating the building was probably a good idea.

He leaned across the reception desk. "Get everyone out of here. Tell them it's for unscheduled maintenance."

The receptionist blinked but responded to his air

of authority with a nod. As he opened his laptop, he could hear the front desk staff following his instructions. Once he had the plan of the gallery on the screen, he enlarged the basement area. *There.* On the outside of the building, at street level, there was what appeared to be a set of double trapdoors. There was a note alongside it that read *Original delivery chute. Preserved but no longer in use.*

His mind was jumping several steps ahead as he left the office and called Trey, relaying what he'd discovered.

"If the chute is not in use, it will have been secured to prevent unlawful entry," Trey said.

"Don't worry about that." Rylan was already on his way out to the parking lot to get his bolt cutters. It was probably better for the sheriff's peace of mind if he didn't know about the various pieces of equipment that Rylan kept in the trunk of his car.

"I don't like the idea of you going in there alone." Trey's tone held all the caution Rylan would expect to hear from a law enforcement officer.

"Trust me. I am the best person to do this." Rylan wasn't being boastful. This was his area of expertise. Going into the unknown, facing a volatile offender, rescuing hostages… They were all situations he'd been in before. Having snagged up the bolt cutters, he was on the move toward the trapdoor entry to the basement. "Just be ready to come through that door fast."

"My deputies will be here any minute with the battering ram and pry tools," Trey said.

When Rylan reached them, the double trapdoors were larger than he'd expected. Made of heavy wood, they were flush with the surrounding sidewalk. He pursed his lips as he studied them. Squatting, he verified his first impression. There was no need for the bolt cutters. The doors weren't locked.

Unsure what to make of this new development, but unable to spend time analyzing it, he stashed his bolt cutters behind a nearby bush. The doors opened easily, almost as if the old iron hinges had recently been oiled. When he had them both fully open, Rylan knelt on the sidewalk, leaning into the opening.

The metal delivery chute was long and steep, and he couldn't see the other end. There was a pulley system alongside, presumably for lifting larger items from below. Ducking his head farther into the gap, he attempted to identify any sounds from the basement. Either there were none, or they were hidden by the thick walls of the old building.

Lowering himself into the space, he gripped the sides of the chute. Using his powerful leg muscles to stop himself from hurtling downward like a toddler on a playground ride, he descended slowly into the darkness.

His facial muscles were rigid with tension, his pulse pounding hard in his ears. Cold sweat beaded on his furrowed brow. He knew why. As a soldier, he had been in dozens of combat situations. Since leaving the army, he had faced danger many times, and in many different forms. This was different. This was about Bree.

After what felt like an eternity, Rylan saw a faint glow of light below him. Soon after, his feet slid off the edge of the chute and touched hard floor. Crouching low, he withdrew his gun from its shoulder holster.

There was enough light for him to see his surroundings. He was in a large square room, the walls of which were lined with shelves. Most were stacked with boxes. He figured this was probably one of the places in which the art exhibits were stored. There was no door, just a narrow opening that presumably led to another part of the basement. That was where the light was coming from. It was also the point from which he could hear voices.

Treading lightly so as not to be heard, Rylan moved closer to the opening. His heart soared when he recognized Bree's voice.

"If I'm the problem, and you have to get rid of me, what do you plan to do?"

"Kill you, of course." The matter-of-fact way in which David said the words made Rylan want to burst out from his hiding place and confront the other man. But he couldn't, because he had no way of assessing the situation beyond his viewpoint. David could have a gun to Bree's head, or a knife to her throat. He could have Kasey in a similar situation. Challenging him could have dire consequences.

"But I'm going to have a little fun with you first." The lustful note in the other man's voice made Rylan's insides grow hot and tight with rage. He bowed his head, breathing deep. Losing control wasn't going to help.

"I'd rather you just shot me." *Bree.* As much as he admired her bravery, Rylan wanted to warn her against antagonizing an adversary.

But her words had told him something important. David had a gun.

"You don't get to choose," David said. "Now come here."

Rylan held his breath. If David touched her, the rule book would be ripped up. He would be forced to act.

"I can't leave Kasey. She needs a doctor," Bree said.

"You really don't get this, do you? If I'm going to kill you, why would I care if she dies as well?"

While David's voice was raised, Rylan risked a glance into the other part of the basement. What he saw chilled him. Kasey, who appeared to be unconscious, was lying at the bottom of the stairs. Bree was on her knees next to her with her arms wrapped around Papadum. David was squatting nearby with his back to the wall. His hands were hidden between his knees, but Rylan was willing to bet he had a gun in one of them.

The choice was simple. Would Rylan be able to take David by surprise before the other man could shoot Bree? He would only get one chance to find out.

Stepping forward, he adopted his military fighting stance, knees flexed, arms extended straight out, raising his weapon.

"Get down flat, Bree."

Although he spoke to her, Rylan kept his gaze trained on David, who was glaring at him with fury in his eyes and his lips drawn back. Bree obeyed him instantly, pulling Papadum with her into the space under the stairs. David scrambled to get to his feet.

"Don't move." As soon as Rylan uttered the words, David raised his gun. There was the sound of a shot, the splintering of glass and the basement was plunged into darkness.

Rylan muttered a curse as something brushed past him. At the same time, he heard the battering ram breaking open the interior door. Seconds later, Trey was framed in the doorway at the top of the stairs.

"Careful," Rylan called out to him. "The suspect is armed, and there's an injured woman at the base of the stairs."

Someone handed Trey a flashlight, and he moved to the top of the stairs. "This is Sheriff Colton. Place your weapon down, and step forward where I can see you."

Nothing happened. As Trey began to slowly descend the stairs, one of his deputies took his place at the top and shone a more powerful light, illuminating the scene below. There was no sign of David in the basement.

Chapter 15

Kasey regained consciousness in the ambulance, her eyes filling with tears as she clutched Bree's hand. "I thought David was a nice guy." She managed to make herself understood, despite the injury to her jaw.

"So did I." Bree gently smoothed the hair back from Kasey's forehead.

"What happened after I blacked out?"

Bree hesitated. Kasey had been through enough. She didn't need to know that after he had shot out the single bulb, David had used the cover of darkness to escape from the basement. He must have always intended to exit via the delivery chute. Rylan had pointed out the pulley system that he could have used to make a quick getaway. That was why he had also removed the lock and oiled the hinges on the trap doors. His careful plan was just missing one minor detail. He had never intended to leave Bree alive.

"Rylan and Trey are still finalizing things." The truth was that a Bradford County deputy was following them in his own vehicle. Even more importantly, at least from Bree's point of view, Rylan was also close behind. Trey had remained at the gallery and was using Bree's office to coordinate the search for David.

"My face... How bad is it?"

Bree was saved the necessity of answering when a paramedic intervened and administered a sedative. There were two hospitals in Roaring Springs, one specializing in trauma, while the other dealt mainly with surgery. She had called Kasey's mom, who was already on her way and would meet them at the Roaring Springs Trauma Center.

As they approached the hospital entrance, the rescue team bustled into action. The deputy caught up with Bree as she followed Kasey's trolley toward the assessment unit. A nurse halted them at the entrance.

"Go into the waiting room, please. Someone will give you an update as soon as we've completed our initial assessment."

It was only then that the enormity of what had happened finally hit Bree. She had focused all her energy on getting Kasey the medical attention she needed, but now that her assistant was in good hands, all the horrifying details of what had gone down in the basement came flooding back.

The taut muscles around her mouth began to tremble and she bit her lip, trying to hold back the tears. It was too late. She felt warmth trickling down her cheek and rolling off her chin. First one, then another. Fast and unstoppable, like a rainfall. She went to sit on one of the chairs in the waiting room. Covering her face with her hands, she leaned back, alternating sobbing and sniffing.

A muscular arm slid around her shoulders and pulled her close against a powerful chest. *Rylan.* She sank gratefully into his strength, letting the tears flow.

"It's okay. I'm here." His voice was warm and comforting against her hair. "Let it all out."

After a minute or two, she straightened and sniffed. "I don't have my purse. No tissues."

"Let me see what I can do."

He disappeared for a few seconds, returning with a handful of scratchy paper towels. Bree blew her nose and did what she could to repair the damage to her face.

"Have they said anything about Kasey?" Rylan asked.

"They're assessing her injuries now." Bree got to her feet as a small woman in her fifties dashed toward her. "This is Mrs. Spencer, Kasey's mom."

The two hours they spent waiting for news was like forgotten time. Everything felt too much. The overhead lights were too bright, the hospital smells too strong, the slightest noise hurt Bree's ears. She held Mrs. Spencer's hand and tried to reassure her, without having any real knowledge herself. When a doctor finally came, Bree didn't know whether to be relieved or apprehensive.

"Kasey's jaw is broken in several places, and she is missing a few teeth. She is going to need emergency surgery to fix the initial damage. Longer term, she will require facial reconstructive and cosmetic repairs, plus extensive oral surgery."

"Whatever it takes," Bree said. She turned to Mrs. Spencer. "As Kasey's employer, I hope you'll allow me to meet the full cost of her medical bills."

On the advice of the hospital staff, Rylan and Bree decided not to stay. Kasey, who was heavily sedated, would have her mom with her, and Trey had posted a twenty-four-hour guard on her private room until David Swanson was caught.

When they stepped outside, Bree, who wasn't wearing a coat, shivered. Darkness was falling, bringing a chill wind with it. Rylan shrugged off his fleece jacket and draped it around her shoulders. She pulled it tighter.

"Take me home, Rylan." There was a question in his eyes as he scanned her face. "Back to the ranch."

Rylan cast a few worried glances in Bree's direction as he drove. Her eyes were closed, and she was very still. She could have been asleep, but he doubted it. He knew she would be reliving what had happened. Going over and over it, her thoughts trying to make sense of another person's agenda. At some point, he figured it was likely she would find a way to blame herself for some of it.

As they reached the gates to the ranch, she turned toward him with a frown. "Papadum?"

"Trey had someone drop him off earlier. They brought your purse and coat as well."

When he stopped in front of the house, she exited the car slowly, moving like a person trying to wade through fast-moving water. Rylan took her hand, and, after looking blankly at his fingers wrapped around her own for a moment, she returned his grip. Together, they walked into the house and through to the kitchen.

"You need something to eat." Rylan went to the fridge.

Bree flopped into a seat at the table. "I don't know if I could." She looked around. "Where's Jekyll?"

"I didn't know how long we'd be at the hospital, so I called Dinah and asked her to take him." He looked up from his inspection of the shelves. "How about a tuna melt sandwich?"

"I could be tempted by that." Bree studied the screen of her cell phone. "I should call my parents."

Rylan nodded. "You should, but you don't have to give them all the details. Not unless you want to. Right now, all they need to know is that you are okay, and that Trey is on the trail of the person who has been threatening you. Tell them as much, or as little, about what happened today as you choose."

Her posture relaxed slightly. "I'll just…" She pointed toward the den, and he nodded. After about a minute, he heard the murmur of her voice, and saw her pacing back and forth as she talked.

By the time she returned, he'd made the sandwiches and poured coffee. He scanned her face. She looked tired, but less tense.

"How did that go?"

She returned to sit at the table. "They were worried, naturally, but reassured after we spoke. I decided to tell them that Kasey had been injured, in case the press picked up on it. Particularly with the Colton connection." She bit into her sandwich. "This is seriously good. I didn't even know I was hungry."

"What about you?" Rylan asked. "How are you?"

She ate in silence for a few moments. "Is it okay to say I don't know? Because I just feel numb."

"Or shocked, maybe?"

"Maybe." The golden hue of her eyes seemed brighter than ever as she looked toward the window. "The thought that they are still out there—"

Rylan frowned. "*They*?"

"David talked about someone else." Bree's brow furrowed in an effort to remember. "He was talking about my family, about how the Coltons trample on the little people. I asked him where that impression had come from. He said it was from someone who knew everything. *We're* going to stop you. That was what he said. The plan was to start with me and the gallery. To scare me and drive me out of town. But then he said…" She drew in a breath. "He said he couldn't stop thinking about me."

Rylan's lips tightened into a hard line. "And that was when scaring you out of town changed, and became about his sordid fantasies of you?"

"But when David talked about it, he seemed to be angry. It was as if he'd let someone down by going off track. He said he had to straighten things out by getting rid of the problem." She shivered. "I was the problem, but he didn't want to kill me straight away…"

Rylan reached for her hand. "I think Trey needs to hear about the possibility of an accomplice."

"It sounded more like the other person was the mastermind," Bree said. "David appeared nervous that he'd annoyed him."

Rylan called Trey and quickly updated him on the information Bree had just given him. "David told Bree the plan was to start with the gallery. That means your informant might have been correct when he told you there could be future attacks on The Lodge and The Chateau."

"Yeah." Rylan could hear the disbelief and weariness in Trey's voice. "Another nightmare to add to the list. Let me speak to my sister."

Rylan finished his snack while Bree chatted with Trey for a few minutes. His mind was processing what she had told him. The situation had just gotten a whole lot more sinister. Because if there was another person in the background, directing David's actions, that person had to have deliberately sought the security guard out. David's motive against Bree was clear, but what about this shadowy figure? Was his grudge directed toward Bree or, which seemed more likely, toward the whole Colton family?

Bree ended the call. She sipped her coffee but pushed the half-eaten sandwich aside. "I'm sorry. I just can't manage any more." She raised her eyes to Rylan's face. "I'm starting to realize that I'd be dead by now if it weren't for you."

"I told you I wouldn't let him hurt you, Bree."

"That's right." She gave him a lopsided smile. "It's your job."

"If you truly believe that's the reason, then you don't know me."

Rylan caught the flare of emotion in her eyes before she looked back at her plate. "Thank you."

He didn't know if the words were about him rescuing her, or for telling her that he hadn't done it because it was his job. "I don't want your gratitude."

Her shoulders slumped. "This is too hard. I should still be angry at what you did to me, but I need you to hold me—"

Rylan moved around the table. Kneeling at her side, he wrapped his arms around her waist. Bree bent her head and pressed her cheek to the top of his head.

"This…" Her voice choked up, and she paused before trying again. "You have no idea how much I needed this."

He laughed. "Believe me. I do. It's been on my mind as well."

She framed his face with her hands. "Take me to bed, Rylan."

"On one condition." Bree quirked a brow at him and he grinned. "Not a sexy sort of condition. We sleep. That's all."

"Are you crazy?"

"I might just be." As she started to speak, he pressed a finger to her lips. "Hear me out. You said it yourself. You should still be angry with me. I let you down, and you have every right to never trust me again. Today, you went through a horrible shock. You have no idea how much I want to hear you ask me to take you to bed. If it ever happens again, I want it to be for the right reason. Because you want *me*. Not because you need comfort."

"You've turned my world upside down and destroyed my trust in you. Now, you're showing me that you are a good guy after all." She shook her head. "You're confusing me, Rylan."

He held out his hands and pulled her to her feet. "You don't have to think about any of this right now. Just get a good night's sleep."

"That's another thing." Her face was serious. "I know I will if I'm with you."

The last time they had shared a bed, Bree had been conscious of the invisible barrier between them. It had felt like there was no way back from the damage caused to their relationship. Now, things were different. She was too tired to analyze how, or if the change was permanent. But if it meant she could fall asleep with Rylan's arms around her, she wasn't going to ask questions. Not after the day that had just passed.

Through half-closed eyes, she lay back on her pillows and watched Rylan as he got ready. These tiny things were what she wanted. This closeness. Resting her head on his chest and listening to the steady beat of his heart. Sharing his body heat. Those incredible Rylan morning cuddles. The feeling that nothing could ever hurt her when he was holding her.

As if he could read her mind, Rylan slid beneath the bedsheets and drew her to him. His lips were a feathery touch on her forehead.

"Good night, Bree."

Her eyes drifted closed as he spoke.

She woke with a start. Rylan's side of the bed was empty, and sunlight was streaming through a gap in the windows. Clearly, it was morning. But…what was that *noise*? The high-pitched wailing sounded like the exorcism of a dozen reluctant demons. It was accompanied by wild scrabbling at the base of the bedroom door.

She smiled. *Jekyll*.

The door opened. "I told him not to disturb you." Rylan carried coffee and toast. "But he wouldn't listen."

Jekyll hurled himself desperately at the bed, his little legs flailing. Bree reached down and scooped him up with one hand. He threw himself at her, his body language clearly indicating that he had been subjected to unbearable torture in her absence.

"Breakfast in bed." She smiled up at Rylan. "I could get used to this."

He pointed at Jekyll, who had draped himself across her ankles. "You may have to. I think that means you are never allowed to leave again."

The words hung between them for a moment, igniting tiny reminders of everything that still remained unsaid. Rylan sat on the bed while Bree leaned against the pillows and sipped her coffee.

"Have you heard from Trey?" She almost didn't want to say the words, didn't want any reminder of David Swanson to intrude on this peaceful moment.

"He called to say that they haven't found David yet. When they searched his apartment, they discovered a huge stash of guns, which goes beyond worrying and into frightening. Trey doesn't believe David has the resources or connections to buy the high-powered weapons they found. He certainly doesn't have a permit for most of them." Exhaling roughly, he raked a hand through his hair. "It all comes back to the same questions. Who is behind this, and what are they planning?

Luckily, Trey also found David's laptop. The Bradford County tech guys are at work, trying to get some information from that."

Bree nibbled at the corner of a piece of toast. "If he started out wanting to scare me out of town, he didn't need to stockpile guns."

"Exactly. It looks like attacking you was part of a bigger strategy," Rylan said. "What will you do about the gallery? With Kasey out of commission, you don't have anyone in charge."

"My mom offered to get together with a few of her friends and keep the gallery open until I'm able to return." Bree sat up straighter. "You know my mom. She can do anything if she puts her mind to it. I'm just concerned that it would be a Colton running Wise Gal. Would she be another target?"

Rylan fell silent as he gave the suggestion some thought. "So far, the action has all come from David. With him in hiding, I can't see his mentor, or senior partner, whoever this other person is, coming out of the shadows and changing his role. I think your mom will be safe, especially if Trey puts a guard on the gallery."

"By that reasoning, can't I go back?" Although Bree asked the question, she wasn't hopeful of a positive answer.

"Not a chance." Rylan didn't hesitate. "David could be anywhere. No matter what other plans he and his partner have, we know he is obsessed with you, Bree. That isn't going away just because he's a wanted man. You are staying right here, where I can watch over you."

Bree's stubborn streak made a half-hearted attempt to rebel. But Rylan was right. She had the memory of what had happened in that basement to convince her of that. The look on David's face when he talked about what he wanted to do to her before he killed her...

She was safe here. With Rylan. His presence gave her the security she needed.

"I need to call Kasey's mom," she said. "I want to check on how she's doing, and if there's anything she needs."

"I'll leave you to speak in private." Rylan got to his feet. "Any thoughts on how you want to spend the day?"

She studied him thoughtfully. "The toast has made me hungry. How about we start with pancakes for breakfast?"

He grinned. "I can do that. Anything else milady desires?"

Actually, there was something she desired very much. Rylan, with his rugged good looks and muscular physique, was everything she wanted. Maybe it was because of the danger she had been in. Possibly, it was the memory of their former connection. Right now, all she wanted was to grab the front of his T-shirt and haul him closer...

Whoa. She should probably turn the shower down nice and cold this morning. Aware that Rylan was watching her with a quizzical look in his eyes, she sank back onto her pillows.

"After the pancakes? I want to check in with everyone. Wonkey, Boo, Cindy from Finance...all of them." She became serious again. "When I was in that basement, I thought of the people I needed to see again. My family." She hitched in a breath. "You and your crazy animals."

Rylan went very still. He stared down at her, his eyes appearing bluer than ever. After a moment or two, his lips parted and he raised a hand toward her. As she smiled up at him, his expression changed. It was as if a switch had been flicked and the light in his eyes went out.

He lowered his hand. "You ordered pancakes, right?"

Feeling slightly bewildered, Bree watched him leave the room.

Rylan pushed his body to the absolute edge of its physical endurance. His workout routine was as demanding and difficult as that of a professional athlete, and he stuck to it rigidly. Until now, he had applied the same ruthless precision to his emotions.

Ever since his mother's death, he'd made a conscious decision. He didn't do feelings. By maintaining complete control over his heart, he had built up a facade that proved his father wrong.

Weak? Wimp? Worthless? He had never let anyone get close enough to find out if it was true.

His encounters with women had been brief and casual. The rules were established up front, and both partners had walked away with good memories and no regrets.

Then along came Bree.

And Rylan was learning the hard way that his heart wasn't as iron-clad and compliant as he'd always believed. No matter how much he tried to suppress the need to tell her how he felt, it was there below the surface, like a volcano waiting to blow.

But he couldn't do that to her. She had just gone

through a horrible trauma, and she was vulnerable. The physical attraction between them was already strong, and there was more to it. An emotional connection that went beyond sex. It was only natural that Bree should turn to him right now. She saw Rylan as the man who would take care of her. Deep down, some primal instinct made her want to take shelter in his arms.

What kind of man would take advantage of that? One who had already proven himself untrustworthy? *Unworthy*?

His mind might be whirling in a million different directions right now, but one thing was irrefutable. For the first time in his life, Rylan was truly afraid. Because if he told Bree he loved her, he could only see two outcomes. The first, and most likely, was that she would gently let him know that she didn't feel the same way. The second was that, caught up in a web of fear and anxiety, she might mistake her own heart. He wanted to hear Bree tell him she loved him more than he wanted his next breath, but not because she was looking for a comfort blanket.

And she doesn't know me.

Like the rest of the world, she saw the tough guy exterior. If she knew what lay beneath…

His musings were interrupted as Bree entered the kitchen with Jekyll at her heels. It was hard to believe she'd been through such a stressful incident the previous day. She was wearing jeans with tiny flowers embroidered all over them, a huge baggy fisherman's sweater and biker boots. Although her hair was loose, a floral headband kept it back from her face. She was fresh-faced, bright-eyed and absolutely gorgeous.

"Pancakes." He forced himself to concentrate. "And there's syrup or fruit. There's even freshly squeezed orange juice."

"Heaven." Bree took a seat and helped herself to food. "Kasey was in surgery when I spoke to her mom, but she had a restful night. Mrs. Spencer said she had been talking, she understood what was happening and seemed in okay spirits. Her mom will send me a text message later to let me know how the surgery went."

"From what the doctor said, this is just the start for Kasey," Rylan said quietly.

"I know." Bree's expressive mouth turned down at the corners. "She was only in the basement because of me. When David asked me to go with him to look at paint, I wasn't really suspicious of him, but I remembered what you'd said about not trusting anyone. So I asked Kasey to come with us."

"You couldn't have known what would happen." Rylan attempted to reassure her. "At that point, none of us suspected him."

She ate a few bites of pancake. "Based on your experience, what do you think David will do next?"

"Hard to say without knowing the motive of the mystery puppet master," Rylan said. "If his intention was purely to cause a problem for the Coltons, he may decide David has become a liability. If that's the case, David is on his own. He must know Trey has all his resources focused on finding him. Sticking around Roaring Springs wouldn't be his smartest move."

"So you think he'll leave town?"

"He will if he's got any sense. And if he's thinking straight." Rylan gave her a direct look. "He's already proved he has an obsessive personality. I'm not sure we can rely on him thinking straight."

"This other person seems to have another motive. Stockpiling weapons sounds sinister."

"If we're dealing with something very different, your brother probably needs outside help. I'm sure we can leave it to Trey to deal with that." Rylan leaned back in his chair. "After we've checked on the animals, how would you like a spa experience?"

She raised her brows. "I thought I was supposed to stay here on the ranch? Don't get me wrong, The Chateau is one of my favorite places, but it is all the way back in Roaring Springs."

Rylan grinned at her. "You Coltons are not the only ones who have a hot spring on your property, wise gal."

Chapter 16

They followed the creek on a winding route for about twenty minutes until it reached the spring. It was a single warm pool at the base of a steep cliff, with piled rocks in the form of an oval creating a large natural hot tub right on the edge of the river.

Bree eyed the water suspiciously before studying the surrounding white-tipped peaks. "Are you sure it's warm enough at this time of year? What about the snow from the mountains?"

"Even with the runoff, it's like a warm bath," Rylan said. "Try it for yourself."

When she'd packed her things for a stay at the ranch, it hadn't occurred to her that she might need a bathing suit. The only option for this activity had been the shorts and tank she was wearing under her outer clothing. Sitting on a rock, she pulled off her boots and socks, then tugged off her sweater. Standing, she shimmied out of her jeans.

Stepping cautiously over the rocks and pebbles, Bree entered the pool. Rylan was right. The temperature was perfect.

"Oh, it's glorious." She turned in time to see Rylan heading her way wearing just his boxer briefs, and Bree decided that glowing accolade also described his body to a tee.

The pool was just wide enough to stretch out and float, but its attraction was the rocky shelf on which it was possible to lie flat, or sit with her legs extended in front of her, and be massaged by the thermal bubbles. Bree leaned back, her skin tingling as she closed her eyes and relaxed. When Rylan joined her, he sat opposite her. Legs apart, he rested his feet on either side of her hips.

She sighed. "Perfect." He didn't need to know she wasn't talking about the water.

Bree's own feet were close to the inside of his thighs. Every now and then, the movement of the water caused her toes to lightly brush his skin. Through half-open eyes, she watched his reaction. Smiling, Rylan casually reached under the water and took hold of her foot. Slowly, he ran his thumb from her heel to her toes, then back again. The sensation sent tiny darts of pleasure running through her entire body.

Something in her reaction must have drawn his attention, because he paused. "Should I stop?"

Unsure whether she could trust her voice, Bree shook her head. Rylan continued to rub the bottom of her foot in firm circular movements. The action was soothing and sensual at the same time. Lying back, she let the feelings carry her. Warm water, the sounds of nature, soft bubbles caressing her body and Rylan's touch. She drifted between awareness and bliss.

Reaching a hand to her side, she stroked Rylan's foot. Running her fingernails across his skin, she continued to lie back and enjoy whatever this was without analyzing it. She had done too much thinking just lately. It was time for a bit of acting on impulse.

Opening her eyes, she sat up straighter. Looking into his startling blue eyes, she smiled. "Can I kiss you?"

"Bree…" There was caution in his expression, but she also saw hunger.

"You wanted to be sure this was about you. Let me prove it."

Leaning forward, she placed her lips gently against his. When his mouth opened, she moved her tongue inside, exploring every inch. With a murmur of satisfaction, she pressed her hands against his chest as she deepened the kiss. Gradually, she felt Rylan relax. His hands moved to her hair, her face and the bare skin of her shoulders. Instantly, her nipples tightened with anticipation.

Feeling totally unlike her usual reserved self, she continued to take the lead. Reaching her hands around to his back, she slowly raked her fingernails down his spine, enjoying the shudder that ran through him. Drawing his tongue into her mouth, she sucked it slowly in and out, teasing him with the suggestive action.

Rylan gave a groan of surrender. His hands worked their way down from her shoulders to cover her breasts over the material of her tank. Taking each nipple between his fingers, he lightly pinched the sensitive buds. Bree murmured her appreciation, changing position until she was straddling his lap.

Face-to-face with him now, she could feel his hardness pressing tight against her core. They continued to kiss as he stroked her breasts and teased her nipples. Overcome with pleasure, Bree ran her nails up and down his back and tugged at his hair.

"Okay. You've convinced me that this is not about finding comfort." Breathing hard, Rylan leaned back to look at her face. "So maybe now would be a good time to lose the clothes and get a condom?"

Bree gazed up at the blue Colorado sky, dotted with fluffy clouds, the mountains with their snowy peaks, the gurgling stream and the clear spring water. She pressed another kiss to Rylan's lips. "Sounds wonderful."

While Rylan climbed out of the pool to get the protection from his jeans, Bree tugged off her wet clothes. When he returned, naked, to the pool, he stretched out on the rocky shelf next to her. Lying tight together with the warm water washing over them was a new and pleasant sensation. Rylan's gaze pierced hers, mirroring the same desire she was experiencing.

Using his fingers, he made lazy circles on the insides of her legs, moving upward in tiny stages. His warm breath caressed the cool skin of one exposed shoulder. Erotic shivers were like an electric charge just beneath the surface of her skin. The connection Bree felt to him transcended anything physical.

The only thing she could compare it to was her art.

She could look at a painting with another person and experience a shared moment of enjoyment. But with Rylan it was unique. It was the same deep-seated bond she forged with her own creations. But this was stronger, fiercer, more intimate because she loved him.

When his finger slid inside her, Bree gave a little cry.

"I will never get tired of hearing that sound." Rylan lowered his head to kiss the sensitive flesh of her neck.

Knowing she wouldn't be able to last long, Bree reached a hand between their bodies and encircled his erection, her grip tightening around him. She started with soft caresses, her movements becoming bolder as her fingers moved up to stroke his length before gliding back down again. As Rylan began to move his thumb in a relentless circle around her clitoris while pumping his finger in and out of her, her own movements became faster.

"Condom." There was a hint of desperation about the word as he rose onto his knees and reached onto the rocks above them.

When he was fully sheathed, Rylan kissed Bree deeply as he eased her onto her back. Spreading her legs, he lifted her so that she could wrap them around his hips. Bree pushed up, desperate to feel him. She moved her pelvis against his, offering herself to him. He groaned, then, in one quick thrust, pushed all the way into her. Her heartbeat picked up speed as their bodies rocked together, and soon she was lost to everything but Rylan.

She moaned and arched her back, pressing her breasts to his chest. The difference between his hard muscle and her soft flesh drove the oxygen from her lungs and what was left of any reason from her brain. Grasping her hips firmly, Rylan began to pound hard. It was as if he couldn't get deep enough inside her, as if he were seeking something more than a physical sensation. She looked into his eyes and knew she could get lost in this new connection between them.

Soft quakes started somewhere in her core and rippled upward and outward. She gripped Rylan's biceps, holding on to him as she let go, all conscious thought slipping away as searing heat tore through her. A moment later, her body splintered. She felt Rylan swell and pulse inside her and she clenched her muscles hard around him, her body trembling as she held him tight inside her.

Her action drew a growl from somewhere deep in Rylan's chest. The look of ecstasy in his eyes as he climaxed made her heart pound even more wildly.

He managed to gasp out a few words. "Was this better than a visit to The Chateau?"

"It was certainly different." She started to giggle. "I can't imagine what Aunt Mara's friends would say if *this* was one of the spa day specials."

He turned onto his side, curling up close to her. "Who knows? They might be queuing up to try it."

"No need to brag. Besides…" She tilted her chin to look at him. "They'd have to fight me off first."

"They would?" She nodded, and he tightened his arms around her. "I'm glad to hear it." After a few minutes, he squinted up at the sky. "We should probably head back."

"Do we have to?" Bree pouted.

"Today is your day." There was a gleam in his eyes

as he looked down at her. "Do you have any more special requests?"

She slid a hand down over the muscles of his abdomen, enjoying the way he sucked in a breath. "When you've recovered your strength, I can think of a few…"

Rylan had just started cooking dinner when Trey arrived.

"Tell me you've found him?"

Trey shook his head. "Where's Bree?"

"In the shower." Rylan had practically carried her home and placed her under the jets of water, joining her briefly to soap off the pool water. He looked up from chopping onions. "Are you staying for dinner?"

"Sounds good."

Bree wandered into the kitchen a few minutes later. "Kasey's mom sent me a message to say that the surgery went well." There was a hint of disappointment in her expression when she saw her brother. "Oh. Hey."

"Aw, thanks," Trey said. "I love you too."

She laughed and moved closer to kiss his cheek. "It's just… I know you'll have come here to talk about the case."

"I have. But before I do, did you know there's a bat following you?"

Jekyll had been hiding behind Bree's ankles, and sneaking occasional glances at the intruder. She picked him up and stroked his oversized ears. "Take no notice of the nasty sheriff. The voters of Bradford County would be shocked to learn that this is the man who drew a mustache on my favorite princess doll."

Trey rolled his eyes. "You make it sound like it happened last week."

"Do you two want to continue this fascinating discussion while we eat?" Rylan asked.

He placed plates of spinach and ricotta ravioli on the table, together with a platter of garlic bread and a pitcher of iced water.

After eating a few forkfuls of the pasta, Trey looked from Rylan to Bree. "So how did you spend your day?"

The look Bree gave him ignited a series of fireworks at the base of Rylan's spine. "Uh, we just took it easy," he said. Bree smirked and lowered her gaze.

Trey, who was focused on his food, appeared not to notice the exchange. "Taking it easy, huh? While you were doing that, I was working. Although we have no information on David's whereabouts, we've been able to access his email accounts. He has two."

"Let me guess. A regular account, the sort all of us have. And the one he used to contact Bree," Rylan said.

"Correct." Trey pointed at him with a piece of bread. "We didn't find anything suspicious in his day-to-day account. But he only used the other one to contact two people. Bree and someone whose email address was lonewolf@ponr.com."

"Ponr.com?" Rylan frowned. "I thought I knew most of the dodgy email providers, but that's a new one to me."

"It's quite recent. Ponr is short for point of no return. Its big selling attribute is the privacy of its users. Mail is automatically deleted after twenty-four hours," Trey said. "Of course, our tech wizards were able to restore everything. It was clear from the messages between them that Lone Wolf was the person in charge."

"Were there any clues to his identity?" Although Bree voiced the question, she wasn't hopeful about the answer.

"None. The messages clarified what we had already pieced together. It isn't clear how Lone Wolf first made contact, but he was preying on David's resentment toward Bree. They planned a series of attacks on the gallery, together with the threatening emails, to drive her out of the Diamond and back to our parents' home. After that, they intended to move on and target the Colton family at The Chateau, then The Lodge."

"And the stash of weapons?" Rylan asked.

"It's not completely clear whether the plan was a mass shooting at The Lodge or at The Chateau. They discussed both options," Trey said. "They also considered an attack on the Diamond."

Bree raised a hand to her mouth. "I can't believe I'm hearing this."

"Believe it." Trey's expression was grim. "In his emails, David described how he overheard you and Kasey talking about her keeping a set of keys to your apartment. He knew she kept them locked in her desk, but he had the master key to the drawer. He had a copy of your keys made. He boasted to Lone Wolf that he was able to get into your home any time he wanted. That was how he damaged the pipe under your sink, causing the water to flow into the gallery. He figured you would have to come out of your hiding place to authorize the repair work that needed to be done."

Rylan looked across at Bree to see how she was dealing with that information. Although she bit her lip, she took it well. It wasn't as if it was news to her. She knew the stalker had been in her apartment several times. The fact that he had his own set of keys? Yeah, that was a new level of disturbing.

"It was all there in the emails. The pornographic leaflets tucked inside the programs, the fake attacker, the chocolate hidden in the ceiling." Trey scrubbed a hand over his jaw. "But the friendship hit a rocky patch recently when Lone Wolf found out that David had changed his approach to you, Bree."

Rylan frowned. "How would he know about that if David didn't tell him?"

Trey shrugged. "Who knows? Somehow, Lone Wolf became aware that his plans were in danger of being derailed by David's growing obsession. The more recent email exchange is very much a series of lectures from Lone Wolf to get back on track. David's responses are mostly apologies and promises to put things right. That's pretty much where we were up to when he lured Bree and Kasey into the basement."

"There's one thing I don't understand," Bree said. "I can see how Lone Wolf—whoever he is—was able to prey on David's insecurities and hostility. But what's in it for David? How was a formerly law-abiding man persuaded into a scheme like this?"

"We don't know what he was promised," Rylan pointed out. "If, behind the secret identity, Lone Wolf is a person of influence, he might even have told David he would get his construction firm back."

"What happens now?" Bree asked wearily.

"We'll keep looking for David," Trey said. "He's the

key to all of this. I have no way of discovering Lone Wolf's identity, or what his motive is, without David. There's only one thing I know for sure."

"What? That Lone Wolf hates the Coltons?"

Trey nodded. "Yes. And that he intends to do something about it."

Most things in Bree's life eventually became a comparison with art. It was how she viewed relationships. Many were like a quick sketch. Others represented a more detailed painting, sometimes a puzzling one. Then there were the masterpieces, handed down through generations, their beauty and intricacy evident to everyone who saw them.

Her parents... Now, theirs was an image of true love. Simple, timeless and crafted by a master. Her uncle Russ and aunt Mara? A confusing abstract. The sort of picture several people could view, all walking away with a different opinion of what they'd seen.

She hadn't stopped to view her own life as a canvas. But she wondered what the future held for her and Rylan. Did they have a future beyond what was happening here and now?

Bree knew he loved her. It was obvious in his body language, and in every look they exchanged. When they made love, and there were no more barriers between them, it was there in the honesty of their bodies.

But did *he* know he loved her? Had he even admitted it to himself? If he had, Bree knew the next step—telling her—would be the hardest. And she understood why. *Anything to make me feel worthless.* They were the words he'd used about his father. When Rylan was a boy, the man who should have cared for and protected him had subjected him to unimaginable torture. Knowing he was a sensitive child, his dad had tried to change his personality.

Bree's heart ached for the boy he had been then, and the man he was now. Because his father hadn't suppressed who he was. No matter how hard Rylan tried to hide behind his tough guy veneer, the sweet, sensitive person was still there. That was the man she loved.

The problem was that his father *had* succeeded in another sense. He had convinced Rylan that he was worthless. As a result, Rylan had spent his whole life trying to prove his value to an unworthy parent. But the damage went too deep. Rylan couldn't get past the belief that he wasn't good enough.

When it came to their relationship, things became even more complicated. Bree knew he was eaten up with guilt because he'd let her down once. She didn't like that it had happened, but she understood the circumstances. And while she was willing to give him another chance, he wasn't prepared to let himself off as lightly.

So where did that leave them? Amazing sex, and then they parted ways when David Swanson was found?

I can't do that, Rylan. Can you?

Bree's thoughts remained troubled as she lay awake. Her mind turned from her romantic woes with Rylan to Trey's visit and his revelations about David's emails. Although they had discussed Lone Wolf's identity, it was impossible to guess who he—or she—might be. The Coltons had plenty of enemies in the business world, and any of the individual family members could have stirred up antagonism in their personal lives. Even so, a threat of this magnitude had the weight of a lot of bitterness behind it.

Had Bree been the starting point because she was seen as the easy target? It was possible that someone looking to cause trouble for the Coltons had learned of David's hostility toward her and decided to make use of it to launch a wider campaign. Anyone who knew her family would know the special place Bree held within it. Hurt her and everyone would be outraged. She was still the little cousin they all loved to protect. It didn't matter how hard she fought against it—that was the way it was.

As they'd batted different ideas back and forth, Rylan had come up with a radical new suggestion. What if there was no second person? What if *David* was the Lone Wolf—the clue was in the name after all—and the email conversations were his way of setting up his defense in advance of committing the crimes? Blame it on the shadowy person in the background.

The bad guy made me do it. It was a different twist on *the voices in my head.* Could David be that devious? Bree would have said not, but he'd fooled her into believing he was a mild-mannered, kindly man when in reality he was a vengeful stalker with an unhealthy fixation on her family.

Taken to the extreme, it was even feasible that David had a multiple personality disorder. If he was suffering from a mental illness, he may not know that he had created the persona of Lone Wolf and that both personalities resided within him. Until he was captured, all this was pure speculation, but it raised a troubling possibility.

One thing was for sure, whether his partner was real, imaginary or a convenient invention, the Colton family was not safe while David was still at large. Which was why Trey had left after dinner and gone back to his office to check how the investigation was progressing.

Bree checked the time on her cell phone. Four in the morning. She should follow Rylan's example and get some sleep. A few weeks ago, the biggest thing she had to worry about was the placement of the exhibits in the gallery.

She curled tight against his body and closed her eyes. Life had sure become complicated, but there were compensations.

Chapter 17

Rylan was woken by the sensation of Bree's warm lips tickling his stomach. Either that, or he was in the grip of the hottest dream ever. As her butterfly kisses moved lower, his hips jerked.

She looked up with a smile. "I couldn't sleep."

"So you decided to wake me?" He gasped as her tongue flicked out, tracing the head of his erection.

"Do you mind?"

"I guess I can live with it." He caught hold of her hair, pinning it at the nape of her neck and angling his head to get a view of what she was doing.

Bree laughed, then slowly kissed along his iron hard length. With one hand squeezing the base of his shaft, she wrapped her lips around him and started gently sucking. Slow and steady. She might be trying to drive him insane. At the same time, her tongue applied exquisite pressure all along his sensitized flesh.

Rylan stroked Bree's cheek, wanting to show her the tenderness he felt, even as she was setting his body alight.

"Feels so good." Rylan's hips moved in time with her rhythm.

Maintaining eye contact, she gave him an "I know what this is doing to you, and I love it" stare that almost singed his nerve endings.

"Pull my hair." She lifted her head briefly to gasp out the instruction.

Rylan obeyed immediately, his eyes narrowing as he observed her reaction. Sheer wanton pleasure. Her absolute need for him was apparent in the way her movements kicked into a higher gear and she looked at him like he was the only thing in the world she would ever want. She took him deeper into her mouth, sucking with more force as her head bobbed up and down.

When she moaned, the vibration triggered electric shocks right through his shaft. It was all too much. Rylan felt the first shudder of release and gripped the mattress so hard he thought his fingers might go right through. Bree's nails dug hard into his thighs, and he gave himself up to a climax so intense he almost blacked out.

When his vision cleared, Bree was crawling back up the bed. She kissed him briefly on the lips. "I can probably sleep now."

He growled as he tipped her onto her back. "Sleep? Not a chance. It's payback time…"

She smiled, stretching lazily as he spread her legs

apart and knelt between them. Bending his head, Rylan kissed the inside of her leg, just above her knee. Working his way upward, he licked the soft skin of her thigh.

Bree shuddered. "Nice."

He moved to the other leg, tracing a path with the tip of his tongue, slowing as he got closer to the top of her thigh. Shifting position, he held her legs apart with his shoulders and blew gently on her center. Bree's hips lifted off the bed.

"Rylan! You tease…"

Chuckling to himself, he swept his tongue along her core. Long and slow. Steady and firm. Back and forth. Stopping just short of her clitoris each time. He waited until she was squirming with desire, until he could tell her mind had become suspended, and her body had reached a point where the sensations of pleasure had taken over. She was breathing fast and moaning softly.

On the next lick, he passed over the tiny nub, stopping to wiggle the tip of his tongue over it for a few seconds. He pulled away for a brief count, then did it again. Bree tangled her fingers in his hair.

"Don't stop."

Rylan continued the action, increasing in speed as she cried out and bucked her hips. He could feel her orgasm building. Her back arched and her thighs trembled.

"Yes. Oh, Rylan…"

She cried out, falling over the edge and riding the lightning bolts of her release. It took several minutes for her body to stop quivering. Rylan moved to her side, cradling her in his arms as they both caught their breath. They lay that way for a while, not speaking, just enjoying the warmth of one another's body. Eventually, Bree's breathing slowed and became rhythmic. Rylan smiled into her hair. She had finally fallen asleep.

A few hours later, Rylan leaned over and moved Bree's hair aside, tickling her ear with his breath. "Why don't you get up and come for a run with me?"

"Still asleep," she mumbled.

"You'll enjoy it once you get moving."

"Moving. Ugh." She wriggled farther beneath the bedsheets.

He laughed and headed out the door. Jekyll, who had finally been persuaded to stay in the kitchen overnight, gave him a calculating look before sinking back into his own bed.

"Two of a kind." Rylan shook his head and left them to it.

He enjoyed his early morning runs at this time of year. The smell of the flowers starting to bloom throughout the valley tempted his nostrils, the birds began to sing as the sun rose and the crisp breeze of spring was in the air. April might just be the best time to see this vast landscape. The mountain peaks that fed the rivers below were still dusted with soft touches of winter, but the sun's rays were casting their golden tint.

Stopping by the kennels, he unlocked the doors. A few of the dogs chose to join him. Others pretended not to see him and remained in their beds.

Rylan tried to clear his head when he exercised, focusing on the views, his land and his animals. The only difference today was that Bree would be waiting for him when he got back to the house. It was his dream of how every day should be.

He hadn't been running for long when his cell phone buzzed. Without breaking his stride, he pulled it from his pocket. The message from Trey was simple.

On my way over.

Switching direction, Rylan ran back the way he had come. He tried not to speculate on why Bree's brother would need to come to see them so early, and so soon after they had spoken. Since it clearly wasn't something he was prepared to discuss in a call, it must be important.

Bree was in exactly the same position he had left her. "Wake up, wise gal."

"No." She pulled a pillow over her head.

"Trey is on his way."

She became a blur of movement, leaping from the bed and diving into the bathroom to shower. Rylan headed to his own room to get ready. When Trey arrived, they were sitting on the porch, drinking coffee and eating cereal.

"You look like a man who hasn't slept." Rylan poured another cup of coffee as Trey strode toward them.

"I managed to catch a few hours." Trey pulled out a chair. "But then I got the news that David Swanson was arrested in Canada yesterday afternoon."

Rylan straightened. "You got the word out to international law enforcement already?"

Trey shook his head. "Things don't work that fast. We froze his bank accounts as soon as he went on the run, but we have no idea how much cash he could have stashed away. Or if he has accounts that we don't know about. It's even possible Lone Wolf is bankrolling him behind the scenes. No-fly lists are for hardened terrorists rather than a fugitive like David Swanson, and it takes time to get international law enforcement involved. But I got a call from the police in Winnipeg telling me they had him in a cell."

"I'm not following this story," Rylan said.

"He was picked up by a patrol car for driving erratically, whatever that means." Trey took a long slug of his coffee. "They approached him, asked him to get out of the car and he tried to run. When they caught him, he resisted arrest. He admitted that he was wanted here in Colorado. Even gave them my name."

"Is it just me, or does that sound a lot like a man who was trying to get himself captured?" Rylan asked. If David was running from American law enforcement, surely he would lie low when he reached a new country? Unless the stress of evading capture had gotten to him?

"That's what I thought," Trey said. "Maybe his friendship with Lone Wolf wasn't going as well as he'd hoped, and he wanted some distance. Possibly, he thought the Canadian police would be more lenient. Whatever the reason, the identification papers they faxed through check out. It looks like I'm headed for Winnipeg to interview him."

"Where does this leave me?" Bree's voice was very quiet.

"Of course. You want to go home and get back to work." Trey turned to Rylan. "This changes everything.

With David in police detention in Canada, I don't see why Bree can't go back to Roaring Springs."

Rylan felt like a dark cloud had just swallowed the sunlight.

Think fast. Find a way to make her stay. "What about Lone Wolf?"

"You said it yourself. Lone Wolf may not exist. If he does, he has been happy to stay in the background and do the planning while David carries out the actual attacks. He's certainly not the person who is obsessed with Bree." Trey finished his coffee and checked his watch. He spoke directly to his sister. "As long as you take every precaution, there's no reason why you can't come back to town with me right now."

She raised her eyes to Rylan's face, and everything he wanted to know was right there. He only had to speak now, and she would stay. But how could he, when he didn't know what the right words were? With Trey sitting there tapping his foot, how could he begin to explain that he wasn't the person she thought he was?

Tough guy. *Wimp.* Protector. *Worthless.* Honest. *Fake.*

The silence stretched out between them and the hopeful light died out of Bree's eyes. In those excruciatingly long moments, Rylan found out it was possible to hate himself even more than he already did.

"So, I guess your time as my bodyguard is over." She tried to smile, but her lips trembled too much. "Can I ask you a favor? I'd like to keep Jekyll…"

"You'll be the one doing me a favor." He had to speak quickly around the tightening of his throat. He got to his feet. "I hope you guys will excuse me, I need to see to the animals."

Walking away from her was like walking over hot coals. This was why he'd avoided falling in love. It wasn't the love that hurt; it was the loss. This was the side of loving that should come with a warning. When you gave your heart to another person, you never got it back again. Leaving her drained the color from the world and turned it into a dark, shadowy place.

"Oh." He turned back. The flare of hope in Bree's eyes was a knife to his chest. "Before I forget... I got a call from Blaine. He's being discharged. He told me he'll be back in Roaring Springs real soon."

"Want to talk about it?" The sympathy in Trey's voice almost tipped Bree over the edge into uncontrollable sobs.

"There's nothing to say." She hugged Jekyll, and turned her face away, watching the familiar scenery roll past the passenger window.

Missing Rylan was already a physical pain. She wanted to be alone to ask herself the same questions repeatedly. To seek the answer that she must have missed the first time. What could she have done differently? How could she have shaken a response from him? Only then could she work on the acceptance that he had no place in her life from now on.

How had she tumbled so fast and so hard? From never having come close to falling in love with anyone ever before, she'd thrown her heart and soul into loving Rylan. Usually reserved, she had opened up to him, letting him see every part of her. It was because of the warm, comfortable feeling she had when he was next to her. Now she was lost. Would she ever feel safe again?

"For what it's worth, I think he loves you," Trey said.

Bree was touched. Her big, tough brother had actually taken the time to notice what was going on in her life. Even more amazing, he was prepared to comment on it.

She took a shaky breath, unsure whether her voice would work. "That's not the problem."

"It seems like an important starting point."

She brushed away a tear. "When did you get all wise?"

"Hey. This is as far as I go with relationship advice." He pulled into the parking lot of the Diamond. "Mom will already be in the gallery. It's your call. Do you want to go in there, or shall we take your stuff up to your apartment?"

"I don't feel ready to face Mom or work just yet." Who'd have thought she'd ever say either of those things? "I'll help Jekyll settle into his new home, and maybe head down to the gallery later."

Once Trey had carried her belongings up to the loft, it took Bree a few minutes to persuade him that she really was fine on her own. "I'll call you if I need you," she promised. "But David Swanson is in a jail cell in another country, and Mom is downstairs."

"You could call Rylan if you need anything," he reminded her.

"Stop matchmaking." She pushed him toward the door.

When he'd gone, she turned back to survey her familiar apartment. It hadn't changed, but it seemed different. It no longer felt like home. Although the broken pipe under the sink was a reminder of David's presence, that wasn't the reason. Her thoughts went to Rylan's ranch, and she determinedly pushed them away.

"So, this is where we live now," she said to Jekyll. "What do you think?"

Since the dog had just noticed the rug in the center of the hardwood floor, he ignored her. Approaching the strange object with caution, he sniffed one corner of it. Apparently emboldened by its passive behavior, he growled at it, then ran away and hid beneath the coffee table.

"It's not going to hurt you." Bree laughed as she went into the kitchen.

This left Jekyll with a horrible new dilemma. If he wanted to go with her, he would have to walk across the rug he had just threatened. He tried howling loudly, but Bree just clicked her fingers and offered him a treat. Summoning all his courage, he made a mad dash into the kitchen.

"You funny little guy." Bree picked him up and rubbed his ears. "Dog logic. How does that work?"

She poured him a bowl of water and gave him some food. Trey had set her bags down by the front door, and she studied them with a feeling of gloom. It seemed such a long time ago that she had reluctantly packed them up. Back then, hurt and bewildered by Rylan's betrayal, she hadn't wanted to go with him to his ranch. If she could turn back time, would she do things differently?

"I'd find a way to show him that his dad was wrong," she said to Jekyll. The dog tilted his head as though trying to understand her. "He's not worthless. He's got a heart as big as the sky." Bree choked back a sob. "And I'd make sure he knows how much I love him for that."

She sank down onto the tiled floor, clutching the little dog to her as the tears came thick and fast.

It took a long time, but when she was all cried out, she got to her feet. Going to the bathroom, she grimaced at the pitiful reflection in the mirror. After splashing water on her face, brushing her teeth and tidying her hair, she started to feel more human.

She returned to the living area where Jekyll had resumed his staring competition with the rug.

"Come on." Bree picked up his leash. "I'll introduce you to your grandma Audrey."

While he tended to the animals, Rylan mentally called himself every foul name he could think of. The dogs sensed his mood and either fussed around him or kept their distance. Only Papadum seemed to understand. Leaning against his legs, the big dog forced him into a moment of stillness.

Rylan sat on an upturned barrel and rested his hand on Papadum's head. "You'll miss her too, won't you, big guy?"

Bree loved his animals as much as he did. They would all feel her loss.

Despite his efforts to remain clear-headed, Rylan's mind swam with half-formed regrets. He thought of his frame of mind as he'd started his run earlier in the day. Now, even the colors of spring were drab, the birdsong shrill, grating his nerves. His mood was his personal rain cloud, pouring sorrow onto the perfect vista.

"I suppose you think I'm an idiot." Papadum nudged

his hand. "Okay. I *am* an idiot. But how could I tell her I love her? Think about it from her perspective. When we first got together, I was pretending to be someone else. She forgave me." He managed a ragged laugh. "Although I didn't deserve it, she gave me a second chance. But how do I explain to the most wonderful, perfect woman in the world that I'm *still* pretending to be someone else?"

Papadum grunted and placed a heavy paw on his knee. "That's where we're different," Rylan said. "You'd just slobber all over her face, then eat her soap."

By evening, the silence in the house was unbearable. How had he ever thought *this* was peaceful? He even missed Jekyll. Wandering aimlessly from room to room, he told himself he would avoid going into Bree's bedroom. Who was he kidding? That's exactly where he'd been going all along.

Although she'd removed all her belongings, a trace of her floral perfume lingered in the air. Rylan closed the door and leaned on it, breathing in the delicious scent. It was sweet torture. For a second, he panicked. What would happen when it faded?

His eye was drawn to the bed. Bree had pulled the bed covers neatly into place, but there was an object on the pillows. If she'd left something behind, he would have to contact her…

Ruthlessly, Rylan quelled the burst of optimism. His heart couldn't stand that sort of stop-start elation. If Bree had forgotten something, he would give it to Trey to pass on to her.

As he stepped closer, he saw it was a sketch. A smile dawned when he realized it was a picture of him. He had no idea when she'd drawn it, and it was hardly flattering, but she'd captured him perfectly as he slept. Half squished into the pillow, his face had a softness that was lacking when he was awake. He appeared younger, more carefree…more sensitive.

He realized he was looking at himself as Bree saw him. He'd never fooled her. She'd seen through the tough guy image to the person beneath. The picture revealed the truth. With the strokes of her pencil, she had shown him her heart.

Instead of her usual *B* signature, she'd written *luv, bree* in loopy childish letters. He knew how difficult she found writing, and that simple gesture touched him almost as much as the picture itself.

He'd never moved so fast. Dashing through the house, he grabbed up his jacket and keys, sending a text message to Dinah as he ran. The journey to Roaring Springs seemed to take twice as long as usual. In his head, he'd rehearsed the conversation where he told Bree he was a wimp. Now, he had to start a new one. It began with the words *I'm an idiot*…

When he reached the Diamond, Wise Gal was already closed. Darkness was falling and the Diamond was coming alive. As Rylan raced toward the steps to Bree's apartment, he caught a glimpse of her heading toward the restaurants and bars. She was wearing a long orange jacket and carrying Jekyll.

She was too far away for him to call out her name, so he followed her into the crowded area. Luckily, she stood out easily because of the color of her coat. Just as he got within shouting distance, someone else stepped in front of her. Rylan bit back a curse as he recognized Lucas Brewer.

Remaining in the background, Rylan watched as Bree chatted with Lucas for a few minutes. They were too far away for him to hear the conversation, but when the other man pointed to On the Rocks and mimed getting a drink, he was unable to stop his hands from clenching into fists. He relaxed when Bree shook her head and indicated Sushi Stop, the Japanese takeout place.

As she walked away from Lucas, Rylan's cell phone buzzed. It was a call from Trey.

The sheriff didn't bother with a greeting. "It's not him."

"What?" Rylan covered his free ear with one hand to block out some of the background noise.

"I didn't get to Winnipeg. Before I left, I got a call telling me the guy they have there is not David Swanson." Trey spoke each word clearly. "He paid someone to cross the border with his passport and get himself arrested—"

"Got to go."

Rylan broke into a run. His heart faltered as he drew closer to Bree, his eyes drawn to her back. There, between her shoulder blades, was the bright red dot of a gun target. It stood out clearly, even on the vivid color of her jacket. He knew what that dot meant—someone had her in his gun sights. Wherever that red circle went, so would the bullet. As he watched, it moved up toward the base of her skull…

He didn't have time to call out a warning. Closing the distance between them, he grabbed Bree from behind and pushed her to the ground. Her startled exclamation and Jekyll's yelp coincided with the gunshot. Rylan's right shoulder went numb, then pain seared through it as if he'd been stabbed with a red-hot poker. Warmth flooded down his arm. Staying upright wasn't an option, and he toppled forward onto his face.

When he managed to turn his head, and he saw how much blood there was, he wanted to cry. Not with the pain—although that was bad—but because he could die right now, and he still hadn't told Bree he loved her.

Chapter 18

Bree landed on her knees, twisting to her side to avoid crushing Jekyll. She turned her head in time to hear the shot and see Rylan standing over her. As his features contorted in pain, it was obvious what had happened. Rylan had risked his own life to save hers.

"No!" As she shouted the word, he toppled forward.

Bree crawled toward him, covering the distance between them on her hands and knees. Her progress was impeded by the panic that erupted around them. People were shouting and screaming, running in different directions or trying to find cover.

By the time she got to Rylan's side, he was unconscious. What worried her most was the growing red puddle that was spreading out from beneath him.

"Help me, somebody." She looked up at the circle of

people that were gathering around them. "He's losing too much blood."

A man pushed through the crowd to kneel beside her. She recognized him as the security guard from On the Rocks.

"I need to apply pressure to the wound." He glanced at her. "Give me your scarf." Bree unwound it quickly from around her neck, and he folded it to make a pad. Holding it against Rylan's shoulder, he pressed down hard on the injury. "Did anyone call 911?"

Half a dozen voices answered to confirm that they had.

"The sheriff and a few deputies are already here," a woman said. "They broke into the apartment over the Yogurt Hut just after the shot was fired."

Bree's mind couldn't fully take in what she was hearing. Her brother should be in Winnipeg. Trey *knew* someone would be in David's apartment? Had he anticipated this shooting? Could he have stopped it?

She couldn't think about any of that right now. Her priority was Rylan. The color had drained from his face, and he seemed to be barely breathing. She gripped his hand tightly, holding a shivering Jekyll to her chest with her other arm.

"*Lucky.* That's what they call you, isn't it?" Leaning over him, she whispered the words into his ear. "Be lucky again, Rylan. Do it for me this time." She bit back a sob. "Do it for us."

His selflessness had been the final confirmation of his love. To care enough for someone to be prepared to die for them…that was the ultimate sacrifice. She didn't need any more evidence, but it showed what a truly good person he was.

I need to tell him that. She lifted his hand to her cheek, trying to stem the feeling that her whole world was draining away while she had no way of stopping it.

"Bree!" She looked up through a haze of tears to see the crowd moving back as Trey strode toward her. "Get these people away from him." He barked the instruction over his shoulder to one of his deputies. Crouching beside her, he turned to the security guard, who was administering first aid. "Vital signs?"

"He's breathing, but it's rapid and shallow, and his pulse is weak. As you can see, he's lost a lot of blood."

Trey placed an arm around Bree. "The ambulance is on its way. I told them to speed things up."

She turned her face into his chest. "Rylan pushed me out of the way. He took the bullet that was meant for me."

His fingers tightened on her arm. "David was never in Canada. I got a call from the police in Winnipeg just before I set off. He tricked us. And he was just minutes ahead of us. He can't have gotten far this time."

In the distance, she heard the faint wail of a siren. "I have to go with Rylan, but I can't take Jekyll." She handed the little dog over. "Be nice to him, he's had a fright."

Trey looked slightly bemused as though his large hands didn't quite know what to do with such a small creature. He patted Bree's shoulder awkwardly. "Rylan is tough."

If her facial muscles hadn't been frozen by shock,

she might almost have smiled. *He fooled you too, huh?* "I'll call you when I know anything."

Once they were in the ambulance, the paramedics got to work, stripping off Rylan's clothes, checking his injuries, applying more pressure and fixing an oxygen mask over his face. Bree saw the damage the bullet had done—it had torn straight through his shoulder—and she had to look away as a wave of nausea washed over her.

She heard the driver radioing ahead, telling their colleagues to prepare an operating theater. Phrases like "major blood loss" and "traumatic injury" imprinted themselves in her mind. Everything else passed her by.

When they reached the hospital, it was like déjà vu. Unlike Kasey, Rylan was taken on a trolley past the trauma assessment unit, and straight through to the emergency operating room.

Bree pointed to the waiting room. "I guess I'll head that way."

A nurse gave her a sympathetic look. "It could be a long night."

It *was* a long night. A night of pacing and panicking or sitting still and feeling numb. Every few hours, Bree would find someone and ask how Rylan was doing. The answer was always the same.

"Still in surgery. The doctor will tell you when we have any news."

Trey sent her a few brief text messages. The Roaring Springs Police Department and the Bradford County Sheriff's Department were working together, both forces on high alert to catch David Swanson. So far, he had evaded them.

Don't go anywhere without telling me, Trey had warned her.

Since she had no intention of leaving the hospital as long as Rylan was there, she hadn't replied.

She was the only person in the waiting room. There was a stack of magazines, but reading the articles wasn't an option for Bree. Once she'd flicked through the fashion, food and lifestyle pictures, she was left with the choice between listening to an audiobook or music through her headphones. Neither option suited her restless spirits.

There was an internal window between the waiting room and the corridor. Even in the early hours of the morning, the place was busy, and her eyes were drawn to the parade of medical staff walking past.

In an effort to stave off the boredom, she idly speculated on the roles of the various people. The different colored scrubs could have been a clue, if she'd known what they meant. Most people had their heads covered, and many also wore a mask, so studying faces was difficult. Bree switched her attention to their footwear. Comfortable, waterproof, lightweight, slip-resistant... She was compiling a list of features in her head, when she noticed an anomaly. One of the medics, someone who had walked past several times, was wearing high-top sneakers.

"Ms. Colton?" It was the nurse she had spoken to when she first arrived at the hospital. "The surgeon expects to be finished in about an hour. It was a difficult procedure, but initial indications are that it was successful. There's still a long way to go, but Mr. Bennet is through the worst part."

"Oh…thank God." Bree slumped forward in her seat, relief hitting her with the same impact as shock.

The nurse, whose name badge read *Shirley Cuva*, squatted next to her. "Deep breaths. That's it. Nice and slow." She rested a hand on Bree's thigh, her gaze dropping to take in the torn and bloodied knees of her jeans. "I didn't realize you were injured."

"It's nothing." Bree had barely noticed the ache in her knees. "I fell when Rylan pushed me out of the way of the bullet." Her lips trembled at the memory.

"Come with me. I can't do anything about your jeans, but I can clean you up and give you something for the pain."

Like a weary child following a parent, Bree went with Shirley along the corridor and into an empty room. It was more like a small ward than a treatment bay. There were six curtained-off compartments at one side of the room, each containing its own bed and equipment trolley.

"Take off your boots and jeans, and then get onto the bed." Shirley indicated the first cubicle. Using a key pinned to the waist of her pants, she unlocked the trolley, opening the top drawer to reveal a number of syringes and packs of medication.

As Bree started to follow her instructions, Shirley's pager began to beep.

The nurse clicked her tongue and rolled her eyes. "Can't anyone do anything around here? Sorry about this." She pointed to a folded sheet. "Use that to cover your legs. I'll be back in two minutes."

Bree lay on the bed and gazed at the ceiling. If the fire alarm went off now, the world would be treated to the sight of her bright yellow underwear with the fruit pictures and the word *Peachy* on the butt. Skye always sent the craziest birthday presents. She didn't care. Rylan had made it through surgery.

Perspective. It matters more than dignity.

When the door opened again she was about to comment that Shirley had taken less than two minutes. The words died on her lips before she spoke. From her lying-flat position, all she could see under the bottom of the cubicle curtain was the feet of the person who had entered.

Shirley had been wearing pale blue slip-on shoes that matched her scrubs. This person's footwear was different but familiar. The sneakers Bree had seen walking up and down the corridor outside the waiting room were now inside the treatment room with her.

Her thoughts stuttered momentarily, before completing the picture. No medical professional would wear those sneakers while working. These were regular high-tops, not providing any padding for someone who would be spending hours on their feet. And they were *grubby*.

The reason she had seen so much of these feet became crystal clear. They belonged to someone who had been pacing the corridor, anticipating the moment when Bree left the waiting room.

It took moments for those thoughts to flash through her mind. In another few seconds, she was slipping from the bed. Without any conscious thought about how she would use it, she grabbed one of the syringes from the trolley drawer and quietly tore its packaging open with her teeth.

As she ducked into the next compartment, she spared a thought for her cell phone. Although it was in the pocket of her jeans, she wouldn't be able to use it. Calling Trey would signal her location to the sneaker wearer, and texting wasn't an option. Although her brother would be alerted by a message from Bree, he wouldn't be able to make any sense of it. On a good day, she might be able to type the word *help*. Under stress, even the simplest of spellings eluded her.

Her mind was racing as she stealthily made her way along the compartments. Ducking under the curtains and over the beds. Fast and silent. It was like the deadliest of obstacle courses.

After shooting Rylan, could David have followed them to the hospital in the hope of finishing the job? Or was she about to come face-to-face with his mysterious accomplice? She didn't have to wait long to find out.

"Come out, Bree. You know I'll shoot the nurse as soon as she comes back." David's voice was moving closer. "You're a Colton. I don't expect you to care, but maybe just for once you could take responsibility for your actions. Do the right thing. Don't be responsible for her murder, as well as Rylan's."

Bree had reached the end cubicle. With nowhere else to go, she judged David was level with the compartment next to her. Holding her breath, she waited until she heard him move before ducking under the curtain and doubling back the way she had come. She would only get one chance at this. He had a gun. She had a syringe. The odds were not exactly even.

As David swept back the curtain on the final cubicle, Bree sprang at him from behind. Clinging on to his neck with one arm, she brought the syringe around toward his face with her other hand. As he gave a bellow and tried to shake her off, she felt like a kitten hanging on to an enraged bear.

One chance. That's all.

David squirmed and twisted in fury, trying to grab the syringe from her. It was now or never. Bree sucked in a breath, jabbed the needle into his right eye and depressed the plunger.

Screaming, he fell to his knees, clawing at his face. The gun clattered to the floor and Bree kicked it across the room. Shaking so hard she could barely move, she made it to the door. Staggering into the corridor, she collapsed to her knees and was caught in Shirley's arms before she hit the floor.

Rylan didn't know where he was. All he knew for sure was that every part of him hurt. The worst pain by far was in his right shoulder. It felt like he'd been pinned to the bed by an iron stake. Maybe he had, because there was no way he could move that side of his body.

He was too tired to do more than open his eyes for a few seconds at a time but after a while, he figured he must be in a hospital. Although the room was in near-darkness, the tubes, drips and beeping of monitors were the dead giveaway.

Eventually, he managed to turn his head to the left. Bolts of pure agony shot through him, but it was worth it. The person sitting on the chair next to the bed had fallen asleep, slumping over with her head resting close to his hand. Rylan couldn't see her face, but he knew those curls. He loved those curls.

Lifting his hand with difficulty, he twisted his fingers in Bree's hair. A smile touched his lips and he closed his eyes.

When he woke again, the room was brighter and Bree was gone. He frowned. Was it a dream? What had happened after he was shot? Had David been captured or had he escaped?

"Hey, there." The unfamiliar female voice was overly loud, booming in his ears, and he winced.

Turning his head carefully to the right, he rode the wave of dizziness. The nurse was checking the monitors and recording the results on an electronic tablet.

"Water?" His voice sounded like it belonged to someone else. Someone who had sandpaper in place of vocal cords.

She brought him a bottle with a straw and held it to his lips. Although everything in him rebelled at his helplessness, he knew he couldn't move, and he swallowed the cool liquid gratefully.

"How long?" Just the action of drinking left him feeling weak as a kitten.

"How long have you been here? This is the second day." She returned to her task. "The doctor will check on you later."

When she'd gone, he tried to process what she'd just said. Two days? How was that possible? And what had been happening with the investigation while he was lying here? He needed his cell phone, but he couldn't see any of his personal belongings. Frustrated, he tried to find a call button. Even the slightest movement was torture and left him exhausted. Wearily, he closed his eyes.

When he opened them again, he was in the middle of another dream about Bree. This time she was sitting at the side of the bed, with her headphones on as she checked her cell phone.

"Wish you were real." He managed to croak out the words.

She started and dropped her phone into her lap. Tears filled her eyes as she removed her headphones. Catching hold of his hand, she lifted it to her cheek. "Oh, Rylan."

"Don't be a dream."

She gave a watery laugh. "Okay, I won't."

He blinked hard. She was still there. "Kiss me."

"I don't want to hurt you." She was smiling through her tears.

"Do I have to come to you?" Rylan tried out a growl. The result was more of a whisper.

"Don't you dare move." Leaning over, Bree gently pressed her lips to his.

He sighed contentedly. "Worth getting shot for."

She rested her cheek against his forehead. "There are some things you shouldn't joke about."

Despite the pain and tiredness, her touch brought perfect serenity. Rylan let the happiness soak right through to his bones. This was everything he'd never allowed himself to want. He closed his eyes and savored the moment. For the first time in forever, his mind was at peace with himself. There were no unrealistic expectations being forced on him. He was accepted for who he was.

He opened his eyes. "I love you, you know."

Bree lifted her head and smiled at him. "I know."

"Well, look who's finally awake." Trey's hearty tones from the doorway made them both jump. "The doctor did that whole don't-tire-him-out thing when I asked if I could visit with you."

"One of these days, we're going to have to speak to your brother about his timing," Rylan muttered.

"What are you two laughing about?" Trey asked, as Bree resumed her seat.

"Just happy to be alive," Rylan said.

"*Lucky* to be alive, you mean. You nearly didn't make it." Trey made a move as if to grip his hand, then decided against it. "Thank you for saving my sister's life."

Rylan smiled at Bree. "I had an ulterior motive."

Trey raised his brows in a question, but Bree shook her head. Clearly, she wasn't ready to share something they'd barely discussed. Instead, she deflected her brother's attention. "How's Jekyll?"

"I didn't know dogs could sulk, but that's one moody mutt," Trey said. "I took him back to Rylan's ranch. Dinah said to let you know she'll take good care of him along with all the others. She sends her love to both of you." He pulled up a chair and sat down, viewing the bank of machines behind Rylan warily. "Can your blood pressure stand the strain if we talk about the case?"

"Ahem." Bree moved her chair even closer to the bed. "David Swanson has done enough damage. If I think the discussion is too tiring for Rylan, we stop. Okay?"

Deciding he liked this new bossy side to her personality, Rylan moved his hand toward hers. "Agreed." She entwined her fingers with his.

"Okay." Trey nodded. "A few hours after I left Bree

at her apartment, I got a call from the police in Winnipeg to say the man they'd detained had started behaving irrationally. As soon as they presented him with a list of the charges he was wanted for here in Colorado—assault, abduction, vandalism, etc., etc.—he asked to talk some more. That was when he dropped the bombshell that he wasn't David Swanson."

"I don't understand." Although Rylan's voice was still weak, it was growing stronger. "You said David paid someone to do this. The other guy impersonated him, drove erratically and resisted arrest. He'll face jail time. Who'd take that deal?"

"Apparently, David found himself a homeless guy who looked enough like him not to raise any eyebrows when he used his passport. The down-and-out won't spend long behind bars. Totally worth it if he gets a big payout at the end."

"If David is also in prison, how will he pay him?" Bree asked.

"The money could already have changed hands," Trey said. "Or someone else may be responsible for making the payment."

"So we're back to Lone Wolf? What does David have to say about him?" Rylan was getting tired of his horizontal position, but he suspected he would regret any attempt to change it.

"Nothing." Trey rubbed his knuckles along his stubbled jaw. "He's not saying anything much at all from his hospital bed under police guard. Although the syringe you stabbed him with only contained painkiller—"

"Whoa." Rylan looked from Bree to Trey and back

again. "Back up a bit here. Who stabbed David? When? What?"

Bree gave Trey a reproachful glance. "I was going to lead up to that in easy stages."

"I'd like to hear you break it gently when you tell him that David turned up at the hospital, stole a set of scrubs and cornered you in a treatment room," Trey said.

"What?" Rylan jerked, then groaned as bolts of agony shot through him.

"Now see what you've done?" Bree was like a tiger protecting her cub. She smoothed Rylan's hair back from his face. "As you can see, I'm fine. I stabbed him in the eye with a syringe."

"She did," Trey confirmed. "While it's not the action I'd have recommended, it worked. My kid sister faced the bad guy and won."

Rylan relaxed slightly. While he didn't like the idea that Bree had been in danger while he was under anesthetic and helpless to protect her, he was glad David had finally been beaten. And if he'd been injured in the process—by Bree, of all people—well, karma had a habit of putting things right in the end.

"When it comes to the emails, David denies all knowledge of any of them, and insists he knows nothing about this Lone Wolf person," Trey continued. "As for the stockpile of weapons, he alternates between saying he found them, or that they were left in his apartment by a friend. Anyway, going back a few steps… I headed toward the Diamond as soon as I knew David was still on the loose. That reminds me. How come you were already there, Rylan?"

Rylan coughed. The action sent fresh sparks of agony

ricocheting through him, and he took a minute to get his breath. "There was someone I needed to talk to." He squeezed Bree's fingers. "I found your picture."

Her gaze was the best painkiller. "So that was what it took to make you see sense? A rough sketch that I did in half an hour?"

Ignoring the pain, he leaned closer. "Maybe that was the excuse I needed to come after you."

"If we can just focus for a bit longer? Because I think that doctor will throw me out once he gets here." Trey forced their attention back to him. "So, I figured David had laid his plans carefully and he would be watching the gallery, and Bree's apartment, for signs of her return. Sure enough, he made his move as soon as she was out in the open."

Bree shuddered. "If Rylan hadn't been there…"

"I *was* there. That's all that matters."

"David was preparing to fire more shots when we broke into his apartment. He knows he's facing life imprisonment for attempted murder, but he's adamant he doesn't have an accomplice." Trey shrugged. "It makes me wonder if you were right, Rylan. Was there ever another person or does he have multiple personalities?"

"If David doesn't talk, we may never know," Rylan said. "Even if Lone Wolf exists, he can slink away now and never be caught."

"Is it wrong to just be very glad that David is going to jail?" Bree asked. "To finally feel that we can get on with our lives without constantly looking over our shoulders?"

"I don't think I'll be looking over my shoulder any

time soon." Rylan winced at the thought. "But I know what you mean."

"Still here, Sheriff?" A voice from the doorway made Trey roll his eyes. "I thought I asked you not to tire my patient."

"Just leaving, Doctor." Trey got to his feet. "Can I drive you home, Bree?"

"No, thank you." She raised Rylan's hand to her lips. "I'm not going anywhere for a very long time."

Chapter 19

Bree watched Rylan as he endured the doctor's poking and prodding. Although his expression didn't change, the lines of pain were etched deeper, and his complexion grew gradually paler. By the time he lay back on the pillows, his face was bathed in sweat and the dark circles beneath his eyes stood out like bruises.

"Will I lose any of the movement in this arm?" he asked. Although his voice was calm, Bree could tell how much it cost him to ask the question.

"I trust not." The doctor pursed his lips. "The bullet passed straight through, fracturing the shoulder joint and causing considerable soft tissue damage. Those issues were addressed in surgery. We also dealt with injuries to the nerve structures that supply to the upper body, arms and hands. What follows now will be a lengthy period of rehabilitation. I can't rule out further surgery, but I'm hopeful that it won't be necessary."

"When can he come home?" Bree asked. She wanted Rylan back in his own environment. On his ranch, where he belonged, surrounded by his own land and his beloved animals. From now on, that meant *their* home.

The doctor looked at her over the top of his glasses. "If he behaves, and follows instructions, it will be a week. If he doesn't, it could be two."

"Do you hear that?" Bree said to Rylan. "You are going to do exactly as you are told."

When the doctor had gone, he turned his head toward her with an obvious effort. "Where were we? Oh, I remember. I said *I love yo*u. You said *I know.* I'm still waiting to find out whether you love me too."

She gave a soft laugh. "You have doubts?"

His smile was teasing. "Not quite the three little words I was hoping to hear."

Bree moved until her face was inches from his. "I love everything about you, Rylan Bennet. I love how you rescued Papadum from a dumpster... How when you heard the story of a cat belonging to Cindy from Finance, you took her home with you. And I love that even though other people left Boo, the brokenhearted goose, at the side of the road, *you* refused to leave him there to die."

"I did what any decent human being in the same situation would have done."

She shook her head, brushing a soft kiss across his forehead. "That's debatable. But in any case, those animals got a new life because of your big heart. It takes a special kind of tough guy to show his sensitive side and make a home for the world's waifs the way you've done. But it's about more than how you care for your misfits. It's how you care for *me* and how you make me feel…" She ran a finger along his arm. "All the time."

He groaned. "Maybe not the best time for that sort of information."

"You asked." She gave him a mischievous grin. "But we have plenty of time for the physical stuff when you're all mended."

"I'm going to hold you to that."

She laid her head next to his on the pillow. "As long as you hold me, I'll be happy."

"I never believed in love at first sight," Rylan admitted. "When other people talked about it, I figured they were describing an intense attraction that happened when they met someone. But the first time I saw you, Bree…my heart was overflowing with the most genuine emotion I'd ever known. Suddenly, the whole world made sense. It was wonderful, and scary at the same time. It was even more meaningful because it was so out of character for me. In case you hadn't noticed, I like to be in control."

"I noticed."

Bree could see his eyelids drooping as he talked. He'd been through so much, and she was amazed at the strength with which he'd clung to life. After the surgery, the doctors had admitted that, in those first hours after the shooting, they had been unsure if they could save him. Hearing that, she'd gone on a roller coaster of emotion, alternating between happiness and might-have-been.

Alongside everything else, she had been dealing with

a hefty should-have-been-me dose of guilt. How did you thank a man who had taken a bullet for you? She knew the answer to that question now. You didn't. Not when that man loved you. She would have done the same for Rylan. That was the magical give-and-take of real love.

"I wasn't looking for love." His voice was sleepy now. "Never thought forever was for me. But when I first saw you, it was like a buzzer went off inside my brain. It told me the search was over. Didn't even know I was looking, but I'd found you."

"We found each other." Bree lifted her head to watch over him as his eyes closed. "And we have our own forever."

Epilogue

Four Weeks Later

"It was my shoulder that got injured, not my legs," Rylan grumbled.

"And you lost a lot of blood," Bree calmly reminded him. "The doctors have said you still need to take things easy."

"I don't think a walk on my own ranch is going to do me any harm."

They were seated on the porch, eating a late lunch and watching a few fluffy clouds scurry across an otherwise perfect sky. The whole pack of dogs were dotted around the lawn, while Jekyll curled up beneath Bree's chair. Nance's ducklings were old enough now to leave her protection, and they bobbed about on the pond. Their cat mom lay in a shady spot on the bank, watching them.

The peacefulness was in such sharp contrast to everything they'd been through. Lightness lifted Bree's heart, invading her senses and making her spirits soar. "If you really are ready for a walk, I have something I want to show you."

Rylan smirked at her over the top of his coffee cup. "I've seen it all. In bed last night, and just now in the shower."

She shook her head sorrowfully. "I always suspected you were a wicked man. Now, I know it for sure."

He reached for her hand. "But you love me." There was quiet contentment in his voice as he said the words.

"Every wicked part of you."

"We could skip the walk while you explore my most wicked parts," he said hopefully.

Bree burst out laughing. "For someone who is supposed to be taking it easy…"

"Honey." He drawled the word, while giving her an exaggerated leer. "With you, I'll take it any way I can get it."

She got to her feet. "Maybe you do need a walk. You have *way* too much energy today."

Hand in hand, they slowly followed the creek toward the boundary with the disused ranch. The dogs streamed after them. Although Jekyll tried to stop the others from getting too close to Bree, his behavior was improving. The little oddball was calmer, and less aggressive.

"It's because he knows he's loved," Bree said.

"Does he?" Rylan raised a brow. "I wonder what gave him that idea?"

When they drew close to the edge of Rylan's land, Bree pointed toward the abandoned ranch. "Remember when we first came out here, and you talked about all the things you could do if you had that land?"

"Sadly, it was just a dream."

"Maybe not." Instead of stopping at the boundary, she carried on walking. "This is our land now."

He smiled down at her, his expression bewildered. "I don't understand."

"After what happened with David, I learned the hard way about using my own name in real-estate transactions. I spoke to my uncle Russ while you were in the hospital, and he got his attorney to approach the owner of this ranch. He kept the Colton name out of it, but he also made it clear we wouldn't be paying over the market value. We agreed on a price, and the contracts were signed a few days ago. I didn't want to tell you until it was finalized in case it fell through." She turned a half circle, sweeping a hand in front of her. "This is my contribution to our animal sanctuary."

Rylan stood very quiet and still, his lips slightly parted, and his eyes narrowed against the bright sunlight.

"Say something." Bree felt suddenly nervous. Had she done the wrong thing? Would his pride lead him to say he couldn't accept a gift of this magnitude?

When he turned to her, his eyes were overly bright, his voice thick with emotion. "You didn't have to do this."

"I didn't *have* to. I wanted to." She placed a hand on his arm. "We're a team now, remember? I want this sanctuary as much as you do."

He used his good arm to draw her close. "What about the gallery?"

"Wise Gal will always have a place in my heart. And I will always be a painter. I visited Kasey a few times while you were in the hospital. She couldn't talk because her jaw was wired, so our conversation was me talking, and her texting me her replies." Bree laughed. "Luckily, it wasn't the other way around, or I'd still be there composing the first text. I asked her how she would feel about managing the gallery. Obviously, her plastic surgery will take some time, but she was excited at the prospect. I can take on a more executive role, perhaps spending a day or two a week there."

"That's my wise gal. You have it all figured out," Rylan said.

"When I thought you might not—" She shook her head. Those negative thoughts had no place anymore. "After you got shot, I reassessed a lot of things. I know how lucky I am to have found you, and I want to spend as much time as I can at your side."

"Hey, I'm the lucky one, remember? It's my nickname."

"Oh, yes." She looped her arms around his waist, pressing her face to his chest. "From now on, we can be lucky together."

"Mr. and Mrs. Lucky." She nodded. When he spoke again, his voice was slightly hoarse. "That was a proposal, Bree." She looked up quickly, her mouth forming a silent *O* of surprise. "I was going to wait. Do it properly. Get a ring. Go down on one knee... But this seemed like the perfect time."

"Any time would be perfect." She rose on the tips of her toes to kiss his lips. "And my answer, of course, is—"

"Bree? Rylan? I've been looking everywhere for you." Trey strode across the overgrown grass toward them.

"Say it quick, or I'll have to get Papadum to sit on him while we run away," Rylan said.

"Yes." Bree dissolved into giggles.

"I'll never understand why you two always start laughing whenever you see me," Trey grumbled.

"Just high on life." Rylan's expression was pure innocence. "You can be the first to congratulate us. We just got engaged."

"It's about time. I don't know what took you so long," Trey growled, as he swung Bree off the ground and hugged her. He shook Rylan's left hand. "Congratulations."

"You haven't come with bad news, have you?" Bree asked.

"No, just the opposite. I heard from my informant last night. He confirmed that those whispers of an attack on The Chateau or The Lodge have gone quiet."

"This, among other things, calls for a celebratory root beer float," Rylan said.

Bree linked a hand through Rylan's uninjured arm on one side and Trey's on the other as they walked back toward the house.

Trey frowned as he watched the pack bound ahead of them. "You do know one of your dogs is a sheep, right?"

* * * * *

SPECIAL EXCERPT FROM

◆ HARLEQUIN®

ROMANTIC suspense

*Tessa Wilkes has trained to become a Special Forces
operator for her entire adult life...that is until she's
unceremoniously tossed out of the training pipeline.
But the gorgeous spec ops trainer Beau Lambert offers
her the chance of a lifetime: to become part of a highly
classified, all-female Special Forces team called
the Medusas.*

Read on for a sneak preview of the first book in
New York Times *bestselling author Cindy Dees's
brand-new Mission Medusa miniseries,*
Special Forces: The Recruit.

Hands gripped Tess's shoulders. Lifted her slowly to
her feet. Her unwilling gaze traveled up Beau's body,
taking in the washboard abs, the bulging pecs and broad
shoulders. A finger touched her chin, tilting her face up,
forcing her to look him in the eyes.

"We good?" Beau murmured.

Jeez. How to answer that? They would be great if he
would just kiss her and forget about the whole "don't
fall for me" thing. She ended up mumbling, "Um, yeah.
Sure. Fine."

"I don't know much about women, but I do know one
thing. When a woman says nothing's wrong, something's
always wrong. And when she says she's fine like you
just did, she's emphatically not fine. Talk to me. What's
going on?"

She winced. If only he wasn't so direct all the time. She knew better than to try to lie to a special operator—they all had training that included knowing how to lie and how to spot a lie. She opted for partial truth. "I want you, Beau. Right now."

"Post-mission adrenaline got you jacked up again?"

Actually, she'd been shockingly calm out there earlier. Which she was secretly pretty darned proud of. Tonight was the first time she'd ever shot a real bullet at a real human being. At the time, she'd been so focused on protecting Beau that it hadn't dawned on her what she'd done.

But now that he mentioned it, adrenaline was, indeed, screaming through her. And it was demanding an outlet in no uncertain terms.

"I feel as if I could run a marathon right about now," she confessed. She risked a glance up at him. "Or have epic sex with you. Your choice."

Don't miss
Special Forces: The Recruit *by Cindy Dees,*
available May 2019 wherever
Harlequin® Romantic Suspense books
and ebooks are sold.

www.Harlequin.com

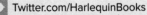

Love Harlequin romance?

DISCOVER.

Be the first to find out about promotions,
news and exclusive content!

 Facebook.com/HarlequinBooks

 Twitter.com/HarlequinBooks

 Instagram.com/HarlequinBooks

Pinterest.com/HarlequinBooks

ReaderService.com

EXPLORE.

Sign up for the Harlequin e-newsletter and
download a free book from any series at
TryHarlequin.com.

CONNECT.

Join our Harlequin community to share
your thoughts and connect with other
romance readers!
Facebook.com/groups/HarlequinConnection

**ROMANCE WHEN
YOU NEED IT**

Earn points on your purchase of new Harlequin books from participating retailers.

Turn your points into **FREE BOOKS** of your choice!

Join for FREE today at
www.HarlequinMyRewards.com.

Harlequin My Rewards is a free program (no fees) without any commitments or obligations.

MYR18